KILLER MOTIVES

KILLER MOTIVES

A HUDSON VALLEY MYSTERY

BONNIE L. TRAYMORE

Charleston, SC
www.PalmettoPublishing.com

Killer Motives
Copyright © 2022 by Bonnie L. Traymore

First Edition

Paperback ISBN: 978-1-68515-908-5
eBook ISBN: 978-1-68515-909-2

For my two favorite mystery book lovers:
Dad, my chief protector and Rick, my chief supporter

TABLE OF CONTENTS

PART ONE

"All these, however, were mere terrors of the night, phantoms of the mind that walk in darkness."
The Legend of Sleepy Hollow

ONE

As Angie made her way to the bedroom, resigned to a night alone in her empty, chilly new house, her imagination was playing tricks on her. The creaking floorboards reminded her of skeleton bones knocking together and the wind whistling through the windows called out to her like spirits in the night. She didn't mind a little fear, though, because it was the only thing keeping her from succumbing to the urge to kill herself. If she felt fear, didn't that mean she wasn't quite ready to die?

She looked down at her outfit, the red fabric clinging to her firm, sexy body that men loved to conquer. It wasn't easy being a woman who every man wanted to sleep with but few really cared to know. Then she heard a car pull up and her heart leapt. Maybe he'd had a change of heart! She dashed into the bathroom to clean the runny mascara off her face. She heard a knock at the door and started down the stairs, trying hard not to get her hopes up only to have them crushed again.

———

Although he knew what to expect as he drove the last curve of the dark road to his destination, he was uncharacteristically nervous. It was not very late—just about nine in the evening—but the crescent moon offered up little in the way of illumination. The thick fall foliage that lit up the sky by day now veiled the area in darkness and shadow. He dimmed his lights on approach and scanned the area looking for other cars or some sign that he'd been spotted, but only one car was in the driveway—hers—and the lights were all out. He slowed his car to a stop as he pulled it in behind hers, hovering between park and reverse, letting the engine punctuate the silence as he observed his surroundings. Nobody else was here. Nobody else knew. He was just being paranoid. He sat there weighing his options, unable to shake the unsettling feeling that someone was watching him.

———

"Is that you, Nick?" Victoria feigned concern as she heard her husband coming through the doorway from her perch atop the staircase, holding a laundry basket in front of her like a shield. The faint smell of oil and garlic from their uneaten dinner lingered in the air.

"Of course it's me. Who else would it be? I ran out to meet my client. The Shady Hill property."

"Why didn't you tell me you were leaving? I was worried." She made her way down the staircase, curious to see how this would play out.

"I didn't know where you were. I got a text from her. She couldn't get her key to work. She was locked out. I had to run over. It's all good now." Nick stopped to hang his keys on the holder. A grocery bag hung from his forearm.

"Getting a key to work? For over two hours?" She walked past him as she spoke, struggling to play it cool although her stomach was in knots.

"Come on! You know how she is. I stopped over there, gave her my spare, she had all kinds of issues, as usual. Then I stopped by the store. We needed coffee. Dutiful husband. See?" He held up his shopping bag and waved it back and forth.

"Well, you could have texted me. You missed dinner." She walked into the living room and placed the laundry basket on their accent chair, stopping to pick off a stray piece of lint that had landed on one of its navy stripes.

"I'm trying to be more focused on my work, bring in more money. This is a big sale. Don't I even get a 'congratulations'?" He ambled to the sofa, mumbling something under his breath, as the bag ripped a bit and dangled from his arm. He plopped down and stretched his arms across the back, giving the soft Italian leather a squeeze. "Speaking of which, did you go somewhere? Your car was in the driveway when I left."

"Me? No. I was doing laundry. Dutiful wife." She motioned to the basket. "I pulled it into the garage when I took out the recycling." She didn't really remember pulling the car into the garage, she'd been so rattled.

"You didn't leave me much space. I could barely get my door open." He reached into the shopping bag. "And I also happened to pick up a bottle of champagne." She looked at him, confused. "To celebrate?" The closing?" He lifted it out of the bag and showed it to her, as if she'd never seen a champagne bottle before. "I wanted to surprise you."

"I don't like surprises, Nick." Was she supposed to feel guilty now? Did she ruin his little celebration?

He smiled in that sly, sexy way that used to send tingles through her body as he stood up and walked over to her. His voice was warm now, inviting. "Come on. You used to like my little surprises, as I recall, at least at certain hours of the night…" He went in for an embrace. When she tensed up, he backed off, keeping a light hand on her shoulder. "Something wrong, Victoria?"

She had no choice but to look at him. In their ten years of marriage, the only signs of the decade on him were some gray flecks in his dark hair that added a measure of gravitas to his boyish affect and matching stubble that accented his square jaw and olive skin. If it was possible, he was even more attractive than when they'd first met. Too bad it was wasted on her. "It's late." She backed away.

"Right." He looked genuinely defeated. "But really Vic, we could try harder to get some of that back. I want to try harder. I really do."

She turned from him and made her way back up the curved wooden staircase, down the hall, and into their spacious master suite to shower and get ready for bed. She had liked it in the beginning, the casual way he called her "Vic," the freedom it gave her to break free of the dead weight of her heritage. "Nick and Vic," he'd laugh. Now it just annoyed her. But she didn't want to think about that now. She was drained. Ready for a hot shower and sleep.

She peeled off her clothes and jumped in the shower, trying to avoid any further interactions with her husband. As she stood under the pulsating jets, her tense neck and shoulder muscles started to relax. Then a sharp pain jolted her as some of the water dripped onto her scraped up forearm. Damn it! It had just stopped hurting too. She cut the shower short and toweled herself off, lightly dabbing the moisture from her throbbing arm. The gash had closed up pretty nicely but the scrapes, although not very deep, were still really raw.

She heard him come in their bedroom as she embarked on her nightly skin care routine. He walked up to his matching sink to brush his teeth, keeping his distance as he grabbed his toothbrush from its holder. They stood side by side, in a sort of stand-off, not looking at each other, not talking. She could see in the mirror that he was sneaking glances at her.

"So, how's that deal on the Cole painting going?" He reached over into her territory to grab the toothpaste. "Didn't you say there were some problems?"

"I think we got it figured out. Foreign buyer, cash, ran into some issues. Charles is working on it with the IRS or the KGB or whoever it is he has to placate. I'm out of it. He'll make it work." She continued to dab her eye cream into the crevices, dotting and pressing as directed.

"At least I hope he makes it work. This buyer doesn't like to be disappointed."

"Charles," Nick said in a garbled British accent, his words obscured by the electric toothbrush in his mouth. "Charlie boy needs to get over himself. He's not very street smart. He's gonna get himself in trouble one of these days with those foreign buyers. They don't screw around."

She ignored him, immune to his constant digs about her upper crust background. Funny how he didn't seem to mind the perks it afforded him.

He stopped brushing and rinsed. "What's with that scrape on your arm?"

"Oh, I was running at Rockefeller. My toe hit a rock. Sent me barreling into a tree branch." She continued her routine, moving on to her neck cream.

"It looks nasty." He put his toothbrush back in the holder, wiping the excess foam from his mouth with the back of his hand. He turned to her with a look somewhere between admiration and curiosity.

"Why are you looking at me like that?" she asked.

"You don't need all that stuff, you know. You're only thirty-five. And you're still the most stunning woman I've ever seen." Nick offered up his best lover-boy smile, and she failed to suppress an eye roll. "What? Don't roll your eyes! I'm serious. And you know it's true, too, I'm not just saying it."

She believed him, which somehow made it even worse. Sure, her complexion was flawless and it complemented her sensibly cut, medium-length honey-blonde hair with subtle highlights perfectly, but she thought for a moment that she looked very pale and bland next to her dark and handsome husband. Maybe that's how he saw her. Boring. Vanilla. She quickly quashed those thoughts. This was his problem, not hers, and she was done with his head games. He should have stuck to talking about business.

"I don't look like I need all this stuff because I have all this stuff and I use it religiously. Ergo, I need all this stuff. But thanks." She really hoped he would just give it up and go to bed. Finally reading her signals, he turned and made his way out of the bathroom.

"And don't forget we have my function tomorrow," she called after him. "You can make it, right? It's the first one in a long time. We need to make an appearance together." She was looking forward to her charity event this year, even more than usual. It was the first one in a long while and she was hungry for some social interaction.

"Yeah, I can make it. I told you. I'm all yours now. Don't worry. The house closed. It's a new chapter. It was a nightmare, drilling a new well, all the crap we had to do to make this work. I'm surprised it wasn't on an Indian burial ground. All to live on that creepy hillside. I hate it up there. I should get a double commission." Was he expecting her to commiserate?

"Well, the customer's always right, as they say." She was running out of face creams. Would he just go to sleep already?

"I'm getting sick of real estate anyway. I might want to do something else. I need a change. You were right, it's a grind, even at the high end." His Catholic guilt was on steroids. Was he regretting the affair? Time to do some damage control?

"Let's talk about it another time, okay? I'm tired." After a few minutes of glorious silence, she felt the coast was clear enough to head to her side of the bed.

She listened to the familiar sound of Nick's rhythmic breathing and the steady pattering of the rain outside. An earthy smell wafted through the window which she had forgotten to close. The cool air felt nice on her face. When she was confident he was down for the count, she pulled the covers over her head and looked again at the images on her phone. She finally had the proof she needed to get rid of him with minimal damage to her bottom line. She should have felt jubilant, but she just felt empty. Maybe that was to be expected? Ten years of marriage, and it hadn't been all bad. She wanted desperately to sleep, but the throbbing from the scrape on her arm kept her awake as her restless mind replayed the events from earlier that evening—over and over and over.

She'd been cooking dinner when she heard Nick's car start. The next thing she knew, she was in her car, driving. She wasn't angry. It was like she was looking down on herself as this other person drove her car mindlessly into the night. She wasn't thinking about what she would do when she got there. As she turned to drive up the dark, winding road, reality started to seep in. She was more careful now as she drove around the bends on the way up the hill. She parked her car on the side of the access road on the way to the house. Her phone was on the passenger seat. She took it in her right hand with her keys in the left. She hadn't thought to grab her purse, but she remembered turning off the stove.

She started walking towards the house, down the short access road. It was pitch black. No streetlights. She used her phone's flashlight to guide her. She was wearing flats which were a little too big in the cooler weather and her feet lifted out near the heel. The shoulder was rocky and uneven so she slowed down. About half way down the road, she stumbled on a rock. She lost her balance and fell into the brush, grasping for the spiny tree branches with her right hand. They broke her fall but she dropped the phone and her keys. Why hadn't she left her keys in the car? The phone was easy to find in the dark, but not the keys.

As she searched for the keys, it dawned on her that she could have just hired a private detective. She could certainly afford one. But she had come this far, and she needed to know the truth. Now. Tonight. Soon she was at the house. Nick's car was in the driveway. She waited a bit, not sure if she could actually bring herself to go in and confront him. Then she looked up. It must have been fate. She could see them now in an upstairs window, locked in an embrace. They started kissing. She was snapping away on her phone—photo after photo after photo. She felt a rush of excitement as adrenaline coursed through her veins. Her heart was ticking like a metronome. She had him, dead to rights!

Then they moved out of her view and her mood shifted. She felt a rush of panic and her face flushed, realizing how desperate she would look if someone saw her or spotted her car. What would her mother think? It felt creepy here now, surrounded by the dark woods, like she could disappear into them and never be seen again. She retreated, heading back to her car, careful to watch her footing this time. When she was inside her car, she locked the doors and took a moment to compose herself before she started on her way back home. It wasn't until she was driving down Bedford that it was light enough for her to notice the nasty gash on her forearm, bleeding into the teal silk of her three-quarter sleeved blouse. She pulled over and started to sob.

TWO

A body was found at the bottom of the stairs at a home in Pocantico Hills, off Bedford near the border of Sleepy Hollow. It looked suspicious so they'd called in Major Crimes. That's about all he knew. He and Lexi had gotten the call about fifteen minutes earlier and it was now just past eight in the morning. Already all hands were on deck. Jack had expected this to blow up fast, but not this fast.

"Watch out, Jack!" A media van almost backed into them while Jack was trying to park the car. He swerved a bit to avoid it and blasted his horn. Lexi could be a bit of a backseat driver but it didn't bother him too much. Besides, he hadn't actually seen the van. Parking was already tight. There were two police cars, the media van, and the forensics team vying for turf, in addition to what was probably the victim's car in the driveway. It was almost impossible to turn around, so he just parked the car where it was, blocking in the van. He had little tolerance for the press.

The property, although a short drive from town up the hillside, felt more isolated than it was, which was fine for some people but not likely for everyone. It was the kind of place about which urban legends would circulate, like sightings of

Washington Irving's ghost at nearby Sunnyside or the famed spirits of Estherwood Mansion in Dobbs Ferry. Even in a region rife with spectral speculation, this property stood out—not great for a murder investigation.

"The media's here? Already? We don't even know for sure if there was a murder!" Lexi's voice went up an octave as she spoke. A reporter and her team were setting up. This was their first homicide call in a while, and it was squarely in the high rent district.

"It's a dead body two weeks before Halloween on the Sleepy Hollow border. What do you expect?" Jack knew it would be harder if the press got involved this early, but there was not much they could do about it now.

Lexi shook her head, registering her disapproval. She didn't seem to like it too much in Westchester. She had been here just over a year—a promotion. Maybe it would grow on her like it had on him. They were both veteran New York City cops and had endured much more unfortunate beats—gang and drug infested—where murders were so common place, they didn't even make the news. It was a luxury to have so few that they became spectacle, but people around here wouldn't get that, and neither would the press. The uniformed officers had already taped off the crime scene and the press knew better than to think that they would comment this early in the investigation, but that didn't stop them from trying as they got out of the car and headed for the house.

"Was this a homicide?" "Do you have any leads?" They weren't taking photos or video just yet. Jack held up his hand as if to shield the two of them as they headed for the front door.

It was a larger house by most people's standards but under-sized for the area. It seemed pristine at first glance—recently fixed up—but he could tell it would be a money pit, an older home solidly built but set on a sloping hillside surrounded by tall hemlocks and mature black oaks that blocked the sun. It looked to be about three thousand square feet, with the lot about twenty thousand. There was a realtor's sign in the yard. Had it just been sold, or was it still in the process? He recalled that there had been a string of real estate agents murdered years back, before his time, a serial killer who had never been caught.

They made their way up the entry stairs to the front door landing. There was no screen door, just a large dark wooden door—high end—with a dead bolt and handle lock combination. Jack thought that it seemed inadequate protection for the caliber of the home, but then this wasn't a particularly high crime area. Still. As they entered the foyer, he noticed a side table with some real estate flyers, business cards of various agents, and some booties under the table. To his left, a body was lying at the bottom of the stairs, appearing to be a woman, with an officer looking down on her. He whipped his head around toward them when he heard them approach, protecting his turf.

"Jack Stark and Lexi Sanchez. Major Crimes." Jack waved to him and smiled as they logged in and donned their gloves and shoe coverings. Officers here weren't normally very territorial, but he made an effort to be gracious just the same. The officer motioned to them to come over.

"Gary Johnson." He offered them a quick raise and lowering of his hand. "Thanks for getting here so quickly."

"So what do we know?" Jack was taking inventory of the surroundings while trying to keep his distance from the body until the Medical Examiner arrived. It was a pretty gritty crime scene. Lots of blood, typical of a head wound, and some twisted limbs from what was apparently a nasty fall. He turned to look at Lexi. She looked a little peaked. It never really got any easier.

Officer Johnson filled them in. "Female, forty-two years old, Angela Hansen. Found at the bottom of the stairs. Looks like she was hit with a blunt object and she tumbled down the stairs. I guess there's a chance the injury could have come from the fall, but I don't think so. And see that bruising on the neck? That's certainly not from the fall. It looks like she was hit from behind and then fell down the stairs. My best guess is it happened last night sometime. The temperature was pretty consistent in here, so it shouldn't take too long to get time of death. We wanted to call you in right away." Jack had already noticed a thermostat on the wall set to 68 degrees.

"Thanks for looping us in so quickly." Jack studied the back of the victim's head from his vantage point, trying not to contaminate the body. She had landed face down with her head to one side, dressed in a tightly fitting red dress, not the kind of outfit a woman wore for a night home alone. Long, flowing dark hair fanned out all over the stairs and the landing. He moved in closer. He could see there were some marks around her neck, but they weren't consistent with strangulation as a cause of death, at least not ligature strangulation.

Then his eyes focused out from the body to its immediate surroundings as he got his bearings. He took a look around the first level. The front door led into the foyer. To the right was a den and laundry area, a full bathroom, and an attached garage filled with boxes. There was another door to the backyard in the mud room by the laundry. Built to accommodate the slope, the main living area was on the second floor. He made his way up the stairs and took a spin around the second level which consisted of the kitchen, living room, the master suite, and two other bedrooms with another full bath. Only the master suite had furniture in it. He went back to the kitchen and saw that a few necessities had been unpacked. There was an open bottle of wine, about two-thirds full, with one wine glass in the sink.

He went up and down the stairs a few times, observing the blood spatter and the angle of her body trying to imagine the crime. From the spatter, it was clear she was hit at the top of the stairs with something hard before she fell. Maybe a fight at the top of the stairs? A crime of passion? It didn't look premeditated. Not likely a serial killer. He was getting ahead of himself, but then that was to be expected. It had been a slow few months in homicide.

"Does it look like anything was stolen?" Lexi looked around at all the boxes and general disarray. It was sort of a mess, but an organized mess.

"Hard to tell. It looks like she was moving in. There's stuff everywhere. Lots of boxes, all over the house. Some half empty, but it doesn't look ransacked. Looks more like she was in the middle of unpacking, but hard to say for sure. It'll be hard to see if anything was stolen with the state it's in. Records show the sale recorded two days ago. Nice housewarming, huh?" Johnson's voice was a little shaky, even a bit emotional, which seemed odd to Jack. He looked too old to be a rookie. Maybe she looked like someone he knew.

"New owner then. I wonder if she even changed the locks. We need to talk to the agents, see who might have had access." Jack made a mental note.

"One thing is, we found her purse but no cell phone so far. Johnson motioned to the purse on a table in the den, the contents of which were being cataloged by the crime scene unit. "There's about fifty dollars in the purse, credit cards, license, all that stuff. But we can't find the cell. We'll keep looking. I guess it could be anywhere."

"Good to know, that's significant." Jack scribbled something barely legible on his notepad which was about the size of a deck of cards. "Any signs of a break-in? How did you even get the call?" He was asking too many of the questions, as usual. He reminded himself that he needed to back off a bit and let Lexi break in, build her confidence.

"No signs of a break-in. The plumber called it in. She had someone scheduled for early this morning. When she didn't answer the door or her cell, he got concerned. He tried the door and it was unlocked, so he came in and found her, called nine-one-one and here we are."

"What woman doesn't lock her door?" Jack pulled on his chin with his thumb and index finger, deep in concentration. Johnson nodded in agreement. Lexi was listening while sketching the scene, a specialty of hers. "And how did those vultures find out so fast? Smelled it in the air?" Jack pointed his thumb back towards the door and the reporters outside.

"No idea. Police radio? Tip from the plumber? You know how this place is. News like this travels fast. You better think of something to tell them. It'll help if we can control the narrative a bit." Johnson was absolutely right about that. He certainly knew this area pretty well.

"Does she have any family?" Lexi finally chimed in.

"She's the sole owner of record. We found an ex-husband in Orlando and her parents live in Brooklyn, but that's about it so far. She seems new to the area, used to live in the city. Looks like she worked in finance. I'm gonna go check with the teams in the other rooms, see if they found anything useful."

"We'll wait here with the victim. Thanks for the update, Officer Johnson."

"Gary."

"Thanks Gary."

While he and Gary were bonding, Lexi had been taking copious notes in her notebook along with her detailed drawings and sketches. She was a total type A which worked to his benefit. He could see she already had almost two full pages.

"How's your thesis coming?" Jack liked to needle her. Their banter may have seemed callous to people who didn't understand their world. It was a way to blow off steam, a way of keeping a part of their humanity in the face of all the horror they saw on a regular basis. It probably kept them from going insane.

"Let's compare notes." Lexi snatched his notepad from his hand without missing a beat. She was younger. Quicker.

"'Cell?' 'Locks?' Wow, very observant, Jack. Bravo. You've practically solved it."

"I don't like to get bogged down in the details."

She shot him one of her looks. "If she just moved in, she probably has a moving inventory or an insurance policy we could check to see if anything of value was taken."

"Great thinking, Lex. Why don't you get started on that and I'll try to track down her real estate agent while we wait for the ME's report to come out." The Medical Examiner's report was a just formality to Jack. He already knew it was homicide. A beautiful single woman murdered in her home in a safe, up-scale neighborhood. They needed to get some answers—fast!

THREE

Nick was driving to his office in Tarrytown when his cell buzzed, an unknown caller. He was still reeling from the night before. He hesitated for a moment and almost didn't answer it, but that was considered bad practice in his business. It might be a potential client. All he wanted was for things to go back to normal. He picked up. "Hi, this is Nick." A click and a pause.

"Nick Mancusio?"

"Yes, Nick Mancusio." Another longer pause. What the hell. Say something. "Hello? *Hello?*" He was about to hang up. Probably a scam call. Then he heard the phone cutting in and out and someone talking. For such a swanky neighborhood, they sure had crappy cell phone reception. The caller spoke up again, louder this time.

"This is Detective Jack Stark with the Tarrytown Police Department. Are you there?"

"What? Yes, I'm here. What is it?" He felt his heart race as his hands gripped the steering wheel a little tighter.

"Do you know an Angela Hansen? I think she was your client in a recent real estate transaction?" The detective's tone was neutral, not threatening, but there was something about the way he disclosed the fact that he already knew something about him and their relationship that made Nick more nervous.

"Yes, yes I know her. We just closed on a property, up on Shady Hill Lane. Why?" What could he say? He couldn't lie about that.

"She was found dead in her home this morning. I'm a homicide detective. We'd like to talk to you as soon as possible. See if you can shed some light on this." He slammed on the brakes to avoid running a stop sign, although his was the only vehicle at the intersection. Coffee spilled on the console and his folders on the passenger seat went flying. His mind was blank. It's not like he couldn't think of anything to say. It was more that he couldn't find his words. This was a detective trained to pick up on cues. He didn't have time to mull over how to play it. He was taking way too long. Finally, he spoke.

"Dead? What? Oh my God. What happened?" The car behind him honked. He turned right and pulled over.

"I can't get into that right now. I can explain more when I see you. We could come to you or you could come down to the station." Down to the station? That sounded ominous.

"Can you give me half an hour? I have to rearrange my schedule. I can call you in thirty minutes with a time and place."

"I'll call you. Be sure to pick up." The detective hung up.

Nick dialed another number. It went to voicemail. "Jeff, it's Nick. Call me. It's an emergency."

———

"What are you doing here?" Jeff was visibly annoyed, standing tall behind his desk, his arms folded like a sentry. Nick had driven straight to his office unannounced, and had interrupted him while he was on a call.

"It's my client. Angie Hansen. The police called me. Jeff, she's *dead!* They found her body this morning. In the new house." Nick started to pace, trying in vain to dispel some of the nervous energy that was clouding his judgement.

Jeff's jaw dropped. He came around his desk, walked a few paces over to the door, and shut it. He turned back to Nick. "You mean *my* client, the client *I* gave to *you*, is dead? What the hell happened?" Right. In all the chaos, Nick had almost forgotten. She was his client too, a big law suit.

"I have no idea. The police want to meet with me. Some homicide detective called. I didn't know what to do, so I came here. They're calling back soon. I'm supposed to tell them where and when I can meet. What should I do?!" Nick rubbed his neck as he continued to pace, thankful that it was spacious enough in the office to distance himself from Jeff.

"Homicide?" Jeff walked across the room and stood by the window, gazing beyond the town a few floors below them out towards the Hudson River. He turned to Nick. "So she was murdered?"

"I guess? I don't know! They wouldn't tell me much. They said they'd explain later. I'm freaking out."

"Why? Did you kill her?"

"Of course not! What kind of a question is that?" Nick knew that Jeff had a sick sense of humor, but this was pushing it.

"Then what are you so worried about? Seems like this is a much bigger problem for me than for you." Typical Jeff.

"I was there last night. Maybe they know I was there. Do you think they know?" Nick's palms were sweaty and his heart was still racing, not just because of the detective, but also because he was anticipating Jeff's reaction to what he was shortly going to disclose.

"So? You're her agent. You can explain that pretty easily. I still don't see the problem. And will you stop pacing and sit down? You're freaking me out." Nick stopped his pacing and sat in an armchair, as requested, his head in his hands. His leg was bobbing up and down, shaking the seat. He let the information sit with Jeff for a moment.

"Wait. Please. Tell me you weren't sleeping with her. For Christ's sake, Nick. Tell me!" His voice was getting louder and Nick motioned to him to keep it down. "Even you can't be that stupid, right? *Right?*"

Nick looked down at the carpet, trying to avert Jeff's signature death stare. He could hear that Jeff was now the one pacing around. He wished he could make himself invisible. Nick looked up and continued.

"I'm sorry Jeff. I don't know how it happened, it just did. It was a big mistake! I've been trying to break it off for weeks. She was still calling me, texting me. There were some issues about her key not working last night. I went over. We talked more. She wasn't happy, but she was calmer. She seemed to be getting it. She was alive when I left, I swear. Upset, but alive."

"Are you *insane?* This was a big case for me! A clear-cut harassment suit, worth millions. High profile. I could have made a fortune, not to mention the publicity. I told you it was a delicate situation. That she was vulnerable. Unstable. And you *slept* with her? You're supposed to be my friend! I went out on a limb for you and you screwed me."

It was all true. Jeff had warned him, and Nick could see just how screwed Jeff was. He had already put a ton of hours into the case, all on contingency, and now he would get nothing. Nick would still get his commission. It was totally unfair. And there was nothing he could do to change it.

"I'm so sorry. It was a major screw up. I'll make it up to you. But Jeff, I slept with her. I didn't kill her! It's not my fault your client's dead. Can we table this until later? Please? Just tell me. What should I do?"

"You should get yourself castrated." Jeff had a right to be upset, Nick knew, but he was hoping that decades of friendship would count for something. They had been friends since college, both disappointing each over the years, and up until now, he figured they were about even. Nick waited, knowing that anything he offered in the way of an excuse would just piss him off more.

"I'm a civil litigator, not a criminal attorney. I don't give that kind of advice." His voice was calmer but his look was still menacing.

"I need something. Now. Please. Anything. They're calling, any minute now. Should I meet with them? Or should I get a lawyer first? What should I do?" He hated feeling this desperate, being at people's mercy. How had it come to this?

Jeff looked at him and shook his head. Nick waited. Finally, he spoke. "Meet them at your house. You'll be more relaxed. The station is too intimidating. Come clean about the affair. To everyone. If you didn't kill her, there's no evidence, so you should have nothing to worry about. Prints in the house, DNA, whatever, it can all be explained. But if they catch you in a lie, you're toast."

"If I tell them about the affair, it'll destroy my marriage."

"That's the least of your worries. If they ask you and you don't tell them, it'll look worse. Way worse. That in and of itself could be a crime." Jeff's advice was solid. Still, Nick found himself trying to recall if there was any evidence of the affair now that Angie wasn't alive to disclose it.

"You wanted my advice, that's my advice. Take it or leave it. Now I have to get back to work. You can see yourself out." Jeff shooed him out the door. As Nick made his way down the hallway to the elevators, his phone rang, right on schedule.

———

Victoria was home working off some nervous energy as she put the dishes away and wiped yesterday's smudges off the white Shaker cabinet doors. Out the kitchen window, the sun sparkled magically on the Hudson River reflecting the scarlet and gold of the fall foliage clinging to its steep banks. Her melancholy mood from the evening before had turned to excitement, bolstered by a bit too much caffeine on an empty stomach and her Alanis jams playing in the background. She had already called her attorney and had an appointment for next week. She would put all that out of mind until then. Today, she had a meeting scheduled at her office at eleven this morning, an important one, and her benefit dinner tonight. It was now half past nine and she needed to get going. She was almost finished emptying the dishwasher in her methodical manner—only a few cups were left—when her cell phone vibrated against the granite island countertop, its dark surface blending in with the stone. She reached over to grab it. There was a text from her husband: It's an emergency. Call me.

There were also three missed calls from him and a voicemail. Nick was not given to hyperbole. Quite the opposite. He was actually a bit too laid back, never worrying much about anything. He had never sent a text like that before. She called immediately, not bothering to check her voicemail, putting it on speaker as she finished her chores.

"Vic?" His voice was soft, almost apologetic. He didn't seem hurt or in danger.

"Nick. What is it?" She felt mildly annoyed, already.

"I have something to tell you, and I'm warning you it's pretty shocking." Was he actually going to confess about the affair now? Over a cell call? That was totally unlike him.

"I have to get to work, Nick. What's so urgent?" She was starting to wish she'd ignored his text.

"My client. From the Shady Hill property. The one I went to see last night? The police called me. She was found dead. At her house. This morning."

Victoria placed the last clean mug on the counter. Dead? A heart attack or something? No. The police wouldn't call Nick for something like that. There had to be more to it. She picked up the phone and took it off speaker.

"What happened?" She wasn't sure she wanted to know the answer.

"I don't know, but a homicide detective is meeting me at the house any minute now. They called and wanted to meet with me in person. 'See if I could shed some light on it,' was how he put it. Jeff told me to meet them at our house, not at the station."

"Homicide? She was murdered?" Victoria had to hand it to Nick. This certainly reached the bar of 'emergency.'

"They didn't say that, exactly. He said he'd tell me more in person. I don't know much more than you do at this point. What if I was the last person to see her alive, Vic?" Nick's voice was shakier now, almost panicky.

"So? You're certainly not responsible for her death?"

"That's what Jeff said."

"What does Jeff have to do with this? You called Jeff before you called me?" She thought that sounded like the actions of a guilty person, reaching out to your attorney friend. But guilty of what?

"He's an attorney! And he knows her! I told you, remember? They had that law suit going. Let's not do this now. *Please!*" His tone was harsher now, devoid of sentimentality. "I just wanted to give you a heads-up. The detective might get there before I do. They'll probably want to question you too. Tell them I'm on my way. I'd appreciate some support. I'm your husband, Victoria, please try to remember that." He hung up.

She picked up the mug she'd left on the counter, looking out to the sun's rays sparkling on the Hudson, her thoughts suspended in the timeless currents of the flowing river. It was all starting to hit her now, just what a disaster this was. The photos that were supposed to liberate her from the marriage were now a liability, potentially placing her at a crime scene. What do detectives look for? Means, motive, and opportunity? She had two out of three for now. Should she be worried? And what about Nick? He was acting strangely last night, and she'd attributed it to a guilty conscience. The affair, she assumed. But could it have been more? She knew Nick wasn't overtly violent, but anyone could commit murder given the right circumstances. What if the woman had gotten pushy? Demanding? Threatening? How far would Nick go to protect what was his? She needed time to think, consult with an attorney. But she didn't have the luxury of time.

The gate buzzer sounded, jolting her out of her stupor, and the mug slipped from her hand, shattering into pieces on the travertine tile floor. She quickly picked up the big chunks, but the shards of porcelain would have to wait.

FOUR

Jack and Lexi waited at the door of the Mancusio residence for a minute or two before it opened. It was Victoria Mancusio who stood in front of them. Jack had heard her name before. It clicked after the husband gave him the address in Briarcliff Manor and he'd done some digging. It looked a bit above the pay grade of a real estate broker, even a successful one. She was a well-known art dealer specializing in the Hudson River School painters and a respected art historian. He also discovered that she traced her lineage to the original Dutch settlers and had a connection to some Revolutionary Era friend of John Adams, both of which gave her valuable social clout and likely a sizeable trust fund. An address like this would be modest for such a person.

The setting was magnificent, sitting along a dead-end street near Sleepy Hollow Country Club on the edge of the Hudson with views that rivaled the mansions of centuries past, the house itself large but not ostentatiously so. The style was unusually modern for the area, a contemporary Mediterranean, stark white with large windows designed to accentuate rather than compete with the raw beauty of nature.

"Hello, Mrs. Mancusio. I'm Detective Jack Stark, and this is my associate Detective Lexi Sanchez. Is your husband home? We're supposed to meet him here regarding an investigation." Either she had a great poker face or her husband told her they were coming. She was petite and beautiful but not in a flashy way. It was more like she couldn't help attracting attention to herself if she tried.

"Good morning, Detectives. Nick isn't home yet but he asked me to tell you he's on his way. Please come in. By the way, I go by Dr. Mancusio." She said this in friendly tone through a pleasant smile, as if she wasn't reprimanding him but simply pointing out a fact. That confidence was mirrored in her gait as they followed her inside. She had the posture of a recent charm school graduate.

"Please, have a seat." She motioned to the sofa. "Nick told me about his client. How awful. He said to tell you he's on his way. Can I get you anything while you wait? Some coffee, maybe?" She stood there, frozen like a statue, waiting for their response.

Jack and Lexi sat. "Sure, some coffee would be nice." Jack noticed that she wasn't asking any questions about what happened. Most people would ask. Maybe it was just her polite society upbringing, but still. Anyone would be curious. It seemed odd to him.

"How do you take your coffee?"

"Black for me," Lexi said.

"Light and sweet for me." Jack was a New York City deli guy when it came to coffee. He realized after he said it that she might not get his lingo. Then he remembered she'd gone to Columbia for grad school.

"I'll just be a minute." Victoria headed to the kitchen, seeming a bit too eager for the escape. The inside of their home—spacious with a few large pieces of furniture, some tastefully placed pieces of art, and not much else—looked more like a model home than a place where people actually lived. He ran his hand over the buttery soft white leather and looked down at the pristine hardwood floors, free of scuffs. They obviously didn't have any kids.

Lexi was using the lull to look through her notes in more detail. Jack got up and started nosing around the house. They could hear Victoria grinding coffee beans in the kitchen. This might take a while. At least they would get some decent coffee.

"So, what do you think?" Jack flipped into mentor mode. He had been assigned to train Lexi after his last partner retired. It wasn't a job he'd wanted to take on. She was young, eager to learn. She deserved better. She was also pretty enough to be a distraction. But she had grown on him, like a pesky kid sister. She was smart, had great instincts, and extensive training as a profiler but little actual experience at it. Cracking a case like this could take her to the next level.

"She's pretty calm considering we came over here to talk about a dead woman." Lexi was combing through her pages of notes, flipping her dark bangs out of her eyes. He'd filled her in on the way over about Victoria's background, but they hadn't talked too much about other aspects of the case. They both agreed that it was homicide, although technically they were still waiting for the ME's report.

"Maybe it's not that she's calm. Some people freeze up when they get really nervous. What else?" He hung back and let Lexi's wheels turn. The familiar smell of freshly brewed coffee was making its way from the kitchen to the living room but still no sign of Victoria. He heard her clanking around in the kitchen like she was cleaning. Who does that with two detectives in the house?

"The killer. It looks like it was someone she knew. There's no evidence of a break-in. It seems like a crime of passion. It happened at the top of the stairs. She was dressed for a date. She probably let the perp in. So maybe she was heading to the bedroom with someone and changed her mind? It went bad from there?" Lexi added something to her notes and then continued.

"But here's what doesn't make sense. The front door was unlocked, so she probably let the perp in the house. They didn't think to lock it when they left. Not a planner. Not thinking straight. But would someone think to grab a cell and not lock the door? That doesn't make much sense. Maybe they'll find the cell somewhere, but I don't think so. Most people leave their cell phones in plain view. It'll be interesting to see what prints they pick up."

"Yeah. Keep playing out all the scenarios." Jack was standing by the fireplace mantle. Above it was a stunning painting of the Hudson at sunset. A few tastefully framed photos sat on its surface. There was one from Victoria's younger days that caught his eye. It looked like she was in Central Park, the upper part near Columbia. Her long blonde hair was blowing in the wind and she was wearing a flowered sun dress, a retro number. She looked like a model from the seventies. She was looking right into the camera with a smile that could light up the city, the kind that only comes from total abandon. Who was she smiling at? Her husband?

There were other photos of both of them. A wedding photo of the perfect couple. The husband looked like the leading man in a rom-com, for sure her equal in looks if not status. There were a few others of the two of them over the years, one that looked like it was on a beach in Maui he thought he recognized and one in Paris in front of the Louvre. They looked like a happy couple in the photos. But didn't everyone?

"Is she milking a cow in there? She's taking forever." Lexi was biting her bottom lip, tapping her pen on her notebook as she stared at its pages, searching for answers. They heard the click of a doorknob and turned towards it. Nick Mancusio rushed through the front door wearing a movie star smile, apologizing for making them wait. Damn. He'd wanted some time to talk to Victoria alone before her husband arrived.

————

"Detective! I'm Nick Mancusio. Sorry to keep you waiting." Victoria heard Nick introduce himself and decided it was safe enough to make an appearance. She headed in from the kitchen with their refreshments. The two men were standing by the mantle, looking at their photos. Nick was all smiles, his charming self. He didn't look too rattled. Of course, when he got uncomfortable, he could sometimes be too friendly and overly chatty. That would be bad.

"Jack Stark, thanks for coming so quickly. And this is Lexi Sanchez, my associate."

"Lexi Sanchez, nice to meet you, Mr. Mancusio." Sanchez stood up, waved, and relocated herself from the middle to the far end of the sectional.

Victoria proceeded to the living area, placing the silver tray with their coffees and a plate of biscotti on the coffee table. She positioned herself on the other end of the sectional, which would force Nick and Stark to sit kitty-corner. She didn't want to be the center of attention during this inquiry.

"This photo, it's stunning! That's Central Park, up near Columbia, right?" Stark pointed to the photo but stopped short of touching it. He reminded Victoria of that detective her mother used to like. What was his name? Columbo? She'd gotten Victoria to watch a few reruns with her when she was growing up. Although Stark was taller, he gave off the same disarming vibe with his hunched-over posture and quirky, charming affect. She figured it was a contrived persona, crafted to get people talking.

"Yeah, I took that years ago. A hundred-tenth and Central Park West. Good eye! Have a seat, Detective." Nick ushered him to the sofa. The two of them sat, almost simultaneously, Nick close to her and Stark a respectable distance from his colleague.

Nick started in. "So, I know you probably can't tell me much, but this is such a shock. I mean, what happened? Can I even ask that? I'm new to this sort of thing." He shrugged and leaned back a bit, looking totally at ease.

"It's a natural thing to ask." Stark glanced Victoria's way for a moment, then back to Nick. Should she have asked?

"First, Mr. Mancusio, Dr. Mancusio, we really need you both to keep this quiet. I'm sure the press will get wind of it soon enough and all hell will break loose. But we'd like to get a head start before that happens. And this is a friendly chat, of course, but as her realtor, Mr. Mancusio, you're an official part of a police investigation. Anything we disclose should be considered strictly confidential. Understood?" Stark looked serious but friendly, like a doctor telling you to cut back on red meat for your own good. Nick readjusted himself in his seat and cleared his throat. Victoria's stomach grumbled but she didn't move a muscle.

"Understood." Victoria offered.

"Of course," Nick confirmed.

"Detective Sanchez, why don't you fill them in?" Stark leaned back and folded his arms, relaxing into the sofa as he gave his colleague the floor.

"Sure. Ms. Hansen was found dead this morning at the bottom of the stairs in her home, around eight o'clock this morning. She was dressed in what one would assume is evening attire: a fitted red dress and high heels. Her make-up was still on. Not the way a woman dresses for an evening home alone, and not like she was getting ready for bed. We're awaiting cause of death and time of death from the Medical Examiner's office, so that's all we can say for sure right now. I can tell you it does look suspicious, and not like a slip and fall, which is why they called in homicide." She looked over her notes as if searching for something else she could say, and then closed her notebook. She looked up at them. "That's about all I have."

"Nick was just there. Last night." It slipped out, almost as a whisper. Victoria could feel her heart pounding in her chest and wondered if anyone could hear it.

"Last night? Wow, that's lucky for us! Maybe not so much for you, huh?" Stark chuckled and took a sip from his coffee mug as he eyed Nick over its rim, then turned his gaze to her. "This is perfect, Dr. Mancusio. Well worth the wait." They locked eyes momentarily and then he turned back to Nick. "So, why were you there last night, Nick?"

Nick started right in. "Well, I'm Angie's agent, as you know. I went over because her key wasn't working. She was locked out, sort of. I mean, you just have to jiggle it, but she was nervous. She couldn't do it. It was dark. So, I went over to give her mine which works fine. It's newer. The one I gave her, from the seller, at my office earlier that day, it was a little rusty. So that's why I went over. Around seven, I think." He was rambling.

"And why did you have her key?" Stark leaned forward, keeping his gaze on Nick.

"She was still in the city, a lot of the time. We had all kinds of repairs and things to do, so I was always going over and handling things for her, checking on repairs the sellers were doing, stuff like that. The sale was a lot of work, to tell you the truth."

"Well yes, but why did you still have her key? After it closed? I mean, why didn't you give it to her at the office with the other keys?" Stark had his hand on his chin now and was rubbing it with his thumb.

"Um, I left it at my house, I think? Or I just forgot?" Nick was bouncing his leg up and down, shaking the sofa. Victoria placed a hand on his knee to steady him.

"Which is it, you left it at your house or you forgot?"

Nick paused for a moment. "I guess both? I forgot it at my house?" Nick shrugged and threw up his hands.

Stark leaned back again and crossed his arms. He took a pause and sipped his coffee. Sanchez was taking notes, but not him. "And how was she dressed when you arrived?"

"Exactly like you said. Red dress, heels, make up done. I assumed she was coming back from meeting someone, but I didn't ask." Why was Nick volunteering more information than he needed to?

Stark turned to Sanchez. "That's a little early to come back from an evening out, don't you think, Detective Sanchez?" She nodded and flashed him a semi-smile, finally pulling her head out of her notebook. "She's younger than me. She would know. Me, I don't get out much! Okay so, what time did you leave her house?"

"About seven-fifty I think?"

"It took that long to get her in the door?"

"She had some questions about the well and the water pressure, who was responsible now. We were about to close a few weeks ago and then the water ran out. They had to drill a new well. It happens sometimes. There were some problems with the pressure. She was having a plumber come in the morning. I told her it was probably her problem now. She'd signed off."

Stark nodded his head. "And what state of mind was she in when you left?"

"She was fine? I guess? A little on edge. She's from the city. The house is a bit isolated for a woman living alone. I tried to warn her about that, that it would feel different at night, alone, but there was hardly anything else available and she really wanted it. And she's the customer, right?" Nick flashed Stark his best realtor smile, in spite of the fact that anyone could see Stark was immune to that kind of overt manipulation.

Nick continued. "She was planning to do some security upgrades. Soon. Add a security gate, and some other features. We'd gotten quotes but I don't think she'd hired anyone yet."

"So she was fine but little on edge. Understandable. And then what? You came straight home?"

"I stopped at the store. Got some coffee. And champagne. So we could celebrate. This sale was a real nightmare. I haven't been around much lately." Nick looked toward Victoria and she met his glance.

"Yes, you mentioned that. And did you?" Stark took another long sip of his coffee, stopping this time to take in the aroma but keeping his eyes planted on Nick.

"Did I what?" Nick met his stare.

"Celebrate!" A cocky smile lit up Stark's face as he lifted his hand into the air.

"No actually, it was too late by then."

"What time was that?"

"I think I got home around nine?"

"That seems like a long time to run to the store and drive home, over an hour, doesn't it?" Stark looked over at Sanchez again who now seemed riveted by the conversation.

"Yes it does, Detective Stark," she replied.

Nick sat up and leaned forward, his smile morphing into a tight-lipped grimace. "Look, Detective, I wasn't using a stop-watch. It wasn't a race. I guess it could have been earlier. I'd already missed dinner. What difference would it make anyway if I rushed? I think it was around nine when I got home." He pushed back into the sofa and crossed his arms.

Stark sat back, his relaxed posture offering an apology of sorts. "Mr. Mancusio, we're not accusing you of anything, I can assure you. This is standard police procedure. We have to establish a timeline, and unfortunately you are a valuable lead right now. Maybe your wife remembers?" Stark turned to her.

"It was actually a bit past nine when you came home. Maybe nine-fifteen?" Victoria looked at Stark as she spoke, keeping her gaze away from her husband. She couldn't face him just yet. Her mouth was so dry, she barely got the words out.

"Maybe he's particular about his champagne, Jack." All eyes turned to Sanchez. She was sitting up stick straight, glaring at Nick with a stare that could pierce concrete. "Mr. Mancusio, just how well did you know Ms. Hansen?"

Nick squirmed in his seat, fiddling with his hands. "How well? I mean, as well as any realtor knows a client, or maybe a little more. She was new to the area. I spent some time showing her around. She's divorced, no kids, family in Brooklyn like me." Nick sat for a minute with a faraway look in his eyes and then suddenly his face brightened.

"Oh! One thing you may want to know. She was suing her company! She worked as a trader at Jackman Capital, a hedge fund in the city. A big harassment suit. My friend Jeff Malone was handling her case. He referred her to me, actually. That's why she moved away from the city. To get some distance from that situation. She was pretty upset about all of it. Nervous. Her boss was a real bastard, from what she told me."

"That is very helpful information, Mr. Mancusio. Very helpful. It could be important. Could you give us your friend's contact information?" Stark finally jotted something down on his notepad. "And do you have any contact information for her family in Brooklyn?"

"No, I don't even know their names. Jeff might. I'll get you his information."

"That would be great. I think that'll be about it for now. Unless you have something?" He looked over at Sanchez who shook her head. "If you think of anything else that could be important, call me. Anything at all. We're just getting started, folks. We'll be back in touch when we get time of death, hopefully to clear the both of you and put this whole thing behind us. I really do appreciate your cooperation. And I'll grab a few of these for the road, if you don't mind. No breakfast!" He grabbed a few biscotti from the tray. "Thanks again, Dr. Mancusio. That was a nice touch." They all stood up.

As they exchanged information and made their way to the door, Victoria excused herself, taking the dishes with her into the kitchen. She hoped they hadn't noticed her trembling hands which she was trying to steady. All she could think about while they talked was the photo of her husband and the woman in the upstairs window. *She was found at the bottom of the stairs?*

She could still hear them at the front door from her hiding place in the kitchen. "We'll be in touch. Don't leave town or anything!" She pictured Stark's cheesy grin, turning the screws ever so slowly, as the front door closed with a soft bang. She reached for the phone on the kitchen counter, picked it up and dialed. She waited. One ring. Two rings. Pick up, please, pick up. Finally, a click.

"Victoria? What's wrong?" Her mother always seemed to have some sort of sixth sense when it came to her. Mother's intuition, she called it. Or maybe it was the timing. Victoria didn't call her much these days, and never on a weekday. Today she found herself willing to endure whatever came next as she uttered the words her mother lived to hear.

"Mom, I need your help."

———

Nick closed the front door and leaned back against it, finally breathing a sigh of relief. The tip about the law suit seemed to placate Stark, for the moment. It seemed reasonable to him that someone from her company might be out to get her. Hopefully it would seem that way to Stark too. He was certain that they considered him a suspect, even if they didn't put it that way but surely he wasn't the only one. A lot of people could have wanted her dead. How did Jeff put it? She was vulnerable? At first glance maybe, but that vulnerability hid a darker side. He should have listened to Jeff. His ears perked up when he tuned into Victoria in the kitchen, talking on the phone. It sounded like the office. Right, Victoria. His wife. They should probably talk. He headed for the kitchen.

"Yes, Charles, I know how important this meeting is, but I'm telling you I'm not going to make it. It's in five minutes! It was an emergency. It couldn't be helped." A pause. "And I already told you I can't tell you what it is, okay? Just trust me. Please?" She was not quite yelling, but her voice was a few decibels above conversational level. For Victoria, this was frazzled.

"That's a fair point. Okay. Tell Sergei it has to do with something that happened in our neighborhood. A detective wanted to talk to us about it. He'll understand that, right?" A pause. "Yes, of course it's true! Do you think I'd make something like that up? And no, I can't tell you what it's about so don't ask me."

She put the phone on speaker as she poured some coffee in a travel mug and threw some biscotti in a baggie. "And switch the tables. Put him at table two, next to me."

Nick could hear Charles now. "What? He's at table ten now. Do you realize the statement you'll be making?" In their world, this was a big deal.

"Yes, I know what kind of statement I'm making. But what choice do I have? This will soften the blow of my standing him up. Trust me."

"I think I can find a better way to shuffle it. But he'll be at table two. Don't worry. Nate and I will figure it out. Table shuffling is a bit below my pay grade, but I'm sure you'll find a way to make it up to me. I'll see you tonight."

"You're the best. Thanks. Now, I need to go."

"Bye, Victoria."

"Bye, Charles. You're a doll." She hung up, looking a bit calmer now. Nick was full well expecting them to debrief the insanity of the morning. Instead, she grabbed her purse and keys and headed for the door.

"Victoria? Where the hell are you going?" Nick was dumbfounded.

She spun around to face him. "Nick, if you have something to tell me, now is *not* the time. Be ready to go by five. I'll see you later." She grabbed her provisions and headed out the side door to the garage. Nick stood in the doorway as the garage door opened and the car engine started, watching his wife back the car out and drive away to who knew where.

FIVE

Victoria pulled up to the circular drive that fronted her mother's Scarsdale estate. The stately structure stood as it had for a century, tucked away on a country road, an imposing Georgian fortress of brick and stone. She wondered how she could live like this, alone in this expansive and secluded space with her father gone. Wasn't it lonely? Empty? Maybe she should come by more often.

She parked her sporty Mercedes in the circle, shut off the engine, and took a moment to admire the grounds with their meticulously manicured gardens that her mother loved to tend. Despite their issues, her mother was the only person Victoria completely trusted to have her best interests at heart, willing to use all the resources at her disposal to help her. As she started towards the house, she could see her mother waiting at the front door in anticipation.

"Victoria!" Their embrace was a little forced, as usual, but it still felt good. They held it a bit longer this time until her mother released her and stepped back, looking Victoria up and down, taking inventory. "Let me get you some food. You look famished." Her mother was dressed in her usual outfit, slacks and blouse which seemed to hang off her thin frame, her hair tidy and her make up sparse yet flattering.

"I'm not hungry right now mom."

"Humor me, Victoria." She seated herself in the living room as her mother went into the kitchen to get them some refreshments. Perhaps food was a good idea, if not for her then for her mother. Maybe she needed to experience the simple comfort of breaking bread with another person. Her mother could afford more domestic help than she had, but like Victoria, she preferred to tinker around the house herself, in private, and had never opted for live-in help even when Victoria was small. Victoria realized how much she missed her father, sitting in the quiet home that his big personality used to fill. He was the conduit between the two of them, and with him gone, the wedge between them had widened into a chasm. As an only child, she should probably do more to bridge it. She'd just been so wrapped up in her own life these days.

Her mother returned and placed a tray of fruit, cheese, and warm scones on the table, along with two coffees. The smell of the warm pastry brought out her latent hunger. Her mother was right. Again. She reached for a scone and took a bite. She looked around, reminding herself how totally opposite their tastes were. She could be sitting on the set of Downton Abbey.

"So, what's going on?" Her mother didn't look too concerned. She probably thought it had something to do with Nick and the marriage. If only things were so simple.

"I don't know where to start." She felt her heart start to race again as she thought about the visit this morning from the detectives.

"Start at the beginning." Her mother leaned back and folded her arms.

"I mean, I'm not sure how much I can tell you." She took another bite of her scone, feeling her blood sugar return to a more stable place.

"You can tell me anything, Victoria."

"Legally. I'm not sure what I can tell you. Legally."

"Legally?" Her mother's eyes widened. "I don't understand. This isn't about Nick? You and Nick? Your marriage?"

"Not in the way that you think." She bit her lip and looked down.

"I don't know what to think! I wish you would tell me because what I'm imagining is probably far worse!" Victoria doubted that.

"I'll try to tell you what I can, but I need to talk to Harrison before I say too much. To protect you. Do you understand?" It was one of the only times in her life she'd seen her mother speechless. Her mother nodded, finally seeming to grasp the gravity of the situation.

"The police were at the house this morning, questioning Nick. About a client of his who was found dead this morning in her home. Possibly murdered. The home she just bought. From him. And he was there last night. He might have been the last person to see her before whatever happened to her, um, happened."

"Victoria! My goodness. What has that husband of yours gotten you into now?

"Mom, please, let's not do this now, okay?" The last thing Victoria needed was her usual 'I told you so' talk about Nick.

"So you're telling me Nick's a suspect? In a murder?" She stood up as if she was going to walk away but then settled back down again.

"No! I mean, I don't know. He was there last night. The police came by. They questioned him. They haven't ruled it a homicide just yet, but they said it looked suspicious. He's her real estate agent so they wanted to talk to him. The house just closed a few days ago and she's new to the area. He was one of the first people they questioned. But when they found out he was there last night, they got more aggressive."

"And this client of his, she's just a client?" Victoria looked away from her mother into the spacious living room. "Victoria?"

"That's all I can say right now mom."

"But what does this have to do with you? Why do *you* need an attorney?" Victoria turned back to look at her, eyebrows raised. "And you can't tell me."

"Right, mother, I can't tell you."

"Okay then. What? We try to enjoy our coffee and refreshments and change the subject? While we wait?" She took a sip her coffee and tucked a stray hair behind her ear. She seemed to be taking it pretty well, on the surface.

"I guess," Victoria said. "What else can we do?"

"So how are the arrangements coming for your function tonight? You were really looking forward to it. What are you going to wear?"

"I was looking forward to it. Not anymore." What to wear! She hadn't thought about the scrape on her arm. Nothing she had would cover that up. Maybe she could borrow something from her mother.

"You still can be. Looking forward to it, I mean."

"In the middle of all this? I'm not so sure about that." Victoria shook her head. Her eyes felt full and her head was heavy from lack of sleep.

"I'm sure," her mother said, catching her gaze. "I know what you're made of. You're stronger than you think, Victoria. We all need to compartmentalize our lives. You know that."

"I know, mother. Compartmentalize. It's what we do. I've heard it my whole life." At least she'd finally stopped asking about grandchildren. Their fertility issues had caused a big enough strain on their marriage. The pressure of knowing she was her mother's only hope for a grandchild didn't help.

"Victoria, I want to help. I do. Trust me. I know you. I know you didn't do anything wrong, whatever it is you're worried about, and that's all that matters. You'll talk to Harrison. He'll tell you what to do. You'll get it all straightened out. You'll go to your dinner with your husband. You'll give your speech. You'll get through this day. And tomorrow is another day. One day at a time, that's how we get through things."

Victoria was trying to steel herself and live up to her mother's expectations but her lip started to quiver and soon the deluge broke. "It's all such a mess!" Victoria's gut wrenched and she started to cry. It came from a place deep inside her. Her mother reached over and pulled her in, hugging her tight, a real hug this time, like she was trying to keep her from falling into oblivion, as she let her daughter release all of her pent-up emotion.

"It's ok. Let it all out, here, where it's safe." After her sobbing slowed to a trickle and then gave way to acceptance, she sat up, sniffling, her eyes swollen but her mind clearer. There was something purgative about a good cry. Her mother wiped the remaining tears from under her eyes and brushed the stray hairs away from her face in a rare moment of tenderness. It felt nice, like she was a child again.

She got up and went to get a tissue, stopping to look at some photos on the wall of her family. They were all happy ones, the face they showed the world. She turned back to look at her mother, a hint of who she might become. She could see the resemblance now more clearly. She sat back down and forced herself to eat some fruit.

"Why does my function have to be tonight, of all nights? On the heels of all this chaos?"

"It's not our place to question these things. We just do our best to carry on. It's an important evening. You've worked so hard for everything. Don't let this incident tarnish you."

"Right, mother. I won't do anything to tarnish the family name."

"Victoria! Is that really how you see me? What do I care about the name? I have more money than I'll ever spend. I don't concern myself with what people think for my sake. I do it for the greater good. You still don't see this? Families like ours, we're the bedrock of civilization. We have to set an example. It's a weighty responsibility, and you're old enough to understand that now. People are counting on you. Keep your troubles in the shadows. Whatever your problems, people have bigger ones." Maybe, but hers weren't exactly trivial. Victoria knew she would pull herself together and go, but she wished her mother would be a bit more empathetic. She thought about Nick's mother. She was so warm. So cozy and affectionate. Even when they'd first met.

The buzzer sounded. Harrison was at the gate, and her mother got up to let him in. As she watched her mother walk away, she wondered if she ever allowed herself any private moments of weakness or vulnerability. Victoria's mind flashed back to a time years ago when she'd buried her troubles in the shadows. What if she had done something about it back then? Would things have been different?

"Harrison, it's lovely to see you. Come in! Thanks for coming on such short notice."

"Of course, Sandra! Anything for you and Victoria. So, ladies, what seems to be the trouble?" Victoria asked her mother to excuse herself and proceeded to give Harrison the run down. She hoped her mother's total faith in him was well placed. Stark was pretty street smart. A white shoe like Harrison might be a bit out of his element in a situation like this.

———

It was now after one o'clock and Jack was famished. He strapped himself in and started the car. While they were in the interview, the Medical Examiner's office had called and left a message. It was officially being ruled a homicide. Time of death was between 8:30 and 9:30 the night before. Cause of death and lab results would take more time. There was no sign of a sexual assault or sexual intercourse of any kind.

A phone call with Jeff Malone confirmed what Mancusio had told them. The victim was suing her former company and its principal for sexual harassment and discrimination regarding a promotion she didn't get. The principal was a hedge fund guy named Randy Jackman, an up-and-comer. She was claiming that she didn't get the promotion because she rejected his unwanted sexual advances. Malone mentioned the fact that the firm was represented by big guns who seemed like they were preparing to settle, but they hadn't gotten an offer yet. Overall, it had been a productive morning. Jack was anxious to get back to the precinct and keep the momentum going.

They'd picked up some sandwiches at the deli and as soon as they got in the car, Lexi started right in on hers. The smell made his mouth water.

"Go right ahead, Lex! Don't let the fact that I'm totally starving over here have any bearing on your actions whatsoever."

She mumbled something he couldn't understand with her mouth full of sandwich. Something about camaraderie? She held up her finger, swallowed, and tried again.

"You ate all the biscotti." Ah, now that made more sense. Had he not offered her one? What a Neanderthal. She was a tiny little thing, and he had a lot more to draw on for reserves.

"Fair enough. I'll go first and you eat. It's not good to talk with your mouth full. Just nod if you agree." She shook her head and kept chewing.

"She was dressed to meet someone, and that someone may or may not have been the killer. No sign of sexual intercourse. We know she came home dressed like that around seven, assuming we can believe Nick Mancusio. Who was she meeting? That's the first question." Jack repositioned the car visor as the sun nearly blinded him when he turned right towards the precinct.

Lexi took a break from her sandwich. "Ok, I'll play along. Mancusio was telling the truth. He was there from seven-thirty to seven-fifty last night. He told us he assumed she was coming home from meeting someone. So maybe she had a quick date? Like a dating app meet up? She wasn't into it and left? He followed her home? Not likely, but we could run it down and see. Whoever it is, she probably let them in."

Jack continued. "Then there's the distinct possibility that Nick Mancusio knows her a little better than he let on. He was sleeping with her, but he's got no intention of leaving his wife. I'm sure there's a prenup. He goes there last night when she calls. She's expecting some romance. He tries to break it off?

She gets demanding? It goes bad? It's more than plausible. Let's see what he can produce in terms of an alibi."

"I think there's a good chance he was sleeping with her, but I'm not sure about the rest of it. It could have been anyone she was meeting, but since she just moved here, he seems a pretty safe bet. Who else did she know up here?" Lexi looked through her notes. "Malone? I guess he could have been sleeping with her, for all we know, but he's lost a potential fortune now that she's dead, and it looks like he's put in a ton of hours he'll never recoup. Plus, he was flying back from Chicago that night. That checked out."

"She could have met a lot of other people we don't know about. We'll run it all down, tire tracks, camera footage. But remember, the person she was dressed up for, that doesn't have to be the killer."

"Remember Malone mentioned the guy she was suing? He wasn't taking it well. He was angry. I'm sure the firm has insurance, but it's not just about the money. He's high profile. She had the potential to ruin his reputation. That could drive him to try to silence her." Lexi was making a good point. They needed to check him out and fast. But guys like that could usually make problems like this go away with money.

"No shortage of people with motive on this case. And then there's all the other random crazies out there. The house isn't exactly Fort Knox. Someone could have gotten in somehow, so we can't dismiss a random burglary just because there wasn't an obvious sign of a break in, at least until forensics is done. Does that about cover it?"

"You're missing one obvious suspect, Jack!" Lexi looked at him in disbelief.

Jack looked over at her as he pulled into the station and parked the car.

"Who?"

"Come on Jack! Really? The wife?"

"Well, yeah, I guess, sure. She was acting a bit cagey. Maybe she knows about the affair. But wouldn't she just divorce him? I mean she's loaded. Why kill the woman? Seems like she's got a lot to lose." He took out his sandwich and tried to get in a few bites before they headed in. The parking lot was packed already.

"Anyone could commit murder given the right circumstances. She's hiding something, we both know it. Stalling in the kitchen, not making much eye contact. I don't know what it is she's not telling us, but she's hiding something." Lexi wrapped up the rest of her sandwich, put it in her carry bag, and checked her teeth in the visor mirror.

"True. I shouldn't have dismissed her out of hand. It could be anyone at this point."

"You wouldn't be the first guy to be fooled by a femme fatale. Women can be murders too, Jack, especially when it comes to love."

"I didn't dismiss her because she's a woman, I dismissed her because she's loaded. Is an affair really that big of a deal for a woman of her means? Something to kill over?" He flashed back to Lexi's interrogation of Nick Mancusio and instantly regretted what he'd said.

"Is it a big deal? An affair? Yes, Jack! What if she actually loves him? It's one of the biggest deals there is! I mean, what does it say about..." She stopped herself, pausing as if she wished she could hit rewind. "Never mind. Just forget it. It's not that important. I shouldn't be getting so emotional about this." She redirected her gaze out her side window.

It seemed like everyone on the force including Lexi knew the sordid details of his divorce, and he hadn't been personalizing what she was saying, but it was gracious of her to stop herself in her tracks. Gracious, but obvious. He didn't want this to turn into a thing.

"You're right. It's a big deal, Lex. She's an obvious suspect if her husband was sleeping with the victim. Being wealthy doesn't make her immune to emotional reactions. I was blinded by biscotti, what can I say?"

"I like the husband more for it too, or maybe the boss, but I'm just saying, everyone in the victim's circle is a suspect until they're cleared. She deserves that much. I think both of them are hiding something, and I want to know what it is."

"Understood. And I learned another really important thing today."

"What's that?"

"Don't cheat on Lexi." She flashed him an eye roll. Jack's phone rang, and he was grateful for the diversion.

"Jack Stark here," he said, his phone on speaker.

"This is Harrison Dalton from Spencer, Dalton, and Brewster. I'm calling on behalf of Dr. Victoria Mancusio. We would like to come down this afternoon to make a statement. Say around two p.m.?"

"We'll be here."

"Excellent. We'll see you then." Dalton hung up and Jack smiled at Lexi, not quite an 'I told you so' smile, but close.

———

Nick was finishing up a workout on his Peloton. He was drenched in sweat. It was helping him to clear his head as he worked through the morning's events. Victoria was obviously rattled too, although she hid it better than he did in front of the detectives. He'd tried hard not to outright lie to the detectives, but they could probably read between the lines. Jeff was right. He should have come clean about the affair right away. But he hadn't. Could that be considered obstruction of justice? He needed to talk to an attorney. Fast. Jeff had called and left him the name of a criminal defense attorney and he'd already put in a call to her. All he wanted was to put all this behind him. His phone rang, a familiar caller this time. They were practically old friends now.

"Mr. Mancusio?"

"Yes, Detective Stark, what can I do for you?" He was a bit out of breath but he was trying to mask it.

"I'm wondering if you can provide us with some documentation to confirm your whereabouts from the time you arrived at the victim's house to the time you arrived home last night. We're trying to clear you. Do you have anything that can verify the timeline you gave us?"

"I probably have receipts somewhere. I paid with a credit card. Around eight-thirty last night? Would that work? I can get that over to you this afternoon."

"That would be very helpful. Can you come in at three-thirty this afternoon?"

"Yes, that works." What else could he say? Nick really wanted to talk to Victoria first, but he had no idea where she was and she wasn't answering his calls or texts.

"What about GPS on your car? Or phone? Anything like that?"

"I can get that for you. It doesn't work very well up the hill by her house, but I can give you what I have."

"That's fine. We're in the process of gathering any camera footage in the area near her home too. We're trying to corroborate your story. If you think of anything else that could verify your whereabouts, let us know. In the meantime, we'll also be checking camera footage of your route, so please write that down for us."

"I'll do that." Nick felt his stomach sink.

"I'll also need you to gather the clothes you were wearing that night, and your shoes. We're processing the scene. We already know you were there, so your shoe prints and fibers are there, but we need to be able to separate the wheat from the chaff. I also need the make and model of your tires so we can eliminate your tire tracks from the mix." Stark's tone was friendly, more friendly than before. Did that mean anything?

"Of course. I'll bring them in the morning. Were you able to meet with Jeff Malone? About the law suit?" Nick thought back to Stark's expression when he'd told them about it. He'd seemed excited to get that tidbit of info.

"I'm not really able to comment on that."

"Right. Well, I'll see you at three-thirty with everything you requested."

"Perfect. See you then."

Nick wiped off the sweat with his towel and took a long swig from his water bottle. He went to look for his shopping bag from the night before. It wasn't lying around anywhere but he didn't remember throwing it out. He went to the kitchen garbage but it had been recently emptied. He proceeded to the trash bin in the garage. The kitchen bag was on top but it was only half full. He opened it up and his bag was there, pretty much intact, along with the receipts, one for the coffee stamped 8:20, and one for the champagne at 8:31. He was about to close it up when a bright teal item caught his eye, looking out of place among the muted tones of their kitchen refuse. He gingerly extracted it from the coffee grinds and egg shells. It was Victoria's blouse.

He was slowly unfurling it when his eyes focused in on the blood stains on the right sleeve, hitting him like a gut punch. He thought he'd seen Victoria's car that night, near Angie's house. This validated what his intuition had been telling him. She was hiding something. She certainly hadn't been wearing that on her trail run at Rockefeller. Just what the hell was going on? He placed it into his shopping bag and proceeded to sort through the rest of the kitchen waste. Satisfied that there was nothing more of interest to him, he closed it up, placed it in the bin and put the trash out to the curb. As he was walking back into the kitchen, his phone buzzed with an alert: Death of woman found this morning in Pocantico Hills ruled a homicide. Police chief to brief public shortly.

SIX

The phone hadn't stopped ringing at the Tarrytown police station since the press briefing. The quaint brick building sat on the edge of the Hudson River across from the train depot near the center of the village. Lexi was inside, leading a team handling the influx of calls. They'd also been hosting a steady stream of walk-ins. Jack had been interviewing a select few of them for nearly hour. Only one had provided any useful information, the proprietor of a local coffee shop in Tarrytown— The Hollow—who mentioned that Angie Hansen had been in a few times a week, alone, over the last month or so. She would sit for hours, working on her computer. She was described as friendly but reserved, seemed like a nice lady. Maybe she was waiting for a lover. Or she was hiding from her former employers in the city. Or maybe some stalker was watching her and followed her home. All three were plausible at this point, and not mutually exclusive.

Mostly, it was neighbors coming by looking for information, concerned about random violence. Then there were the more imaginative folks, an inevitability in an area whose spectral history was as much of a tourist attraction as its physical one: an elderly man who claimed he had proof that the house had a history of being haunted by a previous owner who'd died there, a local medium who posited that the victim was a reincarnation of one of the Van Tassels—a local family with historical roots, fictionalized and made famous in Irving's *The Legend of Sleepy Hollow*. One more and he would take a welcome break from this.

A tall, lanky man made his way over, and Jack took the opportunity to take a sip of his acidic, lukewarm cup of office coffee. The rancid liquid burned his throat, reminding him of his upcoming meeting with Victoria Mancusio and her smooth dark roast which went down like velvet. She'd spoiled him forever.

"Detective Stark, I'm Wade Higgins. I have information about this case that might be of value to you." He was thin with sandy brown hair, mid-twenties, dressed in jeans and a brown tweed coat that looked like it had come from a second-hand store. He didn't appear wealthy enough to be the victim's contemporary, but then you never knew these days. Jack didn't dare hope for anything major, but it would be nice to get something—anything—of value.

"Thanks for coming by Mr. Higgins. So how exactly can you help us? Did you know the victim? Did you see something?"

"I didn't know her, exactly. And I didn't see anything, exactly. But I know something." Higgins paused for a moment and Jack forced himself to play along.

"I'm not sure what you mean by that. Have you seen her around? Did you see something at her home on the night in question?"

"Detective, I'm a respected member of the community. I have a real job. I'm in the tech business. I'm a programmer. I'm not a lunatic. But I have certain other, well. . . talents, if you will, and some people are more open to considering them than others. I don't use these talents for profit." His neck twitched as he ran his hand through his hair.

"And what kind of talents do you have?" Jack fought to suppress an eye roll.

"I get feelings, about people."

"What kind of feelings?"

"I feel their feelings. It's not like I read their minds, but it's like I'm inside their heads, I can sense how they feel. I can't see the future, but I can feel what they feel. So, in that way, I can somewhat predict their actions. It's actually very similar to how an algorithm functions, so it's probably not a coincidence that my job is connected to my...um...unique ability."

"And you felt this about the victim? Is that what you're saying? You felt her feelings?"

"No. Not the victim. The killer. I felt the feelings of the killer." Higgins looked away and then back at him, as if he was trying to remember it more clearly. Jack was all ears now.

"Okay then. What did this killer look like? Can you tell us anything about that?"

"I don't know what they look like. I don't see visions of them, Detective. I just feel their feelings. Sometimes I don't even know who it is or why I'm getting the feeling, so I just ignore it. But this time, when I heard about the case, it clicked. I felt his feelings last night. I'm sure of it."

"And what exactly did this killer feel?"

"Well, it's hard to put it into words exactly. But I'll say this. It's a male. He knew what he was doing was wrong but he couldn't stop himself. He's losing control. He will strike again. I know this might sound crazy to you, but please, consider what I'm saying. Give my information to a profiler. Let them work on it. It can't hurt, can it?"

"No, it can't hurt. I'll pass on what you told me, Mr. Higgins, you have my word. And I'm so sorry. I'm going to have to cut this short. I have another meeting. But do you have a card or anything? I'd really like to follow up with you and pursue this further. Truthfully, I'm a little skeptical about this sort of thing as a general rule, but you're correct, there's no harm in checking it out to the degree we can. Would you be willing to help us if we need more information?"

"Sure, but chances are, that's all I'm going get. I've told you all I know. It's not like I can control it. It comes when it comes. But here's my card. Call me any time. I live right in Tarrytown. I work from home."

Higgins made his way through the crowded office and left out through front door. Jack went to find Lexi and found her finishing up a call. He filled her in on their conversation.

"Run down everything you can find on Higgins. Put a tail on him and start a work up. This nut job just become our newest suspect. Can you start on this while I get the Mancusio interview going? Sorry, it'll be recorded. But I don't want him to get away from us."

"Are you kidding? Give me that card!" Lexi was beaming, eager to finally put her extensive profiling training to use, and Jack chuckled to himself. *Well, Wade Higgins, I'm a man of my word. I gave your information to a profiler.*

"So what else did you find out?" Lexi asked.

"The owner of The Hollow came in. He said that Angie Hansen used to hang out there. She would sit and work on her computer for hours at a time. Started a few months ago. But she wasn't there the day of the murder. She pays with a credit card and he claims there was no record of her coming in."

"You think someone could have seen her there? Fixated on her? Followed her?"

"It's more than possible. She was attractive, in a way that would stand out. Maybe not in Manhattan, but here for sure. The owner gave me a list of regulars that come in. We can start with the ones who sit and hang out." He handed them to Lexi. "Why don't you run background on them? I'll make time to stop by and interview them when we have time. We can both spend some time there observing people, see what develops."

"Did she ever meet anyone there that he knew of?" Lexi asked.

"Nope. Not that he saw. She mostly sat by herself."

"Well, it makes sense if what Mancusio told us is right. If she was moving here and she didn't want to hang out in the city, it's a logical place to sit and work."

"Especially if she was having a relationship with someone. Or even an affair, perhaps?"

"Perhaps." Lexi said.

"What about you? Did you get anything useful?" Jack asked.

"No. Just a bunch of panicked neighbors worried about a serial killer. It's a good thing we didn't release the information about the choking. We'd have full on hysteria."

"Let's look over the details again." Jack looked over his notes as he rubbed his chin with his thumb. "Time of death was between eight-thirty and nine-thirty. They think she died almost instantly, based on the wound and the blood loss. If Mancusio is telling the truth and he left before eight, someone came to the door. Sometime between eight and nine. She opened the door and let them in. But she didn't lock it behind her. And her prints weren't on the knob. Nobody's prints were on the inside and only the plumber's prints were on the outside. Would someone think to wipe the prints and not lock it?"

"Maybe?" Lexi pursed her lips. "And she was drinking a glass of wine. Alone? Some people do that. But what if there was another person there and they took the other glass with them?"

"It's possible. Let's check the moving inventory and count the glasses. See if you can find a missing wine glass. Even if they don't list the number of glasses, if there's an odd number of the same style, then it's likely she had company."

"Good idea."

"Having the inventory really makes it a whole lot easier. We can tell what's missing. We can see if her valuables were taken. And you realized that right away. Good work, Lex."

"Thanks. I'll stay on the inventory and Higgins and you go do the interviews. It'll go faster that way. I can review the tapes later."

"You got it." Jack went out to greet Victoria Mancusio, trying not to get his hopes up of finding anything useful. Over the years, he'd learned to manage his expectations but not his insomnia. This was exactly the kind of case that would keep him up at night. He could feel it already.

SEVEN

"Dr. Mancusio, it's nice to see you again. And so soon! Please have a seat." Stark had his friendly face on. Victoria wondered how long that would last.

"I'm Harrison Dalton from Spence, Dalton, and Brewster and I represent Dr. Mancusio. She's here to make a statement. This isn't a social call." Harrison was in his late forties but he had the countenance of an older man. That might annoy a guy like Stark.

"Understood, Counselor. Whenever you're ready, Dr. Mancusio." They all sat down.

"What I'm about to tell you is highly personal." She felt for a moment like she might be sick. "And this is difficult for me. I'm a very private person, Detective Stark. I would appreciate your discretion."

"Take a moment if you need one." Stark looked to her, and then to Harrison, like he could wait all day.

"What Dr. Mancusio means is that we understand it's a murder investigation, but she would like to avoid any gratuitous disclosing of information that's not directly related to the crime." Harrison came across firm but respectful.

"I appreciate Dr. Mancusio's position, but I can't make any guarantees. We'll do our best. Would you like to get started?" Stark was leaning back now, relaxing a bit, like he was trying to make her feel more comfortable. She nodded back at him.

She took a deep breath and sat up straighter. "My husband was having an affair with the victim."

"And how long have you known about this?"

"I've suspected it for a few weeks, but I confirmed my suspicions more recently." She paused but tried to stay very still. She thought fidgeting would make her look guilty of something. "Last night, in fact. I found out last night."

"Last night? And how did you find out last night?" Stark sat up and leaned in.

She suddenly felt a bit claustrophobic, like her collar was too tight. She put her hand to her neck and stroked it. The air in the room was stale, the smell of sweat lingering under the cleaning fumes. The bright lights beamed down on her.

"I was there. At the victim's house. I heard Nick leave our home, a bit after seven. I made a spontaneous decision to follow him over there. I didn't really have a plan for what I was going to do, but I needed to know the truth. I arrived at the house around seven-thirty. I saw his car was there. I waited for a bit and then I saw them in an upstairs window. Embracing. Then kissing. I was able to snap some photos. I needed them as proof, to trigger the prenuptial agreement. After I got the photos, I left and drove home, a bit before eight. I got home about eight-fifteen." She felt relieved to finally get this off of her chest.

"Did your husband see you?"

"No. Well, not that I know of. I parked on Shady Hill Road and walked in. I got a nasty scrape, on my arm. It was dark. I fell. I'll show you." She took off her jacket, rolled up her blouse sleeve, and showed him the scrape. "Right here. I grabbed some tree branches to break my fall when my toe hit a rock. That's how I got this."

"And then you came straight home?"

"Yes. Well, I had to pull over for a bit. On Bedford. I was very shaken up. I had suspected up until that point, but I didn't know for sure. It was emotional, more emotional than I expected to tell you the truth. I needed to compose myself. I got home around eight-fifteen. Detective Stark, I was there, I saw them, but I had nothing whatsoever to do with her death. My objective was to obtain proof of the affair so that if I chose to file for divorce, my assets would be protected."

"And you have documentation to verify all of this?"

Harrison took over. "Yes, here's a file with everything we have. It includes time stamped photos, her GPS records, phone records of her call to her attorney making an appointment for next week, along with a signed affidavit from him confirming that Dr. Mancusio wanted to meet to discuss the terms of the prenuptial agreement and possibly file for divorce. We also brought along the shoes she was wearing that evening so you can match it with her shoeprints on the road." He handed them the file and a bag.

"And, Dr. Mancusio, why didn't you tell us this when we were at your house this morning?"

"Isn't that obvious, Detective?" Harrison's tone was firmer now, protective.

"Maybe, but we still need an answer. Dr. Mancusio, why didn't you tell us this when we were at your house yesterday?" Stark leaned forward, ramping up the pressure. Sweat beads formed at her temples.

"When you said that she was found at the bottom of the stairs, I decided it was in my best interest not to disclose this in front of Nick. Not until I had more information."

"That's understandable given the situation." He leaned back. "Did you see anything at all to indicate that your husband and the victim were arguing or having any kind of altercation?"

"No, I didn't."

"And your husband was still there when you left?"

"Yes."

"And you didn't see him again until he came home?"

"Right."

"And what time was that again?"

"About nine-fifteen."

"So you left her home at about seven-fifty-five and you didn't see your husband again until nine-fifteen?"

"Yes, that's correct."

"And I have to ask you this. Dr. Mancusio, do you think your husband could have committed this crime?"

She didn't hesitate. "No, I don't. He's never been violent with me. We argue, of course, but he rarely gets angry. He's never been in a rage or out of control. I've never been afraid of him…" The last statement come out almost as a question.

"But? I sense a 'but' in there."

She took a deep breath, looked down, and then looked back up at Stark.

"I don't think he's capable of it, but I can't be certain until you catch whoever did this and clear him. My primary objective in coming here was to clear myself. And I'm also willing to aid in any way I can to help you catch the real perpetrator. I really don't think he did it, but I need to be certain and so does the public, or this will hang over our heads forever, especially with a family background like mine. I'm prepared to make an anonymous donation of a hundred thousand dollars towards a reward for any information that leads to the arrest of her killer, whether it's my husband or not. For the victim who deserves justice, for my peace of mind, and to protect my reputation."

"We can circle back to your generous offer in a moment. But I can tell you that if all of this checks out and nothing turns up to the contrary at the crime scene, you're out of the time of death window. We'll also need to check your car to try and match the tire tracks. I'm afraid I need to ask you one more question and it's a bit personal."

"Personal? This whole matter is personal, Detective Stark," Harrison said.

"Yes, but this is a bit more, how can I put it, indelicate? We have our reasons for asking, rest assured." Stark swallowed and then resumed. "Dr. Mancusio, have you and your husband ever engaged in any sort of rough sex?" She looked at him, puzzled. "Let me be more specific. Have the two of you ever engaged in a form of choking as foreplay? Some people are into that. No judgement! But it is relevant in terms of the state of the victim's body. And this time I'm asking for your discretion, as this is not something we plan to release to the general public but it's relevant to our investigation."

"No! Nothing like that. It wasn't like that at all." She paused as the implication sunk in. "At least not with me." She looked down. It was awkward for all of them.

"Okay. I'm sorry we had to ask you that. I really am." Stark looked sincere.

"Getting back to your offer of a reward, I'm not sure now is the time. People are coming out of the woodwork with erroneous information. You know how people are. I can't stop you from offering it, but I would ask that you wait a bit. See what we can find out on our own. We're running down a number of leads. Maybe one of them will pan out. In the meantime, there is another way you might be able to help."

"How is that?" She already felt like this was going to be a no, just based on the way he said it, and he hadn't even asked her yet.

"Well, are you going to tell your husband about what happened here today?"

"Yes. As soon as I get home."

"Are you worried about your husband's reaction when you tell him?"

"Not really."

"Most people in your situation would be concerned."

"I've taken a few precautions. To check against any kind of negative reaction on Nick's part." She tucked a stray hair behind her ear and looked to Harrison.

"What kind of precautions?"

"Go ahead," Harrison said.

"I changed my will today, and my life insurance. The house is our only marital asset, and whatever is in our joint checking. The rest of my trust, the bulk of my wealth, is separate. We don't live on that money. We maintain our lifestyle on what we earn. In the event of a divorce, my other assets would be protected by the prenuptial agreement if I could prove infidelity. But today I realized that in the event of my death, he would have a valid claim to it. We have no children as of yet. I changed that today. Nick inherits nothing except the house in the event of my death, and my life insurance pays out to my foundation."

"I see. And you're planning to tell him this when you tell him about the photos? And about your coming down here? And you're not the least bit concerned?" Stark's eyebrows raised as he held her gaze.

"Well, yes, I was planning on it. He's been caught cheating. I know him pretty well. I expect he'll be contrite."

"When you tell him, would you be willing to help us solve the case and protect yourself at the same time?"

"How would I do that?"

"Wear a wire? If we could hear his reaction to your revelations, it would give us a good read on him and how we feel about his guilt or innocence. We would also be right outside, in case it went bad." Stark must have been considering Nick a strong suspect. This line of questioning seemed like more than a formality. Maybe he had some kind of evidence he wasn't sharing with her. Even so, she couldn't bring herself to wear a wire. There was just no way. There would be no turning back from a move like that, and she just wasn't ready. Besides, the thought of people sitting in a van? Listening to her most private moments?

"No. I can't do that. A conversation like that is highly personal. I'm not comfortable having people listen in. Surely you can understand that." There was no way.

"We want to look out for your safety, Dr. Mancusio. What if it goes bad?"

"First of all, I'm sure Nick didn't do this. He couldn't! And he's not foolish. He would know that if anything happened to me, it would all be over for him. He has everything to gain with me alive, by his side, standing by him through this. And nothing to gain if I'm dead."

"You don't know what could happen if he snaps. What if he snapped with Angie Hansen? Can you think about it?"

"No, I'm sorry, this is between Nick and me. I need to talk to him in private. Tonight. I can handle him, don't worry about me." She shot Harrison a look. Why wasn't he jumping in? What exactly was she paying him for?

"Detective Stark, my client came here to clear herself and that's all she's required to do. She's given you valuable information about her husband and the victim. If she decides that she needs your protection, she will be in touch. Let us know if you would like to take advantage of my client's generous offer of a reward. Aside from that, she has nothing more to say." Victoria and her attorney stood up and Stark followed suit.

"Thank you, Dr. Mancusio, for your time. We really appreciate it. I'll see you tonight."

"Tonight?" Victoria's heart raced. Was he planning to question Nick? Arrest him?

"Your function. The force has a table every year. Courtesy of the foundation. Or did you forget?" Stark smiled at her reaction, obviously trying to rattle her.

"Of course. Right. It's nice that you can make it." Victoria pictured Stark standing in the sidelines watching their every move. This was a disaster.

"We're very supportive of your work. It's a team effort. In school, off the streets, right?"

"Right! Well, we'll see you there." She needed to find the killer, fast, before this took over their entire lives.

They walked out of the precinct to a swarm of reporters who hadn't been there just an hour before. Flash bulbs blinded her as they made their way to the car—Harrison shielding her as best he could. She couldn't see the reporters but she could hear them loud and clear.

"Are you here in connection with the Shady Lane murder?"

"Was your husband the victim's real estate agent?

"What's your connection to the victim?"

"What kind of relationship did your husband have with the victim?"

Harrison ferried her into his car and turned back to them as he closed the door, tucking her safely away in the passenger seat for the ride back to her mother's house.

"Dr. Mancusio has no comment at this time." Harrison got in and started the car.

As they drove away, she looked back at the crowd, an angry mob hungry for blood. It was too late. This had already taken over her life. Now the question was how could she get it back?

———

It was hard to believe it had all started early that morning. The higher ups were already pressuring them. This kind of high-profile case demanded answers. Faster than they could get them. The timing was terrible, with the region hungry for tourism dollars. Business owners worried about cancellations. Residents worried about a killer on the loose. But he knew an investigation like this would take time. Blunt force trauma was the cause of death, which usually indicated a crime of passion. Their prime suspect was on his way in, an affable real estate broker with no track record of violent behavior.

"Mr. Mancusio, come in. Thanks for coming by today."

"My pleasure, Detective Stark."

"I'm Silvia Murray and I represent Mr. Mancusio. Before you get started with the questioning, Mr. Mancusio would like to make a statement, if that's amenable to you."

"I have no objections," Jack replied. Murray needed no introduction and she knew it. Everyone in their business had heard her name, and Jack had personally faced off against her many times.

Mancusio began. "I was having an affair with the victim. I didn't say anything to you in front of my wife earlier today for obvious reasons. I'd like to tell you everything that happened that night, if that's okay."

"That's kinda why we're here."

"Lose the sarcasm, will you Stark? He's not a hardened criminal. It's not like he does this every day." Murray peered at him over her reading glasses, looking straight into his eyes. He could see the faint hint of a smile.

"Sarcasm? Counselor, you overestimate me!" Jack enjoyed sparring with Murray. She was a worthy adversary. He was sure she felt the same. "Continue, please, Mr. Mancusio."

"I'd been trying to break it off for weeks. I thought she'd finally accepted things. Then Angie called me last night saying she couldn't get the key to work. I thought it was just an excuse, but when I got there, it really was sticking. Then she asked me in. She wanted me to have a drink with her. I told her no, I couldn't do that. But she was really nervous, staying alone the first night. I felt bad. It's kinda creepy there at night. So, I went upstairs with her and we turned on the lights, looked all around, and I showed her nobody was there. Then when we were near her bedroom, she tried to get me to, um, change my mind.

"By that you mean sleep with her?" Jack asked.

"Yes."

"And then what?"

"I told her no. I walked out of the bedroom and we were standing, talking, outside her room in the hallway. She started crying. I felt really bad. I hugged her and told her I was sorry. For everything. But I had to go back home. What else could I do?"

"And then?" Jack tapped his pen on his notepad while he waited.

"That was it. We walked downstairs and I left."

"When you got there, she asked you to have a drink with her but you said no. Was she drinking?"

"No, not that I saw. She'd just gotten in the door when I came."

"What does she normally drink?"

"We'd only been out a few times, so I can't speak to normally. Mostly she drank white wine when she was with me."

"So you were upstairs with the victim around what time?"

"Around seven-thirty." That coincided with what his wife said and with the photos and the time stamps, but that didn't mean much to Jack. Maybe they were in it together, covering for each other. Or maybe he didn't leave when he said he did.

"Did you happen to notice if she locked the door behind you?" Jack asked.

"No, I didn't notice, but I can't imagine that she wouldn't lock it. Why?"

"We're asking the questions here!" His tone was sharper than he'd intended.

"Detective Stark, let's keep this civil, shall we? My client is under no obligation to be here. He's not under arrest, and the Mancusios are practically doing your job for you. One more crack like that and we're gone." Murray was a total shark. A top choice if you wanted to beat a murder rap. The kind of lawyer you picked if you had something to worry about.

"Glad to see you're earning your keep, Counselor. But let me remind you. He was at the crime scene last night and he's already lied to us about his relationship with the victim. You wanna roll the dice with the DA on a charge of withholding information on a felony murder case? Or can I keep going?" Jack was in no mood for games. The pressure was building to make an arrest, and they didn't have time for this.

"Ask me whatever you want, Detective Stark. I have nothing to hide."

"So you left. And what time was that?"

"I guess it was around seven-fifty?"

"And then what?"

"As I said, I went to the store in Sleepy Hollow. I have the receipts here."

"That's helpful, thanks. So we have the photos and the receipts. And your GPS, with some of it in the dead zone. Seems like you left her home for the store before our time of death window, but here's the problem. You didn't get home until nine-fifteen. It's less than a ten-minute drive from the store to your home. We can't verify your whereabouts from eight-thirty to nine-fifteen. So maybe she called you? Threated to tell Victoria? You went back and took care of it, once and for all?"

"No! I was just sitting in my car. Thinking. I was thinking about if I should tell Victoria. Thinking about how I'd messed everything up. I really felt bad about Angie, okay? It wasn't just physical. I cared about her. As a person."

"That's touching," Jack said. Murray shot him a look. "So were you thinking about leaving your wife?"

"No! I cared for Angie, but I love my wife. It happens. Sleeping with her was a mistake. But I didn't hurt her! You have to believe me. I'm not that kind of guy."

"What kind of guy are you?"

"The kind of guy who can care about two women. The kind to have a mistress, like pretty much the entire line of males in my family dating back to the Roman Empire. I know women these days won't put up with it, and I accept that. In ten years of marriage, I've never cheated. Before this, I mean. I play a little catch and release now and then, but that's about it."

"Catch and release?"

Murray whispered something in his ear. "No, I'm not going to stop. He needs to know who I am! Catch and release. You know, go out, flirt, pretend I'm not married. Get a number and then throw it away. It's harmless. But Angie was different. We connected. We're cut from the same cloth. It was comfortable. Victoria's family never thought I was good enough for her. But it was a mistake. I'm married. And I love my wife. Angie knew that going into it."

"Well why did you go back to your wife? If you were so 'comfortable' with Angie Hansen? Was it her money?"

"No! Don't twist my words. I married Victoria because I love her. What do I care about her money? We don't even use it. I earn good money, Detective, I contribute my fair share. Maybe real estate isn't the most prestigious business, but it's lucrative. I'm one of the top brokers in the area. For some women, that would be enough."

"But not for Victoria?"

"That's not what I'm saying!"

"This isn't a marriage counseling session, Stark. Do you have any more questions regarding that evening? If not, we're going to end this. Now." Murray folded up her leather notepad and started to push back her chair.

"Duly noted." Jack changed tactics. "You mentioned she was up here a lot even before she closed on her house. Where'd she stay? Where'd she hang out? Maybe she had an admirer of some kind?"

"Right!" Mancusio perked up. "She had a suite at the Sleepy Hollow Hotel over on Broadway. For most of last month. She was going back and forth between there and the city, waiting for the house to close. She wanted something walking distance to the train. And she hung out at The Hollow, in Tarrytown."

Jack leaned forward. "You didn't tell us about the hotel suite when we were at your house."

Mancusio met his stare. "You didn't ask me where she was staying when you were at my house." They glared at each other for a few long moments.

"Move it along, Stark!"

"Did you ever meet her over at her hotel?" Jack asked.

"One or two times, maybe. Not often. By the time she booked the suite, I was trying to break it off."

"Okay. Just one more question, and it's an important one. Did you see or hear anything unusual that night? Please, take your time, think about this, over the next few days." Jack sat back while Mancusio looked off in the distance. Murray stayed still in her half-pushed-back chair.

"Nothing specific I can point to. But when I left, I had a feeling that someone was watching me. I mean, it was dark, it's that kind of place. But I'd never felt that before."

"Well, something might have triggered that, on some level. A flash in your peripheral vision. Over the next few days, something might click. Let us know if you remember anything.

A smell. A sound. Nothing is irrelevant." Jack stood up, indicating the interview was over, and everyone else followed suit.

"I'll try to think back and be sure to let you know. Angie deserves justice, and I want to clear my name. I'll cooperate in any way I can."

"Thanks for your time, Mr. Mancusio, Counselor Murray. Please see yourselves out." Jack weighed his options as he watched them leave. He could lean on him more, but with Mancusio, it seemed better to just give him enough rope to hang himself while they ran down other leads.

EIGHT

As she drove up to her home, she spotted a smaller cabal of reporters outside her front gate. They parted for her as she opened it and drove in. Only one car was in their driveway and it wasn't Nick's. She took her mother's dress off of the car hook and headed in.

"Jeff! What a nice surprise. How are you?" She shot a curt glance at Nick. It's not that she didn't like Jeff. She did. They'd all been friends for years. But she hadn't expected to find him in her living room, now, with less than an hour to spare before they needed to get going.

"Victoria, how are you holding up?" Jeff gave her a quick hug.

"We've both been better, as you probably know." She looked over at Nick and he looked back at her with a glare that stopped her in her tracks. She'd never gotten a look like that from him before.

She turned to Jeff. "So what brings you over today? I would offer to get you something but I'm afraid I'm behind schedule. I have to get ready for my fundraiser."

"What *brings* him here? Are you serious Victoria? He's here to give me some support, which is more than I can say for you! He got me an attorney. I had to go back to the station to be questioned. And where the hell have you been? I'm practically being accused of murder, and you bolt on me?" Nick's anger threw her off her game.

"I'm sorry Nick, this was all a lot to process. And it's a big day for me. I had to take care of some things."

Jeff looked visibly uncomfortable. "I need to get going now. And looks like the two of you need to talk." He started towards the door.

"Sorry, Jeff. It's a stressful time," Victoria said.

"Yeah, for me too! I was questioned today, you know. She was my client before she was his." Jeff looked over at Nick. "This whole thing is a mess." He shook his head and turned to leave. He seemed to be taking this pretty well, all things considered.

"I guess we'll see you tonight, Jeff? Are you still coming?"

"Yes, we're still coming." He said this with some reluctance. "Sarah's been looking forward to it. And I'll see myself out." It suddenly occurred to her that spending the night alone with Nick would probably be worse than going to her function, so maybe the timing wasn't so bad after all.

Nick turned to her as the door closed, visibly agitated. "You needed to take care of some things? What's more important than this? And you didn't answer me. *Where did you go?*"

"I went to my mother's! To borrow an outfit for tonight. Then I had to run some errands for work."

"Borrow an outfit? Why? You have a closet full of clothes."

"I don't have anything with long sleeves."

"You needed to run out to get an outfit instead of talking to me about what's probably been the craziest morning of our lives?"

"Why? Have there been further developments?"

"Further developments? *It's a homicide!* It's all over the news! Stark called again. I had to go down to the station with anything I could bring showing my whereabouts from eight-thirty to nine-thirty last night to try and clear myself."

"Well, you have nothing to worry about. I'm sure it will all get straightened out. You were at the wrong place at the wrong time, that's all."

"And what about you, Victoria?"

"What about me?"

"Why was your car parked like that in the garage? Did you suddenly forget how to park? Or were you maybe a little shaken up last night? And then you disappeared today after the police left. What's going on?"

She couldn't believe it. He was copping an attitude towards her? "Okay Nick, you want to know why I was upset last night? I was going to wait until after my function to do this, but you want to do it now?" She felt her face get hot as she started to shake.

"I want to know what you're not telling me!"

She wanted to play it cool, but she just couldn't hold it in anymore. "I went there last night, Nick! I was *there*! I followed you when I heard you leave. I suspected the affair for weeks, but I just couldn't take it anymore. I had to know the truth. I parked on Shady Hill and walked in, sneaking along in the dark like a crazy person, doubting my sanity.

But then I saw you, Nick, in the upstairs window. And I knew I wasn't crazy. I was right! I saw the two of you. Hugging.

Then you kissed her. It nearly killed me! We're trying to start a family, and this is what you to do me? What is *wrong* with you? We have everything, and you're willing to throw it all away? For what!? You promised me when I took you back the first time, before we said our vows that are supposed to mean something, that it would never happen again! How could you do this to me? *To us!*" Her body shook as she struggled to hold it all in.

"Victoria…" Nick's voice was softer now but it was way too late to quell her anger.

"*Stop!* This is what you've reduced me to! Stalking you, like a pathetic jealous wife!" She held the photos on her phone up to his face.

He tried to hold her, comfort her, but she started punching at him, not hard but fast, like a toddler having a tantrum.

"*Get away from me!*" Nick backed away. She grabbed a throw pillow and pummeled the sofa with it until she exhausted herself. She took a deep breath and proceeded.

"So now you know. I have photos, Nick. Of the two of you. I was planning to use them to divorce you and trigger the prenup. But then you called and told me about her murder. I didn't have time to process all of it. Then the detectives showed up. I knew I had to tell them I was there. But then they said she was found at the bottom of the stairs, and I just froze." He looked at her, and he finally seemed to understand.

"Victoria, you don't believe I actually killed her?"

"I don't know what to believe! I don't really think you could hurt someone like that, but then I didn't think you could hurt me like this again."

"That's different, Victoria. I'm not violent! You know that. I didn't kill her! I didn't harm her at all. I swear! The affair, I know it was a big mistake. It was brief. And stupid. I've been trying to end it for weeks. But she was still upset. I went over last night to calm her down. I felt terrible. She was crying, nervous in the house alone. I walked her upstairs, showed her there was nothing to be scared of, I hugged her goodbye, and I left. We weren't kissing, not in the way you think. Jeff's furious with me too. I hurt you, her, him. I'm a lousy friend and an even worse husband. But a murderer? Come *on!* You can't actually believe that."

"There's more, Nick. I went to the station today and cleared myself. I told them everything. I gave them the photos of the two of you, in the upstairs window, time stamped at seven-thirty." She took a deep breath as Nick stood there in silence, staring at her. "No, I don't really think you killed her. And I don't need this scandal ruining both of our lives. I'll stand by you until this mess is behind us. We'll deal with our private issues another time." Victoria knew that filing for divorce now would only fan the flames of speculation. She was stuck. For now.

"Victoria. I'm so, so sorry..."

"Save it Nick. I don't want to hear it. I may never want to hear it. And here's another thing. A little insurance policy. I don't think you killed her, but I won't know for sure until they catch her killer. I changed my will and my life insurance. If I die, you get nothing but the house. I'm worth more to you alive than dead. Try to remember that."

"Victoria, I never wanted your money and you know that. What's gotten in to you?"

"I have to get ready for my function. The driver is coming in thirty minutes. We need to get ready. I don't want to discuss this any further right now. Please move your things out of the bedroom and into one of the spare rooms. I'll stand by you until we clear your name and this mess blows over, but we're done. What we have now is an arrangement, not a marriage. Do we have an understanding?"

"Sure. Nice move Victoria. You have me right where you've always wanted me. By the balls."

She turned from him and headed up to get ready, trying to suppress the storm of emotion that was battering her to the core.

———

Jack had to hand it to Victoria. With all she was going through, she was holding up remarkably well. Most people would crack. Her evening dress was elegant, dark brown velvet with cream-colored lace that covered her arms and cleavage, a bit modest for a woman her age but still lovely. He stood on the Grand Terrace looking out at the Hudson and the shiny new bridge that spanned its width, his back warmed by the space heaters, a sharp but not unpleasant contrast with the coldness of his nose. He was enjoying himself a little too much. This was work, he reminded himself, as he took a sip of his club soda wishing it was a scotch. It was probably time to go inside. He took one more long, deep inhale of the crisp, pine scented air and made his way into the ballroom for dinner.

Her organization provided funding for arts education for students with limited means, and the Grand Ballroom, a domed structure with white walls and gold trim, was adorned with their work. He wasn't much of a connoisseur, but it looked as good as anything he'd seen in the local galleries. He spotted Nick Mancusio standing by the bar deep in conversation with another guy around his age. It seemed a bit too intimate for cocktail chit chat. He made his way over, eager to ruffle some feathers.

"Detective Stark? I didn't expect to see you here. Is there some problem?"

"Oh, no! No, not at all. Didn't your wife tell you? I scored a seat at the officer's table. No shop talk tonight, I promise. I'm just here to lend my support to your wife's worthy cause."

"Right! Of course. This is my associate, Jeff Malone."

"Mr. Malone, nice to put a face with a voice. I hope I wasn't interrupting anything, gentlemen."

"No, not at all. We were just talking about how nice it is to be out," Malone said.

"Beautiful weather. You know, for October," Mancusio added.

"Yes, it certainly is." Jack watched as the two of them stood there like a pair of naughty school boys who'd been sent to the principal's office, looking down, shuffling their feet in silence.

The lights flashed off and on, instructing the guests to be seated. "Well, I guess that's our signal," Jack said.

"Yes. Thanks for the support, Detective Stark. And there's my wife, I need to go. I'll see you over at the table, Jeff." Mancusio made his way to the front center table to join his wife.

"Nice to meet you," said Malone. "And let me know if you need anything further."

"Will do, Mr. Malone. Have a nice evening." Jack hung back. He watched as Mancusio walked over and put his hand on the small of his wife's back, pulled out her chair for her, and pushed it in. His view now obstructed and his presence becoming conspicuous, he decided it was time to be seated.

He made his way to their comped table way in the back, stopping at the bar to grab another club soda. A woman around his age was standing to his side, ordering a white wine. She looked vaguely familiar.

"Getting in a last call?" Jack asked.

She turned to him. "I'm not much for these functions, but what kind of mother would I be if I didn't come?"

"You're Victoria's mother?" A striking resemblance, Jack thought.

"Sandra." Her voice was resonant yet feminine.

"I'm Jack. Jack Stark. Detective Jack Stark."

"I know who you are, Detective. And I know why you're here." She tilted her head to the side as she looked up at him. Even in heels, she was barely five-three and he towered over her, yet it was she who dominated the space between them.

"It's nothing personal, I'm just doing my job."

"Everything's personal when it comes to my family."

"I'm sure this is difficult for all of you." Jack took a sip from his club soda as she picked up her wine. They moved in unison to the side of the bar.

"Difficult? Hardly." She smiled. "I come from hardy stock. Don't let this delicate façade fool you." She waved her arm casually along the length of her wispy frame.

"I can tell you're a formidable woman."

"I'm descended from one of the original miller families, you know."

"You don't say."

"I do say." Her smile was as coy as a school girl's, her steel blue eyes deep and intense. "This area was a borderland when my family came to settle here. The wild west. We tamed it. We're on the same side, Detective."

"Call me Jack."

"Jack." That smile again. She was as stunning as her daughter but much more intriguing.

"And I can tell you you're barking up the wrong tree with that Nick. He's a womanizer. That's why I didn't want Victoria to marry him. But a murderer? He doesn't have it in him. Trust me. Look elsewhere, before this murderer strikes again and puts that badge of yours in jeopardy." She brushed the back of her hand lightly across his chest over the spot where a badge would go.

"Thanks for the tip, Sandra." The lights went on and off again.

"Any time, Jack."

"I suppose we should get seated."

"Yes, I suppose so. Enjoy your evening, Jack."

"You as well, Sandra." His chest was still tingling as he made his way to his seat.

———

Victoria was standing to the side of the stage, the hot lights beating down on her, still feeling light headed. It couldn't just be the stress. Maybe she was coming down with something. But she'd come this far, and all she had to do was give her little speech and sit down. The rest would be easy. She watched as Charles glided over to the podium. She hadn't had time to fill him in on everything, but he knew the basics and was trying his best to cover for her. Charles started his introduction, but Victoria wasn't really tuning into what he was saying. Maybe it was something she'd eaten. She couldn't back out now.

"Without further ado, here's Dr. Victoria Mancusio, Founder and Chairman of the Board of Arts for All, to say a few words." That was her cue.

Victoria walked up onto the stage slowly, her head held high. She looked around at the artwork that graced the room and enjoyed a sense of satisfaction and pride that she rarely allowed herself to feel. Looking out to the sea of tables framed in white and gold, she began. She delivered her speech on auto-pilot, hoping she didn't look as bad as she felt. After it was over, she headed back to her table.

"Victoria, you don't look well." Her mother noticed first. Then Charles. Then Nick chimed in.

"Honey, are you ok?" Nick put his hand on her arm. She couldn't do much about it in front of the entire table, but she was annoyed by this invasion of her personal space.

"I'm fine. Can you get me a club soda, Nick? I'll be right back."

She grabbed her purse, and headed for the ladies' room. She hadn't looked at her cell all night. If there were further developments in the case, she didn't want to know about them. But curiosity got the better of her now that she could relax a bit. She powered up her cell and waited in anticipation, touching up her lipstick. She checked her news apps. Nothing. Suddenly she felt a bit odd. Slightly lightheaded. Then her world went blank.

NINE

If there was one perk that Victoria enjoyed about being wealthy, it was having a concierge doctor at her disposal. Luckily, when she'd fainted the night before, an employee of hers had been in the ladies' room and had seen it coming. She saw Victoria go pale, and she knew something was wrong. She was able to catch her and get her into a chair. When she came to, Cindy was putting cold compresses on her face. She had wanted to call for an ambulance, but Victoria wouldn't have it. It was probably just anemia, she'd told her. She'd had issues with that before. Her mother had been called in. They'd decided it could wait until morning, but her mother insisted that she stay the night with her. It was a perfect reason to avoid being alone with Nick.

It was just past eight in the morning, and the doctor had already checked her out. Blood pressure was fine, vitals were great. They would get the lab work in a few hours. She took some iron in the meantime, which made her stomach sick. She felt fine otherwise and turned her attention to more pressing issues, like trying to find out who had murdered Angie Hansen.

"Victoria, I'm headed to the club to play a round. Do you want to come?" Her mother loved golf, and she was actually very good at it. She could hold her own with her father back when they played together. She had some fond family memories of Sleepy Hollow Country Club. The offer was tempting.

"No thanks. Another time. But Mom. I have something to talk to you about, but not right now."

"Again with this? Do you want me to cancel? So we can talk?"

"No, it's ok. I'm not ready to talk about it. But I need to ask you something in the meantime."

"So ask me." Her mother stood with her hand on her hip, waiting.

"But I don't want you to ask me why I'm asking."

"Good grief Victoria! Just spit it out!"

"Do you know a good private detective?" Victoria asked.

"Of course, Victoria. I'm a Vander Hofen." Her mother rolled her eyes and went to get her a name and number. She handed a card to Victoria.

"Sam Coleman. I trust him completely, and so should you. And welcome back to the family. It's about time." Her mother grabbed her clubs and headed out the door. Maybe Victoria had misread her. She didn't seem so frail and lonely to her today.

———

Jack and Lexi had been in since six that morning poring over case files. Only one day had passed since they found the body, and the pressure was mounting. They were preparing for their drive to the city—a full day of interviews ahead of them—still no closer to getting any actual evidence. The insomnia was starting already. Cases like this always brought on the sleepless nights, and this seemed like one of those cases. Although this part of

Westchester was a relatively low crime area, they'd had their share of sensational cases over the years, some of them solved only after decades of painstaking investigative work combined with random strokes of luck. He didn't want this to turn into one of those instances, but this case had all the trappings of such a scenario.

When he'd seen Angie Hansen's body, he thought immediately of the infamous Dating Game Killer. Choking girls had been one of his signature moves. He'd started out in the New York City area with one of the earliest victims found right in Westchester back in the seventies. What if this was a copycat? Or the start of another reign of terror? Nobody knew how many women he actually killed. Some speculated it was over a hundred. Even one more now was too much for Jack as he thought about Angie Hansen and her brutal murder.

He reminded himself to be wary of dismissing someone just based on appearances—like a local multimillionaire who was finally indicted for the murder of his wife, decades after the incident. And there were the crimes of passion, some of them committed by women, as Lexi had pointed out to him. And of course there were the tragic cold cases, the ones yet to be solved—over a hundred of them in Westchester County alone. Jack knew that if he didn't find some answers fast, this case had the potential to go that way. He felt a heaviness inside, the kind of feeling that sometimes made him wonder why he kept at it. But being a homicide detective was all he'd ever wanted to do. He reminded himself that he did it for the victims. Justice for the victims, and their families.

"I think I figured out the murder weapon! And, I think we may have a missing wine glass. There was an odd number of them. Only three were in the house." Lexi snapped him back into the present.

"And?"

"Huh?"

"The murder weapon, Lex."

"Right! There were two brass table lamps listed on the moving inventory, but only one was found in the house. Look at these photos, Jack. It fits with the arc on the wound and the ME's description. She died of blunt force trauma from a hard, cylindrically shaped object." She showed him the photos and it looked like a fit.

"Nice work, Lex. We'll run the other lamp over to the ME before we head to the city. Let's tell them to widen the search area around the house. If someone was on foot, they might have ditched it in the woods. Was anything else missing besides the glass and lamp?"

"Just her cell."

"Jewelry?"

"All accounted for."

"Not likely a robbery then, unless they got interrupted. They thought she wasn't there and then freaked out?" Jack was thinking out loud. "It's possible. How does all that fit with your profile of Mancusio?"

"I still think he's lying about something. But murder? I'm just not sure about that. It's possible, I guess. He's a narcissist for sure. They aren't usually violent, but they'll go to great lengths to protect their interests. He constructs his own moral code, within reason, so the cheating fits. He'll justify his behavior in some way. But he's not a sociopath. He's too transparent. If he killed her in the heat of the moment, he'd feel guilt. Watch for signs of it."

"Good work, Lexi. Great insights."

"We got some interesting intel on Higgins too."

"Oh yeah?"

"He frequents that coffee shop. The Hollow. The one Angie Hansen hung out at. He doesn't sit there much, he's a grab and go guy. He's usually working from home most of the day, according to what I could find out."

"Still notable. Good work. Keep the tail on him." Jack needed hard evidence, not speculation. Forensics hadn't turned up much so far, and he was getting frustrated. The list of possibilities was growing, not narrowing, and they still had one more prime candidate to see, Randy Jackman, CEO and founder of Jackman Capital, the person who probably stood to gain the most from her death.

———

Randy Jackman had agreed to meet with them at his Park Avenue penthouse. In spite of the forty-minute drive, it was nice being in the city again. There really was no place like it, and Jack realized just how much he missed the buzz. A doorman met them in the lobby and took them to a conference room on the first floor where Jackman was waiting, sitting casually in his arm chair, pushed back a bit from the circular conference table, dressed in a black sweater and jeans. It was mid-morning. No attorney, no sign of nerves.

"Mr. Jackman. Thanks for agreeing to meet with us on such short notice." Jack gave him a wave and they both seated themselves across the table from him.

"What can I do for you, Detective? I'm a busy person." He was in his early fifties, a relative new comer to an exclusive list of the most successful New York City hedge fund managers.

"We're investigating the murder of Angie Hansen. I understand she worked for you."

"Are you asking me to confirm something you already know, or do you have a question for me?"

"I have a question for you. Did you kill her?"

"Really, Detective?"

"You said you were a busy guy. I thought I should get straight to the point." Jack leaned back and crossed his arms.

"No, I didn't kill her. Anything else?" Jackman didn't flinch.

Jack leaned in. "Where were you on the night of October fifteenth between eight-thirty and nine-thirty p.m.?"

"Flying back from San Jose. We landed around eleven. Westchester Airport. You can confirm it with my pilot, five other people on the plane, airport personnel, my driver, my wife. Are we done here?" Jackman sat up, like he was about to stand up and go.

"No, we're not done here. She was suing you personally. And your company. That had to upset you."

"It was baseless. She cooked up that lie because she couldn't charm her way into a promotion she didn't deserve. She came on to me, not the other way around. Do I look that desperate?" Jackman held his hands up and looked himself up and down.

"That's not the story we're hearing. We hear there was a tape."

"I don't give a crap what you're hearing. It's over now anyway. She's dead. It's a moot point. We have nothing more to talk about."

"Really convenient, isn't it? She's gone, and so is your little problem?" Jack leaned in further, and Jackman did the same.

"I'm not complaining. But like I told you, I had nothing to do with it. I was on a plane. She probably had a lot of enemies. Girl like that."

"Woman. A woman like that." Lexi said.

Jackman turned to her and then back to Jack. "Right. Well that *woman* and her side kick Malone have been making my life a living hell for the last two months. Our insurance company was planning to settle, just to make it go away. But my reputation? The damage is already done, and having her dead will probably just fan the flames. I'm worth one-point-two billion. Why would I risk prison? For a civil suit I can settle with pocket change? But people won't think like that."

"I can think of some reasons to risk prison. Misogyny? Revenge? Someone with one-point-two billion wouldn't even need to get his hands dirty." Lexi gave him a hard stare.

"You've been watching too many movies." Jackman stood up. "And we're done here. If you have any more questions, talk to my attorney. You can see yourselves out." He walked out of the conference room door and turned back to Lexi. "Have fun at your me-too support group."

"It'll be more fun keeping an eye on you." They locked eyes, and Jack felt a bit protective of Lexi. Her umbrage was understandable, but a guy like Jackman could be dangerous. His tentacles reached into all echelons of society, up and down. Better to play your cards close to the vest with a guy like that. He should have prepped her more.

"We appreciate your help, Mr. Jackman, thanks for meeting with us," Jack called out, but Jackman just kept walking. The ding of the elevator bell echoed through the hallway as they sat for a moment, the silence a welcome respite from the pace of the last twenty-four hours.

"Don't say anything. I know. It was foolish," Lexi said.

"You'll learn. Let's go." Not the hard way, he hoped. They got up and walked to the elevators. "Let's grab a real New York deli lunch before we head to Brooklyn. My treat." It's possible that someone that cocky and that wealthy could commit murder and have the audacity to toy with them about it, but not probable. Still, he was an up-and-comer, likely feeling invincible, like he could get away with murder. More possibilities, but no hard evidence.

"I assume there's no tape," Lexi said.

"Nope. No tape. Can't blame a guy for trying." Jack shrugged.

"So, we have a sociopath with an alibi and a narcissist without one?" Lexi looked at Jack and he nodded.

"Yup. Better than nothing." They had one more stop to make today, the hardest one.

———

Angie's parents, Darlene and Vince Rossi, lived in a modest Brownstone in Bay Ridge, a working-class area of Brooklyn not quite as gentrified as some of the more popular sections. The pizza joints, neighborhood bars, and dollar stores had yet to be replaced by art galleries and brew pubs. The Rossi family had owned their place for decades and it was likely worth a small fortune, but Jack pegged them as the type of people who would be reluctant to cash out and leave.

"Mr. and Mrs. Rossi, thanks for seeing us today. We're so very sorry for your loss." They had met briefly, at the morgue. Jack didn't want to think about that now.

"Thank you, Detectives. Come in." Vince Rossi was a large man, not pudgy but tall and broad. He looked to be in his late sixties. His bald head made him look even more formidable. His wife was on the smaller side and looked to be a few years younger than him. She was attractive with dark hair and an olive complexion like her daughter, the kind of woman who would never let herself go. Their narrow living room was warm and comfortable, filled with dated but tasteful furnishings and photos of Angie, her two brothers, and all their grandchildren. It was heartbreaking.

"First, Mr. and Mrs. Rossi, we need you to rest assured that we're doing everything we can to find out who did this and bring them to justice. We know how difficult this must be for you. To talk to us so soon."

"We want to help in any way we can," Vince said.

"Yes, I can imagine. First, can you think of anyone who might want to harm Angie? Did she have any enemies that you knew of?"

"That bastard boss of hers. Jackman. I wish she never went to work for him. Everything started to change when she went over there," Darlene said.

"How so?" Jack could only imagine.

"It was really high pressure. She got caught up in it. All that money. Nothing is ever enough for people like that. She's always been ambitious but this job brought out the worst in her. In all of them. I warned her about suing too. A guy like that? It could go bad. And look what happened."

"We know about him, yes. We interviewed Jackman today and he has a solid alibi for that evening, but we're still keeping tabs on him. Is there anyone else at the firm who might have had a beef with her? If it was competitive, maybe she made some enemies?"

"She didn't talk much about anyone else. I think they all hated their boss. I'm sure it was competitive, but she didn't get the promotion she wanted, so I'm thinking there probably wasn't much resentment? Of her?" Her father made a good point. "And Jackman, he could have hired someone."

"We're looking into that too. What about her ex-husband?"

Darlene smiled. "Stu? No, he's a sweetheart. I wish she'd stayed with him. He wanted kids, but she was too into her career so he moved on. He's been married for years, has two kids now, lives down in Florida. There were no hard feelings. He still sends us a Christmas card. He's that kind of guy."

"She kept his name?" Jack asked. Darlene nodded. "Any other exes that you know of who might be upset with her?"

"Nobody comes to mind, but I'm pretty sure she was seeing someone. Up in Westchester. She wouldn't tell me anything but I could tell by the way she acted. I was hoping it wasn't her attorney. He's married."

"And how did she meet her attorney? Jeff Malone, right?" Lexi asked.

"Yes. Her good friend Sherry used him in a similar case and she referred Angie to him. He got her a good settlement. Not as large as Angie's would have been, but then she doesn't make nearly that kind of money. She works in public relations at a hotel. She would probably know more about the firm and what was happening in her life. Angie confided in her. They've been close since college." Darlene looked down and he could see tears welling up. She was trying hard to hold it together.

"That's very helpful. Could you get us her contact information?"

"Yes. Excuse me for a moment."

Lexi put her hand on Darlene's arm. "Take all the time you need. We're in no rush." Darlene nodded and left.

Vince stayed with them. "I didn't like the idea of her living way up there in Westchester. In the woods, no less! I wanted her to move closer to us, but she wouldn't have it. She wanted space, she said." He sat for a moment with his head in his hands. "*Space!*" His hands lifted up to the heavens. "And now look what happened! I should have tried harder!"

"Please, don't blame yourself. The neighborhood is generally very safe. This was a terrible tragedy, but I really don't think it was random. There were no signs of a robbery. We think it was someone she knew. Something personal."

Jack struggled with how to tell them about the affair with Nick Mancusio. They would find out eventually, and it was probably better they heard it from him. But how could he do this to them now? Darlene came back looking more composed. She handed them her friend's contact information.

"So do you have any leads?" Vince asked.

"We can't really comment on an ongoing investigation. But there's one thing we found out that I need to tell you because it will probably come out at some point. You might as well hear it from us. Mrs. Rossi, your hunch about her relationship was correct."

"I knew it. So, who was it? The attorney?"

"No. It was her real estate agent. Nick Mancusio. And he's also married. I'm so sorry," Lexi said.

"My poor Angie. Why didn't she come to me? These married men with their empty promises! Do you think that cheating son of a bitch had anything to do with what happened to her?" Darlene's lips were taut, her face now showing the enormous strain that the last few days had placed on her.

"We're looking at a number of possibilities. Anybody who had any interaction with her is on our radar, but I can't say anything more about it right now. I can tell you we've questioned him. We're keeping an eye on him and several others. We will keep you updated on all developments. In the meantime, if you can find out anything more about the work situation, please let us know. And if you can give us the names of any more friends she might have confided in, that would help too. Over the next few days. And call any time. We'll get out of your hair now." Jack stood up and Lexi followed suit. They all walked towards the door.

"Thanks for coming."

"Thank you for seeing us on such short notice. Again, we're so sorry for your loss."

"Mr. and Mrs. Rossi, we'll get justice for Angie. I promise." Lexi put her hand on Darlene's arm again. Never make a promise you can't keep, Jack thought. But he'd let this rookie mistake slide. It was a very sad day.

———

It was late afternoon and Victoria still hadn't been home. She would have to face Nick sooner or later. He'd texted her twice asking where she was. If she was okay. She told him she was. But could she stay in the same house with him? Maybe she should just move in with her mother, start the divorce proceedings. Was it just that she didn't want the media attention, or was she just not ready? It was difficult to sort through all of her conflicting emotions.

She'd called Sam Coleman, the private detective, and given him an overview of her situation. She told him about the civil law suit. Gave him as much information as she had on the case. Coleman was going to start with Randy Jackman and see where it led. She wasn't leaving this to Stark and the Tarrytown Police Department. She had to help find the killer.

The four o'clock local news broadcast was about to start, so she turned on the TV to see if there was any more about the story. The anchors were greeting the viewers when a 'breaking news' banner flashed across the screen. Then they started in on the story.

> There's new information coming in on the brutal murder of Angie Hansen, found bludgeoned to death in her home in Pocantico Hills yesterday morning. It seems that local real estate broker Nick Mancusio may have been having an affair with the victim. He was her agent in a recent home purchase. The Tarrytown police department confirmed that Nick Mancusio is a person of interest in the case, but no arrests have been made. WNBC TV News received exclusive photos of the two of them. We'll bring you more information as this story develops.

They showed two photos, one of Nick and Angie Hanson on an upscale elevator, all mirrors and gold trim, enjoying the ride a little bit too much, and another of the two of them eating in a restaurant, holding hands, looking intimately at each other across the table. She didn't recognize either of the venues. She wasn't really that shocked by the fact that the affair had come out, but she was surprised at how fast it had happened. It was also clear that somebody was out to get Nick. She had to make a decision. She could stand by him and help clear his name, and by extension hers. Or she could cut her losses now.

Her phone buzzed and she didn't even want to look. It was probably Charles or her mother or one of her fair-weather 'friends' calling about the news story, looking for the juicy details. But then she saw it was Dr. Mason calling. She'd almost forgotten about her check-up.

"Hi, Dr. Mason."

"Hi Victoria. Is this a good time?" Dr. Mason obviously hadn't seen the news.

"Sure. Is something wrong?"

"Well, no, not exactly. You're a bit on the low side on your iron, as we thought, but I don't think that's the main reason for your symptoms."

"Then what is it? Just tell me. Please." She couldn't deal with a major health issue now. The universe couldn't be that heartless, could it?

"This might come as a bit of a surprise, given your recent history, but hopefully a pleasant one. Congratulations, Victoria. You're pregnant!"

TEN

Nick had been home laying low like an ostrich with his head in the sand, hoping things would all blow over. He hadn't been into the office for two days, not since the morning of the day she was murdered. He was avoiding the news and not picking up most of his calls. But this one he needed to take. It was his brother.

"Hi Mark." Nick wondered how much he should tell him.

"Have you seen the news?" Mark asked.

"I'm not sure what you mean. What news?"

"*Your* news, Nick. The news that you were having an affair? With your client? The dead woman?"

"Jesus. Hold up a minute." He fumbled with the remote while trying to put his phone on speaker.

"They showed photos of the two of you." Would Victoria leak those photos? No. It made no sense.

He'd missed it. The news broadcast had moved on. "What kind of photos? There's nothing on now."

"You and her in an elevator. You and her at a restaurant."

"*What?!*"

"Pretty damning."

"Let me get online and find them." He dashed into his office and searched up the story. Christ. Just googling his name brought them up. The photos were everywhere. It was that kind of story. Murder. Sex. Beautiful people. Life as he knew it was officially over.

"Those were taken in the city," Nick said. "Over a month ago. When it first started. Who the hell would have photos like that?" Jackman came to mind.

"Who knows. But what the hell were you thinking, Nick?"

"I know! I screwed up!"

"And you're a person of interest? In her murder?"

"I really screwed up?"

"Why didn't you call me?" Mark sounded offended.

"I was hoping it would blow over," Nick offered.

"Well, it didn't. Do you need a lawyer?"

"No. I have one."

"Who?"

"Silvia Murray."

"She's good." Mark paused. "But I do know a few lawyers myself. Why didn't you ask me? I'm your brother."

"I just . . . I don't know! I didn't want to get the family involved. I didn't want to get anyone involved. I didn't think it would turn out like this."

"So, do you have anything to worry about?"

"I didn't kill her, if that's what you want to know."

"That wasn't what I asked."

"That's the only answer I can give you."

"Jesus, Nick. You need to call Mom. And Pops. He's got his connections. They could be useful. We'll all stand by you."

"Thanks. I will. Not now."

"So, what's going on with Victoria?"

"She's at her mother's. She already knew about it. This won't help."

"She must be furious."

"Yeah. I haven't been handling it very well."

"Well, start handling it better. Maybe she'll come around."

"I'm not holding my breath."

"That's too bad. I always thought you guys were the real deal."

"We were. Are. Oh, my God. I don't know! Look, I need to go call my lawyer."

"Did the police know about the affair before this?"

"Yeah, I already told them."

"That's good. Okay bro, I'll let you run. Let me know if you need anything. You have family. Remember that. You're not alone. Call Mom and Pops."

"Not today. I will soon. Tell them I'm sorry." Nick hung up.

He remembered that day. Clearly. The day those photos were taken. Because it was now officially the worst day of his life. He and Angie had spent a lot of time together before then. In his office, looking at property, driving around town. She was looking for something in the area. Single family. Under a million and a quarter. She was okay with a fixer upper. They'd had chemistry right away. It wasn't just that she was beautiful. And sexy. There was also a vivaciousness, a warmth to her personality that was familiar to him. They had a lot in common. She was a lot of fun. And he and Victoria were having a dry spell. Again.

She'd asked him to come to the city that day to meet her. The seller had accepted her offer on the property and she wanted to 'go over things' with him. He knew it was a pretense. He did it anyway. They met for lunch at a romantic place she'd picked out. That's when she told him about her boss. How scared she was of him. The combination of her vulnerability and her sexuality was intoxicating. Not to mention the wine. Her hands were trembling when she talked about Jackman. He grabbed them to steady her. He promised he'd find her a place in Westchester. To keep her safe.

Before he knew it, he was getting a room at the nearby Westin, next to Grand Central Station where he'd taken the train into the city. Both photos were from that day. The physical part was all pretty much a blur. He was buzzed. The make-out session in the elevator. The frantic effort to get the hotel door open. The ripped clothes. The sex itself. All a blur. What happened next was firmly embedded in his memory. They were lying on top of the bedspread. They hadn't even turned down the covers. She rolled over on her side, turned to him, and smiled.

"You're my knight in shining armor, Nick Mancusio." She was looking up at him with doe eyes—wide and hopeful—and it was positively terrifying. In his opinion, she'd come on to him. She was so sophisticated in bed. And such a successful trader. It was a ruthless business. And now she was acting like a teenage girl who'd just lost her virginity.

He knew right away that he was in trouble. Jeff had warned him that she was vulnerable. But this seemed like a bit more than that. Like something was wrong with her. They were both adults. He was married. She knew that. He thought it was all understood. Had he done anything to lead her on? He felt instant regret. And guilt. She was already having a hard time and this would make it so much worse. And what if Victoria found out? He had no intention of leaving her. He should have been stronger. Smarter. What was wrong with him?

Over the next five weeks, he'd tried to let her down easy. Close the sale. Move on. But she wasn't going gently into the night. She even booked a hotel suite for the month in Tarrytown, making it harder to avoid her. He thought about the night he broken it off for good. And then the very last night. Her last night alive. How distraught she was. And how totally unappealing he found her. It was horrible to think that way about a dead girl, but it was true. The mascara running down her face. Her nose red. Her face blotchy. All the drama. He looked at her and longed for Victoria. Calm, cool, collected, low-maintenance Victoria. What had he done? He just wanted Angie Hansen out of his life. He needed his marriage. His wife. His life back. It was all such a mess.

———

Victoria sat on her mother's sofa looking out into the spacious, opulent home she grew up in, trying to absorb this news. She was pregnant. That certainly explained the mood swings. At least she wasn't losing her mind. Even with the horrible timing, she couldn't help but feel a warm glow inside of her. She'd miscarried once, over a year ago, so her happiness was mixed with trepidation. About the pregnancy. About her marriage. Still, she couldn't help but allow herself a moment of joy.

It turned out she took after her mother in more ways than one. Pregnancy didn't come easy to either of them. Her cycle had always been a bit irregular. She envied those women who seemed to get pregnant just looking at a man, the ones who exuded fertility. The ones who looked like Angie Hansen. She'd had a happy childhood, but it was so lonely. Their big house and nobody to play with. She'd always wished for siblings, as far back as she could remember.

She and Nick had been trying to start a family for years. She never thought it would take so long. The stress from trying to conceive had put a great strain on their marriage, and Nick had been nothing but supportive. Sex had turned clinical, timed to her ovulation schedule. No spontaneity or romance, but he never complained. He'd joke with her when it didn't take. "Hey Vic, it's fine! It just means we have to practice more!" His levity grew to annoy her. She withdrew. Shut him out. They drifted apart.

About two months back, he'd surprised her with two first class tickets to Hawaii. Nick's business was booming, and he was happy to be able to do this for them. They had gone there on their honeymoon and had planned to go back for their ten-year anniversary but travel restrictions delayed their plans. She was reluctant to go, but he'd insisted.

He booked the Presidential Suite at the classic Kahala Hotel and Resort, knowing her taste. Presidents, dignitaries and movie stars have graced it since the sixties when it was built, valuing its intimacy, charm, and discretion, the boutique property a stark contrast to the more recently built sprawling resort complexes that dotted much of the island chain. It had been a perfect seven days. They swam with the hotel's dolphins, ordered in and ate together on their ocean front lanai, frolicked in the ocean, ran together. And made love. It all came back to her, in waves, like the ones they had seen from their luxurious suite.

She was looking out the sliding glass door of the bedroom, watching the white caps of the gentle waves punctuate the turquoise blue water that stretched to the horizon, listening to them crash on the shore. A briny smell drifted into the room on the gentle trade winds coming off the sea. She heard Nick. He came up behind her and touched her shoulders, stroking them lightly with his fingers. It set off a hunger in her that had gone dormant. He turned her around and brushed the hair from her eyes.

"Your eyes, they match the ocean. This place suits you. Run away with me?"

"I thought we already ran away."

"I'll send for our things."

"Who needs things?"

"The hell with our things then." He leaned in and started with a gentle kiss which quickly became more urgent. She met his desire with equal passion. He lifted her up and carried her to the bed as they explored each other as if it were the first time. He started to undress her, slowly, making her wait. She was a bundle of nerves. He touched her in all the right places, ever so lightly, building up her desire until she exploded with a veracity she hadn't felt in ages—so lost in herself, she barely registered when it ended. They stayed like that for a while, his full weight on her. It felt good. Safe. Like a warm blanket. They were both silent, neither of them wanting to spoil this perfect moment.

He finally rolled over, propped himself up on his elbow, and looked at her. "So, do you know a good realtor?"

"No, they're all terrible." They both laughed and he kissed her again.

"I love you."

"I love you, too."

But when they'd gotten back home, they'd slipped back into their old patterns. It wasn't just her, it was both of them.

Something about the house. Their bedroom. The empty rooms that begged for children to fill them. Nick was from a big, close Italian family. He loved children. Family was everything to him. It was probably killing him too, but he never let on about it.

That was probably about the time he'd met Angie Hansen. Victoria had met her once. At Nick's office. She was instantly jealous, even though the woman was older than she was. She exuded sexuality in a warm, comfortable way. She could see they had a connection. The way they laughed, talked. It made her grow even more distant. More critical.

She wasn't excusing Nick's behavior, and she was still angry about the affair. But she knew in her heart he could never commit murder. And he wasn't just a husband to her now. Someone expendable. He was the father of her child. Whatever happened with the marriage was of secondary concern to her now. The father of her child could not go to prison. She needed to use all the resources at her disposal to clear his name and protect her child from pain and humiliation.

———

She drove up to her house not sure what she was going to say when she saw Nick. The reporters had multiplied. They didn't part for her as readily this time. She didn't want to honk her horn and fan the flames. She opened her window a crack and tried to appeal to their sense of decency.

"Please, this is a very difficult time for us. We would appreciate some privacy."

She heard some of them asking questions, but most of them responded well to this tactic, backing away slightly, giving her enough room to open the gate and drive her car through it.

Nick's car wasn't in the driveway. She felt a flash of disappointment. Maybe it was in the garage. Then she gasped as she saw someone running through the gate up to her car. His fist flew up in the air as he ran inside the gate!

Bam! Bam! Bam! The young man pounded on her car window as the car sat halfway through the security gate. Her heart raced as she tried to process what was happening. He was waving a business card around, frantically, and she could hear him yelling something through the glass. She was thankful now for the reporters. He didn't look like one of them. She cracked her window a bit.

"*Ma'am!* I have to talk to you! *Please!* It's important! I have information for you." His bulging eyes looked back at her through the glass as he caught his breath.

"This is not the time and place, sir. If you have information, please pass it to the police."

"I've already talked to them but they won't listen. I have a feeling that you're in danger. *This killer!* He's going to strike again. Please be careful. I'm not crazy! I just have a certain gift. Please. Call me sometime. Any time. Here's my card."

"Thank you. Now please step out of my way so I can get home." She drove through and watched as he backed out and the gate shut in front of him, then breathed a sigh of relief. Maybe they needed to get some security. She opened the garage door and saw that Nick's car was there. She pulled in next to him and shut off her car, finally looking at the card, her hands still shaking: Wade Higgins, Computer Programming and Forensics.

PART TWO

ELEVEN

Two weeks later

The sun was just starting to rise and the Hudson was materializing, as if out of nowhere, under a stormy morning sky. Victoria was sitting at her kitchen table, meditating on the view. Off in the distance, she spotted a translucent ship on the horizon poking through the fog. It reminded her of an urban legend she'd heard as a girl about ghost ships on the Hudson. Some claimed that Henry Hudson's ship was still out there, searching for the Northwest passage, and the ethereal ships people spotted in the early morning were the remnants of his quest. Later, she read a *New York Times* article claiming the sightings were actually a trick of the morning light as the cruisers made their way down river and into the city to dock. It didn't really matter to her. It still gave her the tingles.

They had settled into a fairly comfortable pattern over the past two weeks. Nick was staying in a guest bedroom and she was in their master suite. There had been no further drama and no word on the case. He was worried about her health. She told him it was just mild anemia and the stress. She wasn't ready to tell him the real cause.

She knew her husband well. She could see the guilt in his eyes, his hunger for absolution. She knew he wanted to talk, but she wasn't ready. And she appreciated the fact that he was giving her space. For someone like Nick, the fact that he was hanging back and letting her breathe meant more to her than if he were constantly apologizing, begging for redemption. Her husband knew her too. It was a smart move.

"Hey!" She startled a bit. "Sorry. I didn't mean to scare you," Nick said. "I was trying to be quiet." He stood behind her. The wind was whipping the leaves around and a faint whistling sound slipped in through the thick glass. Empty tree branches warned of the stark winter ahead.

"It's okay." She took a sip of her herbal tea, missing her morning coffee desperately. "I think I see a ship out there. Do you see it?" She pointed to her right.

"Yeah, I think I do see it." He put his hand on her shoulder and she politely brushed it away. He walked over to get some coffee.

"Think it's a ghost ship?"

"A what?"

"Never mind. Are you going into the office today?" she asked.

"No. I have some loose ends to tie up. I can do it from here. I'm pretty much radioactive right now as far as securing new business."

"Right. Well, it'll blow over. Give it time."

"Think maybe I should lean into it? Use it in my marketing? *We've got a 'killer deal' today on listings with Nick Mancusio*"

She tried not to laugh but a smile slipped out.

"I saw that."

"You saw nothing."

"So, what about you? Going to work?" Nick asked.

"Yes. Soon. I have a lot of catching up to do. Charles has been covering for me but I have to get back. There's a museum in France that wants to acquire one of my client's paintings. It'll be better if I do it. Their English is good, but it'll go more smoothly if I can speak to them in French. You know how the French are."

"Oui, oui." He actually had a decent accent. Nick had taken some French, but not nearly much as she had. And she'd lived and studied in Paris. They used to play at it. She'd humor him for a while as they tried to converse, and then she'd take off jabbering away, leaving him in the dust, and they'd both crack up.

Nick was in his workout gear. "Going for a run?" she asked.

"Yeah. Wanna come?" He looked hopeful.

"Not today. I need to get going. I'm going to do some Pilates and then shower." She was holding off on the running until her OB appointment, but she couldn't tell him that. Plus, a run together was a little too 'back to normal' for her.

"Okay. Have a good day." He went off somewhere with his coffee, leaving her alone with her view. It was time to get going anyway. She had the meeting with her client and then one with Sam Coleman. She made a mental note to remember to tell him about the strange man at the house the other day. She looked at his card again. Who are you, Wade Higgins? And what did you want to tell me? She tucked his card away in her purse.

She looked out the large picture window and reminded herself to be wary. A killer was still out there. Somewhere. A killer lurking outside the house wasn't even her worst-case scenario, but she tried to push that thought from her mind. She took out the slim Glock 43 that she'd retrieved from the safe. What good would it do her there? She needed to find a better place to keep it. She looked around, trying to think of the perfect hiding place, wishing that she could turn back the clock to two months prior, before all this insanity started.

———

Nick didn't know what to do with himself. He wanted desperately to get back to work. Back to normal. How many workouts could he do? He was still avoiding the office, but he couldn't stay idle for very long. It wasn't his style. At least Victoria had come home, and at least the case seemed to be stalling, as far as he could tell. He wasn't sure where his wife's head was at or what had prompted her to come home, but he was glad that she had.

He was heading out to go for a run when his eye caught a glimpse of the photo he'd taken of Victoria in Central Park. He used to love looking at it. Her smile. The way he could make her laugh. Now it just reminded him of Stark and the mess he was in.

They'd met in the quad at Columbia a few weeks before that photo was taken. He'd noticed her sitting there on a concrete bench, drawing something on a sketch pad. She looked like a princess from a fairy tale. Delicate, with finely chiseled features. Her long blonde hair was whipping around in the wind. He watched as she kept brushing it away from her face, trying to beat the wind at its own game, totally engrossed in whatever she was doing. She finally gave up, grabbed a scrunchy from her bag, and tossed her hair up over her head and into a bun in one fluid motion. It was totally feminine. Sexy. It was then that she noticed him looking at her. He smiled at her and she smiled back. He walked over.

"That's some fancy moves you've got there."

"I'm sorry?"

"Your hair."

"Oh, right. It's so windy today!"

"Yeah it is. Are you an art major?"

"Art history. Master's program. But I'm taking a drawing class for fun. I'm terrible at it!"

"I'm sure you're not."

"No, seriously, I am. I love art, but I'm a terrible artist. Believe me, I've tried! But trying makes me appreciate those who have talent even more."

"That's a positive way to look at it. So, what are you planning to do with your art history degree?"

"Oh my God! You sound like my mother!"

"I didn't mean it like that. Sorry!" She smiled and he felt relieved. He didn't want to blow it with her.

"I'm not sure yet. Museum work? Open my own gallery? And what's your major?" she asked, tilting her head to one side. God, was she cute!

"Business. MBA in marketing. But I'm taking a photography class. For fun."

"A real Renaissance man."

"Not really. I'm terrible at it."

"You're just saying that!"

"You're right. I'm not that terrible, but I still won't quit my day job."

"What do you do for work?"

"I help manage my family's construction business. What about you?"

"I'm working as a TA, grading papers. Doing all the grunt work for Professor Rankin."

"So can I see?"

"See what?"

"Your sketch!"

"Oh, no. Please. I told you. It's terrible." She covered her face with the sketch pad.

"Come on! It can't be that bad. And look on the bright side. If it's bad, it'll make you less intimidating."

"Intimidating? You find me intimidating?" She flashed him a wry smile.

"A little."

"And I find that hard to believe," she said.

"Would you like to have dinner with me this weekend? I mean, if you're not otherwise unavailable for that sort of thing?" He felt a pang in his gut. He wasn't used to hearing no, but for some reason, he wasn't taking this one for granted.

"Don't you want to see the sketch first?"

"Nah. I'll take my chances."

"And you are?"

"Nick. Nick Mancusio."

"Hello Nick Mancusio. I'm Victoria. Victoria Vander Hofen."

His wife walked in the living room just then, snapping him out of his reminiscence. He turned to look at her, as if for the first time. He realized how much he needed her in his life. How much he wished he could turn back the clock to two months before. But he couldn't. The only way was forward.

"What?" she asked, her blue eyes wide and wary.

"Nothing. I'm just glad you're home." He wasn't hoping for much of a reply. She smiled a little. That would have to be enough for now.

———

Victoria stopped in downtown Tarrytown to get some coffees and scones to take to her office. The weather had shifted suddenly. It was colder than the day before. Blustery. A few downed branches and pockets of tree twigs littered the streets. Wet, dead leaves were scattered all over, stuck to the pavement like colored post-it notes. She watched her footing as she walked a few blocks up the steep incline to the coffee shop. Parking was getting tighter all the time, a downside to the village's recent surge in the popularity. It had rained a bit already and it looked like it was going to start up again.

The shops on Main Street were all decked out for Tarrytown's biggest holiday. The annual Halloween block party was this weekend and the town was gearing up. A headless horseman on the corner was tethered to a pole, blowing back and forth in the wind, clanking against the cold metal. Store fronts were decorated with skeletons, ghosts, and carved pumpkins. She thought back to the Great Jack O'Lantern Blaze, an annual event at nearby Van Cortlandt Manor, and the seven thousand hand-carved pumpkins that had stared back at her when she was a child, each one more haunting than the next. She used to love it, even though it chilled her to the bone. But even the smiling ones seemed creepy to her as she entered The Hollow and got in line.

Locals and tourists alike flocked to the area this time of year. Touring Sleepy Hollow just a few blocks away—with its Old Dutch Church, its famous cemetery, Patriots Park. Watching the dramatic reenactments of Irving's famous story, steeping themselves in spookiness. It was all part of the fun. But with a killer loose somewhere and a real fear permeating the town, the decorations took on a more sinister character. She thought about the other night, walking back to her car, surrounded by the dark woods, the tree branches reaching out like arms ready to grab her. And Higgins with his strange warning that she was in danger. It made her shiver.

"Hi Victoria." Mandy, the dark haired and buxom barista called out to her, her voice a tad loud. She startled. It was her turn in line but she was still a few paces back, lost in thought, holding things up. She rushed forward.

"Hi Mandy. Sorry! I'll take three café lattes and half a dozen pumpkin scones please." She looked around at the patrons. Were they looking at her differently? Did they all think her husband was a killer? The simple act of picking up some coffees now put her stomach in knots. Would this ever blow over? She paid for the coffees and put a generous tip in the jar.

"Thanks so much!" Mandy said. She seemed to be the same kind, friendly girl she had been the week before. Maybe she was just being paranoid. Or maybe they just felt sorry for her. Poor Victoria with her cheating husband. Wait until they found out about the baby.

She waited to one side for her order, checking her email on her phone. When it was ready, she grabbed it and was headed out the side door when she caught Stark in her peripheral vision, walking through the front door. He didn't seem to see her. Was he following her? Just pretending not to see her? Or was paranoia now taking over her entire life?

She needed to get centered again. She'd worked so hard to overcome her anxiety for years, and now it was all rushing back. She had to get ahead of this. Last time, it was Aikido that had helped her. Gave her confidence. Centered her. She was sure she couldn't start that up again now that she was pregnant. She couldn't even have a glass of wine! But she didn't dare complain. It was bad luck. And she certainly didn't need any more of that.

As she was walking back to her car, she saw Jeff Malone across the way. He waved to her and walked over towards her, meeting up with her as she got to her car.

"Hey Victoria! Let me get the car door for you." She struggled for the clicker and unlocked the door as the wind whipped her hair around, obstructing her view. He opened the passenger door for her.

"Thanks Jeff." She put the coffees, secure in in their holder, on the floor and placed the pastries on the passenger seat. She stood back up and turned to him, hoping for a short conversation. She wasn't in the mood for small talk.

"So how are you holding up?" he asked.

"I'm fine, all things considered."

"How's things with you and Nick?" That seemed a bit personal. Nick was probably trying to get him to do some detective work on his behalf. She didn't plan to give anything up that easily.

"I guess I could ask you the same thing," she replied.

"He's one of a kind, that one." Jeff rolled his eyes and sighed.

"Thank goodness for that. Well, I'm running behind. I need to go. Thanks again, Jeff!"

"Of course. Hey are you guys going to the block party this weekend?"

"I hadn't really thought about it. Maybe."

"I think it'll be a real blowout this year. Try to make it. We'd love to see you two."

"Thanks Jeff. I'll talk to Nick. We'll try to make it."

The Halloween block party. Maybe they should go. Things were quiet now in terms of the investigation. She couldn't hide away forever. And she could even wear a costume. It might just be the perfect opportunity to do a little detective work herself.

———

Nick was back from his run. Victoria had already left. He had been avoiding this phone call like the plague, but it was time. He dialed. It rang a few times. She picked up, as she usually did.

"Nick?" His mother sounded more worried than upset. That made him hopeful. He was the apple of her eye, which probably explained a lot about the choices he'd made in life. She spoiled him rotten most of the time. Still, this was a big screw up.

"Hi Ma." He didn't really know where to start. "I'm so sorry. This is all such a mess."

"Well, it's not me you have to apologize to, hon. It's Victoria."

"I know."

"How's she doing?"

"I don't really know. You know how she is."

"I know how she appears to be, Nick. And I also know how she is."

"Right."

"She's a lot more sensitive than she lets on. She's probably hurting. Deeply. You've eroded years of trust. It might be impossible to get that back." His mother's words stung. He knew she was right. It had taken them so long to build trust. Victoria was so guarded. Could they ever get it back?

"What should I do?"

"Just be there, Nick. Be patient. Don't push her. And don't be a wise guy!" She'd adored Victoria right from the start, despite their different backgrounds, and the feeling was mutual. They'd taken to each other right away, much to his surprise.

"Right." He knew what she meant.

"And that poor girl, Angie. She was murdered? Her poor parents! My God! They live right in Bay Ridge, I heard. It's so tragic."

"Yeah. Pretty close to Carroll Gardens. We knew a lot of the same places."

"You had that connection, I guess. She felt familiar. Like Gina."

"Yeah."

"And her feelings got hurt too, I imagine? This Angie person?"

"Yeah. I feel awful about all of it."

"Nick, you've lived a charmed life. And I'm probably responsible for it being a bit too charmed. But I have to say I'm disappointed in you right now. *Very disappointed!* I thought you'd learned your lesson. That you'd matured. There's no excuse for what you did, so don't try to offer me one." It was a tone of voice he hadn't heard from her in ages. It made him feel like crap, but he knew he deserved it.

"Ma, I know. I know." He wanted to talk about his real fears. Being arrested for murder. Going to prison. But his mother didn't know the whole story, and he'd already told his father that he'd been cleared. He wanted to spare them. It would kill her to know what a real possibility it was. So, he just took it like a man. She was right, but what good did that do him anyway to hear it? He was still in the same crappy predicament.

"I won't say anything more about it, Nick. Just give Victoria my love. Tell her to call me any time."

"I will. Is Pops there?"

"No, he went out. Try his cell. But he might be out at a job site. He might not hear it. Do you need anything else from us?"

"No, not right now. I love you, mom." Nick's voice cracked a bit.

"I love you too, Nick, but if you're looking for absolution, you came to the wrong place. I'm sure Father Patrick would love to see you though. It's been a very long time.

"I know, Ma. I'll put that on my list of sins for my next confession."

"Very funny, Nick. This is exactly what I'm talking about. If you want to save your marriage, don't pull that crap on your wife."

"Yes, Ma. Take care." She hung up, leaving him staring at his phone, trying to figure out how to save himself from his inner wise guy.

TWELVE

Jack had stopped to grab some coffees for himself and Lexi at The Hollow. He thought maybe he'd see Higgins, or someone else who could have been stalking Angie Hansen. He looked around and didn't see anyone who looked familiar. The case, meanwhile, was going nowhere. It had been two weeks, but the lab was backed up and they still hadn't finished processing the crime scene. Since the house had been on the market and there had been so many workers in it, there was way more trace evidence than usual.

But the things the killer might have touched—the banister, the door knobs, the body—were clean, aside from the plumber's prints on the outside door knob. Investigators were scouring the woods looking for the cell and the murder weapon. He had also been canvasing the neighborhood to get camera footage. The little they could find was very grainy. Nothing of use. He was about to order. He was next in line and about to order when his phone pinged. It was Lexi calling. He stepped to the side, trying to hear above the loud whirling of the coffee grinder.

"Hey. What's up?" It came out way too loud.

"They found the murder weapon!" Finally, a break in the case. They needed this.

"The lamp?"

"Yeah. In the woods. In back of the house, about a quarter mile down the hill. Someone ditched it. It was wiped clean. Did you know there's a path back there? It leads down the hill and back out to Bedford Road, but down near the bottom."

"Interesting. So, do we think the killer came on foot? That would change things a bit." Jack massaged his forehead as he paced around in small circles.

"Well, they certainly left on foot. Out the back door probably. Which could explain why the front door was unlocked. She let the perp in and forgot about it. Then he left from the back." Lexi offered a plausible theory.

"Yeah." He thought about it for a moment. "But still. Why weren't her prints on the doorknob? Somebody wiped it. Then they took the cell. The murder weapon. And forgot about locking the front door? It's possible, I guess."

"Right. So if they came on foot, we're back to square one? Is that what you're thinking? It could be anyone? A robbery gone bad? A stalker?" She paused. "Higgins?"

"Higgins. Interesting thought." Jack flashed back to his strange affect. His weird twitch. His strange 'feelings.' But would he give himself up that easily? And then just vanish? Most people like that tended to insert themselves into an investigation more than once. "Let's try and see if we can get camera footage further down the hill. Maybe the perp walked down and caught an Uber or a cab."

"Mancusio could've run down there and ditched it and then ran back to his car. It wasn't too far down the hill where they found the lamp. He's probably not stupid enough take it with him," Lexi said.

"True. And he probably looked around the grounds with her when he was selling her the house. As her agent, he's more likely to know about that path behind the house than anyone else we're looking at right now. But the timeline was tight to begin with. Add in a jaunt up and down the hill and I'm not sure. Silvia Murray would have a field day with that. And we have no actual evidence tying him to the murder."

"Maybe you can try the route yourself? Drive it? Run down and back? Time it? Before you come in?"

"Good idea. Your coffee will be cold by then."

"I'll heat it up. Bring it still! Anything's better than what we have here."

"You got it, boss." Jack hung up and got back in line.

———

Victoria's morning meeting went well. Business was picking up and she was very happy for the distraction from her personal troubles. Her assistant Nate came in to inform her that Sam Coleman was there to see her. She told him to send Mr. Coleman in.

"Hello Sam. It's very nice to meet you." She stood up and walked around her desk to greet him.

"Hello Victoria. It's nice to meet you finally. In person, I mean. What a lovely view you have here." He looked out past her desk to the view of the Hudson and the Tarrytown depot.

"Yes, we're quite fortunate. It's a great space."

"I've heard so much about you over the years, I feel like I already know you." That seemed odd to her. She'd heard nothing about him until the other day.

"Yes, I understand that you and my mother have known each other for a long time." He was not at all what she'd expected. Maybe she'd seen too many movies. He looked to be in his early sixties and he was overdressed for the occasion. Confident. Polite. Cultured. The James Bond type.

"Yes, we have."

"Did you know my father too?"

"Not quite as well. But I know he was crazy about you." His face took on a look of concern. "I'm sorry, I didn't mean to bring up something difficult for you to talk about."

"Oh, no, it's fine! I like thinking about him. Talking about him. I should do it more. We were very close."

"Your mother cares a great deal too, Victoria. She just doesn't wear it on her sleeve." Why was this relative stranger talking to her about her family dynamics? And why was she letting him?

"Yes, well. Thank you for that insight, Sam. But can we get to the point of why we're here?"

"Certainly. I'm sorry if I overstepped."

"No, not at all. It's fine. I've just got a lot to do today."

"Yes, well then, let's get to it."

"We can meet in our conference room. It's more private." She ushered him out of her glass-walled office and into their larger room a few doors down. Its wood paneled walls were adorned with two paintings she'd kept for herself, a Thomas Cole and a Frederic Church, two of the most famous of the Hudson River School painters. Their paintings had sparked her interest in art, the river, the entire region on a trip to Olana when she was a child, the former home of the artist-explorer Church, designated a national historic landmark back in the sixties and now a museum of sorts.

"Those are stunning. They must be worth a fortune."

"A small fortune. They don't go for as much as you might think. Europeans are still a bit snobby about American art, especially from the nineteenth century. Old rivalries die hard." She smiled. "Please, have a seat."

Coleman kept his gaze on her as he lowered himself into his chair. "Is that why you have a concealed carry permit?"

"I'm sorry. What?" She felt a pang of indignation.

"I understand that you have a concealed carry permit. They're not easy to come by. I was wondering if that's why you have it. Because you are around very expensive art pieces. Or is it something else?"

"Yes, I have it because of my profession. But why are you asking about me? I thought I hired you to find a killer."

"My job is also to clear the two of you, as I understand it." He waited and she looked at him, a bit taken aback. "Isn't it?" His eyes widened and she offered a reluctant nod. "To do that, I need to find out anything the authorities can find out. About you. Your husband. Anything that could be used against you. Aside from investigating the possible perpetrators, that is."

She remembered what her mother said. She should trust him completely. What he was saying made sense. But still.

"I suppose that makes sense," Victoria said.

"Do you know how to use it properly?"

"What?"

"The firearm you own."

"Yes, of course. My father taught me from an early age. But I'm a bit out of practice."

"I suggest you get back into practice. If someone were to overpower you, well, it might be better to not have it at all. If you're not up on your training, that is." He sounded just like her father. Maybe he knew him better than he was letting on.

"I'll take that under advisement." She knew he was right but she still found his attitude a bit paternalistic for a stranger. It was weird. "So, have you found anything out? About Randy Jackman? Or the case?"

"Yes, I have. It was Jackman who leaked the photos to the press. He was having Angie Hansen followed. Well, his insurance company was. To build a case against her and impugn her credibility. To show a pattern of behavior in case it went to trial. I can't prove for sure that he had those specific photos, but I know he had photos of the two of them. He was planning to use the photos as leverage when they went in to make a deal. He preferred to get it settled quickly. Not go to trial. But when she turned up dead, he instructed them to be leaked to the press."

"Can we go to the police? Tell them about this?"

"It won't do much good. We have no hard evidence linking him to the leak or to those specific photos. They might even be upset that you're taking matters into your own hands. But I'm working on getting some evidence."

"But why would he leak them now? There's no trial. Isn't this matter over for him?"

"Not really. He needs to defend his reputation. Even though the suit hadn't hit the news, rumors were flying all over the finance world. People knew about it. He probably wanted to nip it in the bud. He always claimed she was making up the story that he sexually harassed her. An affair makes her look less credible. It also throws the spotlight on Nick and away from him for her murder. I doubt he has anything personal against either of you. But it's perfectly legal for him to obtain the photos and to send them to the press, and it's a smart move."

"Do you think he could have killed her?"

"At this point, anyone could have killed her, Victoria. I don't have an opinion about that yet. I've been trying to find a pattern of behavior for Jackman. Find out if there were any other sexual allegations made against him that were swept under the rug. I've talked to many people and there's nothing so far. He's a difficult man to work for and a ruthless businessman. Everyone says that. He says insensitive things about women. To women. To everyone, really. But nothing of a sexual nature has turned up."

"Well, nothing turned up in most of these cases for years. Women were afraid to speak up. It's possible he wanted to silence her before anything more came out."

"That's true. I know. But that still doesn't mean he'd risk prison and kill her. He could silence her with money, and he has a great deal of it. Still, I'm checking on it. His alibi is solid. He was on his plane when she was murdered. Unless he hired someone, it wasn't him. For now, all I can say is he leaked the photos. But I can't offer you or the police proof of that. That's how my business works."

"Thank you for doing all that. And so quickly."

"I'm just doing my job."

"I also wanted you to check someone else out, if that's okay."

"Of course, Victoria. I work for you."

"This man." She handed him the card. "He was outside my house. Last week. With the reporters. But he wasn't one of them. He was strange. Not quite homeless looking, but close. He came up to my car and pounded on my car window when I drove up. He was saying something about my being in some kind of danger. I told him to talk to the police. He said he'd been to the police already. He gave me his card and asked me to call him. I didn't talk to him for very long. I just took the card and drove through the gate."

"That's very strange. And concerning. Did you tell the police?"

"Not yet. Should I? I'm not sure if I can trust them. I wanted to talk to you first."

"Yes, absolutely. That's something they should know about. I'll check him out too, but you should let the police know. Right away. He could be unstable. Dangerous. Is that why you hired the overnight security? Because of that incident?"

"Yes. I'd been thinking about it. But that incident made my mind up for me."

"Keep the security for now, and with your permission, I'd like to vet your team. Can you give me their contact information?" She nodded. "Anyone else I should check out? What about domestic help?"

"I use a cleaning service once a week. Do you want their info?" Victoria asked.

"Yes, I'm taking nothing for granted. And do you think you'd be safer at your mother's? For now? Her property is much more protected."

She thought about it. "No. I don't want to do that. Not now. I feel like I need to be home. For now. I'll be fine. It's all died down. The reporters aren't even there anymore."

"Your mother's is always an option if you need it. Be careful. Check your surroundings when you drive in. And when you get out of your car. Lock up, even in the day. With stories like this, people come out of the woodwork. Vigilantes. Crazy people."

"Yes, good point." She hadn't really thought about that. Was she not safe anywhere now? Not even in her own home?

She thought about her house with its large wall-to-wall windows and suddenly felt very exposed. She wrote down the contact information for her security company and cleaning service. "Here you go."

"Thank you. I'll check them out and report back." He tucked it in his jacket pocket. "I'll get going now. Again, lovely to meet you in person."

"Thank you, Sam. You too. It helps to know you're looking out for us."

"Always. And Victoria?"

"Yes?"

"Start target practice again. Please. For everyone's sake. The last thing the world needs right now is an out-of-practice jumpy woman with a firearm at her disposal." He got up and left, rendering her speechless as she watched him walk out of the conference room.

———

Jack had just gotten back to the precinct. It was mid-morning. Lexi was in the conference room mapping out the case on a whiteboard when he entered.

"Here's your coffee. I heated it up a bit."

"Thanks." She took a cautious sip. "So, how'd it go on the timeline?"

"Unfortunately, I think this hurts our case against Mancusio. There's barely enough time to drive from the store to the house, park, go in and kill her, get back into the car and then drive back to his house. If you add in fifteen minutes to ditch the murder weapon down the hill and run back to the car, it's pretty much impossible. Unless the time of death is off."

"Well, sometimes it's off."

"Yes, sometimes it is. If we had some evidence that he was up there at that time, we might be able to get a warrant. Bring him in for questioning. But I don't think we can get one with what we have. Plus, this really opens up a lot more possibilities. The idea of someone on foot. We have to be careful. It could be a random crazy. We can't be blinded by the obvious."

His phone rang. "Hi Dr. Mancusio. Is everything alright?"

"Yes, I'm fine. But something happened the other day that I thought you should know about. I should have told you earlier, but it just slipped my mind."

"I can imagine you have a lot on your mind these days. What is it?"

"This man. This strange man, he accosted me at my home about two weeks ago. I was driving through my gate and he was outside, with the reporters, but I'm sure he wasn't one of them. He started pounding on my car window, following me in. Saying I was in some kind of danger. I told him to talk to the police, but he said he'd already done that and they wouldn't listen. He gave me his card. His name is Wade Higgins. Did he come see you?"

"Wade Higgins?" Jack was intrigued. Lexi's eyes widened when she heard the name.

"Yes, he's some sort of computer programmer. Do you know him?" Victoria asked.

"Yes. He came in about two weeks ago, when this all hit the news. Claiming to be some kind of psychic. We've been keeping an eye on him, but we must have missed this. That he went to your house. I'm sorry. I'm very glad you told me," Jack said.

"A psychic?"

"Yes. He claimed to know something about the killer. He said he felt his feelings. We've been getting a lot of wacky leads, but something about him seemed a bit off, so we've been keeping tabs on him. We'll set up a meeting with him. See if we can advise him to keep away from you. In the meantime, I can make sure we have a squad car patrol your street more regularly."

"I've hired private security overnight."

"That's good. We can't afford that level of service. Budget cuts and all that. I'm sure you understand. But I'll do what I can to protect you. And please. If you see him again, let me know. And don't talk to him yourself, understand? He could be dangerous."

They signed off and Jack turned to Lexi. "So now what?"

"Let's take Higgens up on his offer to help. Ask him to meet for coffee tomorrow at his favorite spot. Tell him we want more information," Lexi suggested. "I'll be able to get a good read on him if he's more relaxed."

"Good idea." Jack reached for the phone.

"Let me call him and set it up. He might be more comfortable with me. I think I can get him to trust me."

"What? You're saying I'm not comfortable?" Jack held up his hands and looked himself over.

"Sure. I mean, even a grizzly bear can be comfortable. In certain circumstances."

"Point taken. Call him. Set it up for tomorrow morning. You want to do it yourself?"

"No. Come with me. Just let me take the lead. I happen to know a bit about psychics."

"Oh yeah?"

"My aunt. She claims to have the gift. I've always been skeptical, but I have to admit, she does nail it on occasion. Maybe he's just really intuitive. I don't want someone accused of murder just because they're a little different or maybe have more of an innate ability to read people."

"Right." Jack wondered if Lexi was more of a believer than she was letting on. He would bite his tongue on the psychic jokes. For now.

THIRTEEN

Jack and Lexi arrived early to meet Wade Higgins at The Hollow the next day. They waited inside near the entrance, taking in the local art on the walls. He came a few minutes after them, wearing the same jacket he'd worn to the station. But he'd gotten a haircut and was clean shaven this time. It gave him a much different first impression. He looked like a typical computer geek. That probably was intentional.

"Why don't you tell me what you want and I'll go order? You two can grab a seat," Jack said.

"I'll have an Americano. Black."

"Same for me," Lexi said.

The line was short. Jack watched Lexi and Higgins find a table and sit down. She was right. She would get more out of him by earning his trust. If he could be that patient. It wasn't his strong suit.

He ordered, paid, and then went to join them. As he walked over, he scanned the café, looking to see if he recognized any repeat customers. Anyone who could have been watching Angie Hansen. Stalking her. When he sat down, their conversation ground to a halt.

"Don't let me interrupt! Go ahead. We've got all the time in the world." Jack shot a look at Lexi and her eyebrows lifted in reply. The rustic wood table looked inviting but the bench was hard and uncomfortable.

"Mr. Higgins was just telling me a bit more about the history of the area. He has a blog and You Tube channel where he posts about it," Lexi revealed.

"Interesting. Is this a side gig or your main business?"

"A side gig. I'm really interested in the history and folklore of the region. I'm from Michigan. Originally. I moved to the city for a job out of college. I used to come up for day trips on the train. I'd read a lot about the Hudson Valley. Sleepy Hollow. Tarrytown. Its reputation. I wanted to check it out. I thought maybe I'd meet some more open-minded people here that might be less judgmental about my gift. And I did. So, I got a remote position and moved up here permanently."

"*Jack?* Your order is ready," the barista called out.

"I'll get it," Lexi said. "The two of you can get more acquainted." She walked away, leaving them to try and develop some sort of rapport.

"So how do you like it up here?" Jack asked.

"I like it most of the time. I miss the city sometimes. The buzz. But the slower pace has grown on me."

"I can relate. There's no place like New York City," Jack agreed. Lexi came back with two coffees in ceramic mugs and placed them in front of him and Higgins. Then she went back for hers. The two of them sat there fidgeting, waiting for her to come bridge the silence.

"Thanks for the coffee. I see you ordered it in real mugs." Higgins was leaning back in his chair, eyeing Jack.

"I think it tastes better that way. Don't you?"

"I guess I never thought about it," Higgins replied. Lexi returned with Jack's coffee and sat back down.

"So, Mr. Higgins. About that night. Can we get back to that?"

"Sure. Yes. That's why we're here, right?"

"Right. So, where were you when you had that feeling?"

"I was home. Working on my computer. On a project that needed to be done the next day. I was alone, if that was what you were going to ask me."

"Eventually, but thanks. Is there anyone who can verify that?"

"You can get a warrant and have your computer techs check my IP address. Verify what I'm saying. Or you can take my word for it."

"So that's a no?"

"I'm not stupid, Detective. I know you're planning to take this mug and get my fingerprints and my DNA. Go right ahead. I have nothing to hide." Higgins' look turned sour.

"So do you want to come down to the station and we can get your prints and DNA in a more effective manner?" Jack asked.

"And make it easy for you? No. Now if you had asked nicely, maybe. But now. No."

"Mr. Higgins, we're just doing our jobs here. A woman was murdered. You had to know that coming to us would put you on our radar. This is just how it works. It's nothing personal," Lexi said.

"Exactly. Why would I do that? Come to you and tell you about it? If I was a murderer?"

"Why would you go over to Victoria Mancusio's house and pound on her car window like a crazy person?" Jack shot back.

"Oh that." He blushed a bit.

"Yes. *That!*"

"I got another feeling. That someone was in danger. I didn't get a clear idea of who it was, but I figured it was probably her. After it was on the news. That maybe her husband did it. I wanted to protect her."

"Why don't you leave that to us and stay away from Victoria Mancusio?"

"Because it's clear you don't believe me and that this is all a ruse. You, pretending to be interested in me." He pointed to Lexi and then looked back at Jack. "And you, playing bad cop." His neck started with the nervous twitch again.

"I can see why you'd think that. But it's not true. I swear," Lexi said. "I asked to take the lead. I asked to be the one to call you. I have an aunt like you. She claims she has a gift too. I know how hard it is for her. I know she's not making it up. She believes in herself and it's hard for her when people act like she's crazy. Or a phony. I can empathize. I wanted to make sure you were treated fairly, not judged."

"She's telling the truth. I'm the skeptic," Jack confessed.

"The thing is, all you had to do was ask me. Ask me for my DNA and my fingerprints. I have nothing to hide."

"That's just not the way it works," Lexi said. "I'm a profiler. Sometimes people do insert themselves into investigations. Sometimes people are clever. Psychopaths *are* out there, Wade. We have to assume everyone is a suspect until they're cleared or the perpetrator is caught. It's not about you, it's about the victim. If you try to look at it from that perspective, maybe you'll see things differently. If you really want to catch the killer, that is." Lexi was so calm. So rational. So effective. Jack was impressed.

"It's not like I asked to have this gift. When it first happened, I thought I was going crazy. I can't control it. It doesn't help me. It just haunts me. It's a burden, believe me. And I'm telling you that someone else is in danger now. He's still around. If it's not Victoria Mancusio, it's someone else."

"I believe you," Lexi said.

"About Victoria Mancusio." Jack sat up and leaned in, trying to convey to him the gravity of the situation. "We need you to stay away from her. You frightened her! She doesn't need this right now. And going onto people's property? You could get yourself hurt. You do your job and let us do ours. We'll run your DNA and prints. If you have anything that can clear you from eight-thirty to nine-thirty that night, let us know. And if you have any more visions, call Detective Sanchez. Don't take things into your own hands."

"They're not visions, they're *feelings*." Higgins rolled his eyes at Lexi. Jack's head was about to explode.

"Okay then! That's settled. We all know our roles. Can you excuse us now, Mr. Higgins? Detective Stark and I need to talk." Lexi headed off the explosion.

"Sure. Thanks for the coffee. I'll see you around. Be sure to check out my channel. And if you can't get what you need off that cup, let me know. I'll come down. Like I said, I have nothing to hide." Higgins got up and left.

Jack turned to Lexi. "So he only gets these 'feelings' after he sees a news report? Give me a break. I'm not passing judgement on that aunt of yours, but Higgins is full of crap. He didn't feel anything from any killer."

"Well maybe he doesn't know he's full of crap. Did you ever think of that?"

"Think of what?"

"Maybe he just has some kind of issue, something psychiatric that never got diagnosed. And this is how he copes with it. Or maybe he has a vivid imagination."

"Or maybe he just wants attention. Or maybe he's a killer. Don't let your relationship with your aunt cloud your judgement about Higgins. He's pretty smug. Are you telling me you actually believe him?"

"I don't believe he's in touch with the killer in any way. But I think he believes he is. It's how he sees himself. He's interested in that world. He found kinship with these people. He's convinced himself he's got a gift. But he's no Edgar Cayce."

"Who?"

"Dorothy Allison?"

"Yeah. That one I know. The Son of Sam case, right?

"And she worked on over five thousand other ones."

"From what I understand, not everyone was a fan of hers. There was a lot of controversy. People followed her down some pretty big rabbit holes."

"She had her share of successes too."

"I'll stick to cold, hard facts. Let's get this mug to the lab. See what we can find in the way of actual evidence."

"Do you have the 'feeling' that we're missing something on this case?" Lexi asked.

"Always. Let's go." Jack chugged down the last half of his coffee and proceeded to bag the evidence. "Do you want to take another drive to the crime scene? Speaking of missing something?"

"Sure. Let's time it again. From the store to the house."

"Good idea." It was another cold day but it was clear, unlike the day before. Not a bad time to check out the house. The Halloween decorations downtown reminded him of the upcoming annual street fair. He expected it to be a real scene this year. People were itching to blow off some steam. The town was filling up with tourists, and so far, the case didn't seem to be affecting the festivities too much. As if reading his mind, Lexi brought it up.

"We should go to the fair on Saturday. See who turns up."

"I was just thinking that!" They got themselves strapped in and Jack started to drive. It was a few blocks to the store where Mancusio went that night.

"Okay, you can start it now," Jack said to Lexi. He drove north on Broadway for a bit and then took a right onto Bedford, going about the speed limit as he made his way up. He was taking the turns slowly, more slowly than he needed to in daylight, figuring a person would go slower at night, especially on a rainy one. They wound their way up as Lexi kept her eyes on the timer. It seemed to be taking a long time, with both of them silent and focused on the task. He passed Union Church on the right, a glint of sunlight reflecting off its famed stained-glass windows. After a few blocks, he took a left onto Shady Hill Road. The thick forest of the Rockefeller Preserve that bordered the residential area now blocked out much of the light. He pictured Victoria Mancusio creeping along in the shadows. It must have been humiliating for a woman like her to tell them about it. Then they veered right into the driveway.

"Eleven minutes. In the rain. At night." Lexi stopped the timer.

"And it's at least that long to drive back to their house from here. Plus a few minutes to walk from the store to his car. I think it's impossible. He didn't have enough time."

"It's not enough time to kill her, but it's a lot of time to have unaccounted for. I don't buy his story that he was just sitting in the car," Lexi said.

"Me neither. He's hiding something. But what?"

———

Victoria had gone to work early that morning. Nick was sitting at his desk at home, wondering what to do with the rest of his life when an idea struck him. He'd finally worked up the nerve to go into the office earlier that morning. It was even worse than he'd imagined. Nobody said anything at all about any of it, but the tension was so thick you could cut it with a knife. Even if they didn't think he was a murderer, they knew he'd cheated. With a client. It would never be the same. It was his brokerage, but he'd lost all moral authority. He was there for less than an hour and he knew he had to make a change. He decided he was going to put the firm up for sale.

His commission had hit his bank account the other day. He'd thought about offering the commission to Jeff, but that was small change compared to what he was planning to make off her case, and it would probably just piss him off more. Their friendship was still strained but it seemed to be going in the right direction. Better to leave well enough alone. With the commission, he had about a hundred and fifty grand to play with. He pulled out his phone and dialed.

"Nick! What's up Bro?" Mark was always there for him.

"You know how you always said I should quit selling real estate and start flipping houses with you? And how I'd always said hey, yeah, maybe someday?"

"Let me guess. The day has arrived. Now that your wife and your clients have kicked you to the curb? You'll slum it with your big brother Mark?"

"It's not like that and you know it."

"I'm just busting your balls, Nick. Is this a hypothetical or do you have a place in mind? Prices are high right now. I don't want to get stuck."

"I have a place in mind. It's a fixer I showed to Angie. It was too much of a project for her. Then it went into escrow. But I saw today it's back on the market. It's a good deal."

"In this market? There must be a catch."

"Well, it's not for everybody. It needs a new kitchen. Bathrooms. A roof. All stuff we can do. Easily."

"If we can get supplies. The timing isn't great."

"Let me go look at it again. Take some photos. Call the listing agent. Ask for the disclosure. If it checks out, we can go see it."

"Up there, in the wilds? Can't we find something closer to me?" Mark and his entire family had never gotten used to the fact that he'd moved to Westchester. It might as well have been another planet to them. But to Nick, it had been a fresh start. As the youngest brother, he always existed in the shadows of his siblings who'd both went into the family business. He was expected to do the same, but he'd had other plans. He and Victoria were alike in that way. They both wanted to be their own people, but they both had strong families pulling on them.

"It'll grow on you," Nick said.

"Right. Like moss, or mold. That grows on you too. Look, I don't want something deep in the woods or up in the hills. I don't want to deal with a slope. It's too much risk. Find me something level. With good bones."

"The lot's flat, Mark. I know what I'm doing."

"Then why isn't it selling?"

"Let me go and look at it, okay? Find out why it fell out of escrow. Maybe the buyers went bankrupt. Maybe it's not the house. It'll give me something to do. Get my mind off of it."

"Okay, get to it and get back to me. Run the comps. Run a rough estimate of the work it needs. Give me some hard numbers and we'll talk."

"Sure, Mark." He was one of the most successful real estate brokers in the county, the owner of his own firm, but Mark still acted like he couldn't tie his shoes. But he meant well, and Nick was in no position right now to turn away moral support.

"I'm not making any promises. I'm just wrapping up that project in Park Slope so the timing's not bad. But you know how this market is. Pops and I are making a killing. If the numbers don't work, maybe it's better you just come back. Join back with us." Nick was afraid he would say that. No way. He was not going back to the past. The only way was forward. He would figure something out.

"I'm not asking for charity, Mark. And this isn't just a Hail Mary. I've been thinking about it for a while now. I told Victoria I wanted out, after that last place closed. I've been wanting to do something on my own."

"You could finish your M.B.A. Do something in management or marketing. You'd be great at it."

"You're a career counselor now? *Stop!* This makes sense for me. I know construction. I know the market up here. And I'm not a nine to five guy. You know that. If you don't want in, it's fine. I'll do it myself."

"*Calm down!* I don't know enough about it yet. You may have been thinking about this for a while, but this is coming out of the blue for me. Check it out and get back to me."

"Right. I will. I just need something else to focus on."

"I get it. Look, I gotta get back to work. Maybe I can take a drive up there this weekend with the kids. See the place. See you."

"The Halloween fair is Saturday. You should come! The kids will love it."

"Sounds like a plan. We'll work out the details later. Gotta go." Mark hung up and Nick got to work, trying to move things forward, whatever that might mean. He was looking forward to seeing Mark's kids. He hadn't thought about children since this all started. If he and Victoria didn't reconcile, where would that leave him? It was a terrible thought, so he put it out of mind and went back to work.

FOURTEEN

It was almost one in the afternoon and Victoria was at her office working the day away after an early morning start. She still hadn't taken a break. She was catching up on all the paperwork she had left for another time. Between tasks, she thought about Jackman. About what Sam Coleman had told her. Jackman had leaked the photos. She thought she heard someone breathing and looked up. Charles was standing there in her office doorway. Staring at her.

"Yes?" she said. He walked in and closed the glass door behind him. He sat in the armchair to the side of her desk, crossed one leg over the other, and folded his arms in front of him. And waited.

"*Yes?*" she repeated with a smile.

"What is going *on*? Talk to me!"

"I'm not sure if I can."

"Victoria! This is *me*! You can always talk to me. You can tell me anything." She and Charles had been best friends since high school, an exclusive prep school that had served them well. But Victoria had trouble making girlfriends there. The popular girls were too ruthless for her. She refused to play their stupid games. The less popular ones shied away from her. She was too intimidating for them. She'd made one female friend in ninth grade, but her father was transferred out of state and she moved away.

The next year she'd met Charles in art class. He had just come out at a time when not many people were out. His relationship with his guy friends changed. They weren't mean—they knew better than that—but things were different. They were both lonely. They'd connected right away. He was the only person who had the gumption to tell her she was a terrible artist. He probably knew her better than almost anyone.

"I know, Charles, but things are really complicated."

"Try me."

"Well, you know the broad strokes. The affair, the fact that Nick was at the house the night before."

"Right. And how are you doing about all that? Planning to divorce him? He certainly deserves it."

"It's more complicated than that. Given what's happened."

"Let me guess. You don't think he did it. You feel like you want to help clear his name? And yours? And, hopefully, protect our business?" He motioned to the offices beyond her door.

"That's part of it. I'm sure they'll clear him anyway, but if I file for divorce now it will look worse. I don't want to chance it."

"Is that the only reason you're helping him?" He knew her pretty well and she knew what he was getting at. But she didn't want to go there. She didn't really know herself what her true feeling were, or what she would have done if she hadn't gotten pregnant.

"I don't know. Not really?"

"I mean, couples get past these things, Victoria. If that's what you want, don't let anyone judge you."

"Frankly, I can't even think about that now. Not until this legal mess is over."

"Does Nick have an alibi?"

"Sort of."

"Sort of?"

"There's about twenty minutes unaccounted for."

"What's the implication?"

"I guess that he's still a person of interest? But there's more.

"Regarding what?"

"What happened that night." She paused.

"And?"

"I was there too, Charles."

"You were where, too?" His brow furrowed in confusion.

"At her house."

"*Victoria!* I always knew you had a dark side. Say no more." His hands went to his ears.

"How can you *joke* at a time like this?" Her eyes started to well up.

"I'm sorry! Oh my God! You look like you're about to cry."

"It's just . . ." She reigned in the tears with a few deep breaths.

"I know. I know. It was in poor taste. Stupid me! I'm sorry. It's just a lot to process. So why were you there?"

"I told you that I suspected it. The affair? Remember?"

"Yes."

"So that night, I heard him leave, and I don't know why. I just couldn't stand it anymore! I needed to know. I followed him to her house. I saw him with her. In an upstairs window. I took photos from out front. And then I left. I wanted proof of infidelity. For the prenup."

"What kind of photos?"

"They were hugging. Then I saw them start to kiss. Then they moved out of my view and I left."

"Oh, that's awful. I'm so sorry.

"He claims he broke it off with her a few days before that night. She was still upset so he went to calm her down. He said nothing more happened. He left about ten minutes after me, but I'd already left so I didn't see him leave. I went to the police the next day. Told them everything. They cleared me. But Nick's still a 'person of interest,' whatever that means."

"They'll move on. I'm sure. They're just going for the low hanging fruit."

"I hope so."

"I know so. You need evidence to convict someone of murder. It's not that easy, even today. But that's not the only issue, is it? I mean, what are you going to do about the marriage? It must have been awful to see him. With her."

"I really don't know."

"Take your time. This is all a lot to process." He started to get up to leave, but then stopped. "Oh, and who was that mystery man the other day?"

"A private detective. I'm hiring him to help find the killer. To clear Nick."

"It seems like you're going a bit overboard for a cheating husband. Unless . . are you worried they'll come after you? Like you're not really cleared?"

"No. Not really. But it's gotten a bit more complicated." She looked at him, not sure how much to reveal.

"More complicated than a sordid affair and a murder?"

"I'm afraid so."

"Do you want to tell me?"

"Oh, I don't know! I have to tell someone. And it can't be my mother and it can't be Nick."

"Then tell *me*. That's kinda why I'm sitting here." He pointed to himself, flipped his hands up and gave her a look.

Charles was her best bet. But she was still feeling uncomfortable about the fact that she was telling someone before she told the father of her child.

"Okay." She paused. "I'm pregnant."

"Oh my God! You had me so worried. I thought you were dying or something after what happened at the function. Congratulations!"

"Really? But the timing?"

"What do babies know about timing? They come when they come. Embrace it. It's a blessing."

"It's not just that. It's what happened last time. The miscarriage. I'm so stressed now about everything. I'm worried it's bad for the baby."

"Well, I'm over the moon for you. It'll be fine. You'll see. A lot of women miscarry and go on to have healthy babies. You know that. We'll find ways to manage your stress."

"Do a lot of women find the father of their child a 'person of interest' in a murder?"

"I'd have to check the stats on that and get back to you." They both had a laugh. Charles could always put a smile on her face.

"And can I ask a favor?"

"Anything."

"Come to my doctor's appointment this afternoon?"

"Really? Of course!"

"It would really help to have you there."

"I'm happy to go, Victoria. I'll probably never get a chance like this again."

"A chance to go to an OB? I feel like you're setting yourself up for a big disappointment there, Charles."

"Hearing the heartbeat? The ultrasound? Seeing a baby in there?" He pointed to her belly.

"Oh, right. I hadn't thought of that part." She remembered the last time. The elation. But then the devastation. It could cut both ways. Charles, he'd never even had that chance.

"Don't get me wrong. Roger and I love Chloe like she was our own. But this, I'd never get to experience it otherwise. I'll be here for you the whole way, whatever you decide about Nick. No judgement. You're not alone. Remember that."

He stood up and she walked over to the door. They hugged each other tight.

"Thanks, Charles."

He looked into her eyes, his arms firmly planted on her shoulders.

"This is a blessing, Victoria. A light in a time of darkness. Embrace it. Take the victory." She nodded. "Okay, I'll take the victory."

He propped the door back open and a strong odor came barreling into her office. Was it eggs? She promptly excused herself to the ladies' room, reminding herself not to complain. Morning sickness was by far the most positive feature of her life right now.

———

Victoria and Charles sat in the waiting room, passing time on their cell phones. It was raining again. They could see the rain-drops and hear them tap-tap-tapping steadily on the window outside. It was cozy in the office. They'd put up some Halloween decorations. Not scary ones, just cute ones. The office wasn't very crowded. There was a middle-aged woman to their right and a mother with a sleeping baby and a toddler across from them. The toddler was fixated on the baby, looking anxious for his sibling to wake up and entertain him.

She was having a baby. Finally. She'd wanted a family for as long as she could remember. With lots of kids. A big, loud one—like Nick's. As a child, she'd wanted siblings so much, she'd invented one, causing a bit of a stir. She remembered the day clearly, the day when all the fretting began. She was sitting at her play table, a tea cup in front of her and one placed across from her in front of an empty chair. A copy of *Goodnight Moon* was on the table. She picked it up and started reading out loud, then turned the book around and held it up to the empty chair, showing off the photos.

"Hi Victoria. What are you doing, sweetie?" She turned around and saw her father with a strange look on his face.

"Hi Daddy! I was just reading to Millie."

"Millie? And who is Millie?"

"Daddy! Don't be so silly. She's my little sister!"

"Oh right! I didn't see her there."

"Now she's sad. Don't cry. Daddy, do you want to read to Millie? You've upset her."

"Um, sure honey. I'm so sorry, Millie. I didn't see you there." He sat down and started reading to her imaginary sister. She didn't understand why her parents looked so upset, but she knew enough to stop talking about Millie. Then they'd had her see someone to 'talk about her sister.' She went over and played with Dr. Jane a few times, but it wasn't any fun. Dr. Jane asked her about her loneliness. She didn't understand what she meant. To her, Millie was real. And very good company. But she kept her mouth shut after that and eventually Millie just faded away as her parents started to fill her days with lessons and outings—ballet, piano, art classes. But it didn't fill the void, it just made it worse. She'd since read that many children had imaginary friends. What was the big deal? She vowed she'd never make her own child feel like a freak for having a vivid imagination. Her parents meant well, but they were always so over protective. The burden of being an only child.

"Victoria Mancusio?" the medical assistant called out.

"Yes, I'm here." They walked over. "This is my friend Charles. He's going to accompany me today."

"That's totally fine. Whatever you want." She didn't ask any questions, thankfully, although Victoria had been there with Nick several times before. She'd probably seen the news, along with everyone else in the town. Victoria hoped she could count on her discretion.

Her mind wandered back to the first time they had come. Nick was so excited. Even though she wasn't alone now, she still felt a bit empty thinking about it. The anger that had earlier given her strength had given way to a melancholy reality. The reality of raising a child with two homes. A child who had to choose between Mommy and Daddy for holidays and special occasions. A lonely child with no siblings. Or the reality of choosing to stay in a marriage with a man she didn't fully trust anymore. Why did he have to go and screw it all up? She tried to focus on what Charles said. Take the victory, but it felt a bit like a hollow one right now.

———

Victoria got home and pulled into the garage. Nick's car was there, and she found herself grateful for the fact that he had the gift of gab. She wasn't in the right frame of mind to try and think up things to talk about to fill the space between them, but she knew she could always count on him for that.

She walked in the side door near the kitchen. She hadn't thought about dinner until she smelled Italian food. Nick was in the living room working away on his laptop. Papers were spread out all over the coffee table.

"Hey!" he said.

"Hi. Did you make dinner? It smells great." She hadn't even realized she was hungry until she smelled the tomatoes and garlic.

"No, I got us some take out from Mr. Nick's."

"That sounds great. I've been so busy."

"Don't rub it in."

"What's all that? Are you working on something?"

"Always. You know me. Let's eat first and I'll fill you in."

"I'm actually pretty hungry. That sounds good." Victoria knew Nick liked to work. He loved the buzz of trying something new. He would go crazy sitting around the house all day. It didn't surprise her that he'd already cooked something up.

"Okay, let me get dinner set up for us." Nick was trying so hard to get things back to normal.

"No, I'll do it. You finish up what you're working on." She looked over at him, his nose in his work.

"Really? He looked up at her, one eyebrow higher than the other, looking a bit skeptical of her offer.

"Really! Stay put. I've got it."

"Thanks."

Victoria set the table and took inventory as she put out the food. She was hungry but her taste in food was changing. Cheese ravioli looked good to her. And the salad. The chicken marsala was a no-go, but she could fudge her way through dinner without arousing too much suspicion. She was happy to at least have an appetite again.

"Oh, and do you want to go to the block party on Saturday? Mark and the kids are coming up. They want to go," Nick said as he made his way over to the table.

"That's funny you mention it. I ran into Jeff. He asked if we were going."

"Where did you see Jeff?"

"In downtown Tarrytown. When I went to get coffees for the office. Are you two back to normal?"

"Not really. It's still a bit strained, but we're getting there."

"Give it some time." She went back into the kitchen to get some waters, hoping Nick wouldn't suggest wine, as she mulled over the idea of going to the fair.

"I think we should go to the fair," she called out to him. "We have two days to get costumes!"

"Me too. I mean, what's the worst that could happen?"

"Don't tempt fate, Nick. Let's eat." A sudden flash of light interrupted their plans.

"*Victoria!* Move away from the window!" She ducked into a corner of the kitchen that was less exposed.

"What's happening?"

"Something set off the motion sensor! Out back! Call the police and stay put. I'll go outside and check," Nick said.

"Why don't we just wait for them?" She knew she should stop him. Tell him to take the gun she had retrieved from the safe and stashed in the kitchen for just such an occasion. But for some reason, she didn't. She was much more comfortable around a gun than he was. And she hadn't told him she'd taken it from the safe. How would he take that?

"I'll be fine. Wait here!" Nick ducked out the back door with the baseball bat he kept in the closet. Victoria waited, secure in the fact that she could defend herself if needed. Soon she heard sirens in the background. When the police arrived, she met them out front. After a pretty thorough look around, everyone agreed it was probably a false alarm. There was no trace of anyone and the cameras had picked up nothing. They came back to their cold dinners still sitting on the table, which Victoria proceeded to heat up. This was their new normal, and Victoria wondered just how long she could live like this.

FIFTEEN

The evening of the Halloween fair was damp and misty. A surreal atmosphere permeated the town. The tableau of families with costumed children, picturesque in the light of day, took on a more carnivalesque feel at dusk. The sun was starting to set on the alcohol-infused adults as their children ran around in sugar-fueled abandon. A mom in a witch costume laughed with her friends while the toddler she held on a leash crawled around on the pavement. Her drink spilled as she wobbled in place. A young, single crowd mingled in with the families, ready to party. A band was setting up their equipment. The sudden, loud screeching noises added to the sense of being off balance.

But Jack hadn't come to party. He'd come to observe. The case was stalling and the town was anxious. So was he. So was his boss. Still, he allowed himself a beer. He wasn't officially on duty. Lexi had gone to take a tour of the Sleepy Hollow Cemetery and watch the street theater. She seemed to be getting into the spirit of the place. Jack hoped it wouldn't cloud her judgement. He was sure she was more of a believer than she let on.

Across the way, he finally saw some familiar faces—Nick Mancusio and Jeff Malone. He almost didn't recognize Victoria. Maybe that was the idea. She had on a long black wig. Her face was painted pale and she was wearing bright red lipstick. She was dressed in long black gown holding a dying rose in her hand. Morticia Addams, he guessed. Her husband was at her side in a suit. The Addams Family. How fitting. The Malones and their two kids were with them, along with another couple and two kids he didn't recognize. Nobody else seemed to notice them. Either the scandal had died down or people were too buzzed to care. He let them pass as he waited, enjoying his beer. They didn't seem to notice him either. There was no sign of Higgins so far.

He started walking the few blocks over to Patriots Park—the starting point for the parade—to meet Lexi, taking in the spectacle. Lexi finally arrived, about ten minutes late, just as the parade was getting into gear. "So how was it?" he asked.

"It was really good! Interesting."

"The place seems to be growing on you." Jack remembered how much she'd hated it in the beginning. Funny how things change.

"Making the best of it, I guess." She gave her shoulders a shrug. "I was keeping an eye out. I didn't see Higgins or anyone else. Did you?"

"I saw the Mancusios. They're dressed as the Addams Family!"

"How strange! In the middle of all this?"

"Yeah! They were with the Malones and another couple with two kids I didn't recognize. No sign of Higgins yet. So what did you learn?"

"Well, I never really knew the whole story of Sleepy Hollow. Did you know that the Headless Horseman is based on a local legend? About a Hessian soldier whose head was blown off in the Revolutionary War? He's supposedly buried in an unmarked grave in the cemetery grounds at the Old Dutch Church. And he haunts the area, of course."

"Of course."

"And then there's the legend of Major André. He was a British spy who worked for Benedict Arnold. He was caught and hanged right here. In Patriots Park. It kept the British from taking West Point. That monument marks the occasion. Right there." She pointed in the direction of the statue, her excitement evident.

"Let me guess, he haunts the park?"

"Naturally. Some people claim he got a raw deal. And so now his spirit can't rest. Another thing is. I always thought Irving's story gave this place its supernatural reputation. But really, it goes further back. To the Dutch, even before the British came. Then back to the Indian tribes of the region. African American folklore. It all sort of blended together. And it's always had that reputation."

"And you learned all of this tonight?"

"Not all of it." She looked away, trying to avoid his gaze.

Oh my God! You've been watching Higgins videos!" Jack laughed out loud. "You're so busted!"

"*Whatever!*" Lexi rolled her eyes. "But seriously, isn't that part of my job, Jack? Getting in his head? Watching his videos helps. It doesn't mean I can't find them interesting. I've always liked history."

"And the supernatural?"

"I guess I've always wanted to figure it out. Are people who claim to be psychic just really intuitive? Do they use parts of their senses the rest of us aren't in touch with? Do people like Higgins believe they can help even if they can't? Is it some sort of coping mechanism?"

"I can see that. And what have you concluded?"

"It's an ongoing investigation."

"Right. Well, I do like your newfound enthusiasm for Westchester."

"It's still no Manhattan."

"No place is."

"So, what about the case? Any thoughts?" Lexi asked.

"My main thought is we need a break. Evidence. Camera footage. A witness, some solid prints or DNA. So far, everything Mancusio says checks out. He was there, so the DNA doesn't help us. He said he didn't sleep with her that night. That checks out. He said she told him a plumber was coming in the morning. Check. So, unless we can get a witness or some actual evidence to the contrary, we can't make an arrest."

"Do you think he did it?"

"My gut says no. But with that family, who knows? I met the mother. I told you she's a piece of work. She tried to steer me away from her son-in-law with that veiled threat."

"I thought she didn't like him."

"She still doesn't want it tainting her family name. Maybe they're all in on it together! The wife. The mother. Him. Paid someone to break in and do it. Shut her up."

"Or Jackman got someone to break in and do it."

"Or it was a robbery gone bad. Which really is starting to look to me like the most likely scenario. Someone was watching the house. Didn't know she was living there but knew the stuff was there. Got caught. Killed her in a panic. Ran." Jack thought about how hard it would be to find the person if that were the case.

"Maybe. But the bruises on the neck? Seems more personal," Lexi offered.

"Maybe it was the Headless Horseman. Was he into that sort of thing?"

"*Stop!*" Her eyes widened in exasperation. He enjoyed busting her chops and he was pretty sure she felt the same. As the parade started to roll down Broadway, Jack and Lexi strolled along with it as it progressed from Patriots Park in Sleepy Hollow towards the center of Tarrytown. It was a cornucopia of sight and sound—costumed ghouls on floats interspersed with kids in skeleton uniforms, hip-hop dancers mixed in with school marching bands, and of course a headless horseman to top it all off.

"Hey, look who's here!" Lexi gestured to the trio across the street. Higgins was walking along with two other people, a guy and a girl. Hipsters. Not in costumes. Looking like pretty normal twenty-somethings, apparently headed for downtown. Higgins stopped and looked over at Lexi. He raised a hand to her and she waved back at him.

As they got to downtown and the parade passed them by, Jack scanned the crowd one more time. Some of the families with children were packing it in for the night. Others were still hanging around, letting their kids blow off steam while they enjoyed some much-needed adult interaction. Then there was the crowd of revelers congregating down by the band. Unless Jackman had hired someone to kill Angie Hansen, it was likely the killer was someone from the area. Were they here, in this crowd, hiding in plain side? Or had they already fled? Most people didn't understand how hard it was to solve a crime. How hard it was to prove guilt beyond reasonable doubt. It was slow, imperfect, and frustrating.

"I'm getting another beer. Want one? You can tell me more of your stories. We can call it a night on the case."

"Yes! That sounds great." A full moon rose over the fair casting long shadows across the party goers as Jack and Lexi prepared to join them.

———

Victoria and Nick were driving back to their house. They had just said their good-byes to Mark and his family. It had been a really nice evening. They'd met up with the Malones for a bit and things seemed to be smoothing over between Nick and Jeff. Nobody had bothered them at the fair. Maybe it would all blow over. She allowed herself a sliver of hope. Was it possible that their legal problems would just disappear? Could she learn to forgive Nick?

He was so great tonight with his niece and nephew. He was a natural with them, unlike her. He made them laugh. He'd grown up in a big family with lots of cousins and family gatherings. His interactions seemed effortless to her. She never knew what to say to kids. Maybe it would be different with her own? That was one of the things that attracted her to him in the first place. That and his big, loud, emotional family.

"That was fun." She looked over at him. She knew she needed to tell Nick sooner rather than later about the pregnancy. But not tonight. She just wanted to get the make-up off her face and sleep. She felt exhausted. But maybe the next morning.

"Yeah, it really was."

"What did Mark say about the house-flipping idea?"

"He's still mulling it over."

"You should do it. Regardless. I think it's a good idea."

"Really?"

"Yes. Really. You know about both sides of it. Construction and real estate. And I'm not bad at the design part. I wouldn't mind helping with that." She really did think it was a good idea. And the pessimistic side of her also thought it wouldn't be a bad idea to have a second home nearby. Just in case.

"You did an awesome job with our remodel. Would you really? Like we could partner on it?"

"Maybe. Let's talk it over more when you have all the numbers."

"I'm working on it." Nick drove through the gate and all her hopes and dreams shattered into a thousand pieces as her eyes focused in on the garage door.

"*Nick!* What is that?" Her heart raced so fast, it made her feel dizzy.

"*Oh my God!*"

Spray painted in red, strikingly evident against the white door, was one word: "KILLER!"

———

Jack had gotten the call just as they were about to order their beers. He'd only had the one, but he decided to let Lexi do the driving. She pulled up to the gate and hit the buzzer. There was a squad car in the driveway. The red spray paint stood out, even in the dark. Jack also noticed that house looked different at night. It was still stunning, but the windows reflected everything—the bare and craggy oak tree branches, the street lights, the moon. In this context, it felt a little unsettling, not to mention exposed. It would probably be hard to get good camera footage with all the reflections. And the gate wasn't very high. Someone could easily climb over it. Even a teenager out for a thrill.

Nick Mancusio was at the door waiting for them.

"Hi Detective Stark. Detective Sanchez. Please come in. Victoria is changing out of her costume. She'll be right down." He was still in his Gomez costume, adding to the surreal feel of the evening. They followed him in. Jack noticed another familiar face—Officer Johnson.

"We were just going through the security cam footage taken from the door. We can make out someone. It was one person, dressed in black. With gloves on. He moves into view briefly, two times, going up go over the gate. They were in and out in about ten minutes. Looks like it happened around six-fifteen p.m. Let me show you." Johnson proceeded to show them the footage. He also filled Jack in on an incident from the previous evening that they'd chalked up to a false alarm. Now he wasn't so sure.

"Looks like a male to me. Tall. Lanky. Maybe six-two?" Jack said to Johnson.

"That's what I figure."

"Where was your security team?" Lexi asked, turning to Mancusio.

"They don't come until eight. They should be here any minute now."

"Anyone could probably get over that gate. But if it were teenagers on a lark, there would probably be more of them and they probably wouldn't be in camouflage," Jack said.

They all turned as Victoria Mancusio made her way down the stairs. She was wearing jeans and a sweater. Her face was bare and freshly cleaned. She looked like a teenager.

So it was one person? And they had the presence of mind to not leave any evidence?" she asked.

"Seems like it," Jack said.

"I think it's clear that someone is out to get us. What did you find out about Wade Higgins? Have you talked to him?" Victoria sat next to her husband.

"Yes, we have. I was waiting to get the DNA results back from our lab to fill you in. But we didn't find any of his fingerprints at the murder scene and it wasn't him tonight. We just saw him at the street fair. We don't think he's involved in the murder. He's into the whole psychic supernatural thing. He seems to really believe he has a gift. But we don't think he's out to get you. Quite the contrary. He says he wants to help you. But we told him to stay away. We think he got the message."

"I have another theory. And it's actually a bit more than a theory. I have some information." Victoria bit her lip and sat up straighter.

"Is there something more you haven't told us?" Jack asked.

"Not about that night," she said as she fiddled with her hair. "I hired a private detective. He found out some information that might be useful for the case." She looked down at the ground like a kid caught with her hand in the cookie jar.

"You did what?" Her husband seemed shocked.

"I might ask the same thing." Jack said.

"I hired him to help clear my husband." She put her hand on her husband's thigh and he turned towards her. She nodded.

"Dr. Mancusio, this could really complicate the investigation. We really don't like it when people take matters into their own hands."

"I had to do *something*! It's obvious that someone is out to get us. And I might know who it is."

"Who?"

"Randy Jackman. He leaked the photos to the press. He was having Angie Hansen followed. In preparation for his civil suit.

When she turned up dead, he ordered the photos to be leaked. To try to clear his reputation. Apparently, the news about the law suit was all over the finance world, even if it hadn't hit the press. An affair would make her look less credible. He claims she was making up the allegation about sexual harassment."

"And you have proof of this?" Lexi asked. Jack knew she was no fan of Jackman and would only be too happy to have a reason to go after him. Still, he wasn't convinced.

"Well, no. Not yet."

"This is exactly why we discourage this sort of thing. What good is it if we have no proof? Maybe this private investigator is just telling you what he thinks you want to hear." Jack wasn't really surprised by the fact that she'd hired someone. A lot of wealthy people did. But still.

"He's a former FBI agent and a longtime family friend. He knows what he's doing. I trust him completely. If he says Jackman leaked the photos, it's good enough for me. I called him and told him about what happened tonight. He thought it was time I revealed all of this to you."

"That's very generous of him. May I ask his name?"

"Sam Coleman."

"Sam Coleman. Okay then, Nancy Drew. What's your theory?" Jack jotted the name down on his notepad.

"Jackman is trying to make Nick look guilty. To throw suspicion away from himself."

"He's not a suspect. He has an alibi."

"Maybe he hired someone to do it. The night of the murder and tonight."

"We'll check out all angles but I really think you're grasping at straws here. Even if he leaked the photos—and I'm not saying he did, but even if he did—it doesn't mean he did this. It could have been anyone. And Jackman has no reason to have it in for you. So don't let your guard down. Whoever did this could be much more dangerous to you than Jackman. A friend or family member of Angie Hansen. A vigilante in the area. The real killer, trying to keep the spotlight on Nick." Jack was genuinely concerned for her safety, and he hoped that was coming through.

"I see." Victoria turned a shade whiter. Jack remembered her fainting at the function. The stress was likely getting to her. She seemed the type to internalize all of it.

"I know you want to put this all behind you, but these things take time. Let us do our jobs. Work with us, not against us. Let me try to figure out who might have a better reason to do something like this." Jack's mind flashed back to Darlene Rossi, Angie's mother, and her reaction when he'd told her about the affair. She'd instantly blamed Nick Mancusio. Seen her daughter as a victim. Angie had brothers. And how many other people in the town probably thought he did it? Wanted to see him punished?

"Yes, I understand now. I really do. I'll be careful."

There was a knock at the door. Mancusio went over to open it. It was their security officer reporting for duty, wanting to know what all the fuss was about. They sat down and proceeded to go through the story with him all over again.

———

Nick turned to Victoria after they'd all left for the evening. "You hired a private detective? To help clear me?" He was trying not to think about the fact that she'd been keeping a lot from him these days.

"Yes. Why? Does that surprise you?"

"A little." He took a deep breath. "So you really believe me?" Did he dare to feel a tiny bit of optimism?

"Yes, Nick. I believe you. I believe that you're not a murderer! But we're still in a big mess here. All because of ..." Victoria didn't finish her sentence but they both knew what she was going to say. "You know, I'm really tired. I don't want to do this now. I need to get some sleep. Let's talk in the morning. It's been a long day." Nick noticed the dark circles under her eyes and a pallor that hadn't been there a few days ago.

He walked over and held out his arms. She leaned in, leaving her arms at her sides. He hugged her tight to his chest and rested his chin lightly on her head. He was grateful that she didn't resist. He could feel a few wet tears seeping through his shirt but she wasn't making any noise. They stood there like that for a while. Then she took a breath and stepped back, avoiding eye contact with him.

"I'm going up to bed. I'll see you in the morning."

"Good night."

"Good night," she said. He watched his wife turn and walk over to the stairs, trying to figure out how he could ever make things right again, careful to take these little seeds of hope for what they were, fragile and easy to crush.

SIXTEEN

Victoria could hear Nick in the kitchen as she slowly made her way down the stairs the next morning. The heavenly smell of freshly brewed coffee filled the air, tempting her. She had fallen into a very deep sleep and she was still groggy. Vague remnants of her dreams clung to the edges of her mind. Something about trying to give a talk but forgetting what she was talking about.

"Hey sleepy head!" Nick looked like he was getting ready for a Peloton session.

"I guess I needed to sleep." She was usually up at least an hour before her husband.

"I've been up awhile. I already painted over the garage door."

"That was fast." She went to the cupboard and got an herbal tea bag, still foggy.

"No coffee? You love coffee." He watched as she put on the kettle to boil the water.

"We have to talk, Nick. There's something I have to tell you." She turned to him. There was no need to drag this out any longer.

"What is it?" His eyebrows shot up and his face went pale. "I had a feeling there was something you weren't telling me. After you fainted. Are you sick? *What is it?*"

She took a deep breath. Nick ran his hand through his hair as she stalled. She was trying to find a way to say it, but the words wouldn't come out. "I, um, . . ."

"Just tell me!" His twisted face pleaded with her.

There was no graceful way to ease into it, so she just blurted it out. "I'm pregnant!" She watched as the words connected with his brain.

"You're *what?*" Nick's jaw dropped.

"We're pregnant, Nick." She threw up her hands.

"I heard you. But I mean, how? I thought the doctor said we had to 'go to the next step' and all that jazz."

"She said sometimes when you stop worrying about it, it just happens."

"Well, I guess!" He shook his head as a smile lit up his face. "My God! This is . . . this is *great!* So, how far along are you?"

"About fourteen weeks now." She could see him doing the math.

"Hawaii?"

"I guess."

"So we didn't need fertility treatments, we just needed a vacation?" The kettle started to whistle.

"Apparently." She went over and filled her tea cup with boiling water.

"When did you find out?"

She hesitated, knowing that this would be hard for him to hear. "After I fainted. After the function. I was as shocked as you are now." She knew he'd be a bit hurt that she'd held out this long on telling him, but she was hoping he knew better than to make an issue of it.

"So that's why you came home. That's why you're backing me. The baby." He lowered his eyes.

"Let's go sit. In the living room. And talk about this." He followed her in as she walked slowly with her hot tea. They sat on opposite corners, really looking at each other for the first time in a long while.

"Nick, I absolutely don't believe you did anything to hurt that woman. The baby isn't the only reason I'm backing you on that. I promise."

"But it does change things. Is that the reason you came home?" He was asking the question, but she knew he didn't want to hear the answer.

"Maybe. I don't know. I'm here now. Does it really matter?" That was all she could give him. She didn't even understand her own emotions yet. How could she explain them to someone else?

"I guess not. But let me ask you something."

"Okay?"

"What happened to us when we got back from Hawaii? We had such a nice time. And then we got back and it was like it never even happened. Why?"

"I don't know. I really don't." She realized that it was a fair question, but she just didn't have a good answer.

"But you felt it, right? That things changed?"

"Yes, of course."

"So why? What was different? Why did you freeze me out?"

"*Freeze you out!* Is that where this is going? This is all *my* fault?" She sat up bolt straight and thought about going up to her room.

"Victoria! *No!* Not at all! I'm just asking. I'm just trying to understand. What I did was inexcusable and I'm not using this as an excuse. I just want to know if I did something. Was it me? Could I have done something differently?"

She settled back in, sinking into the sofa. "No. It wasn't you. I think it was just the situation. The house. The memory of what happened last time. All the disappointment over the last few years. The tension of it all." The truth was, she really didn't know why she'd grown cold towards him.

"But why couldn't you talk to me about it?"

"I don't know, Nick!"

"Okay, okay. You're talking to me about it now. So let's try to talk. Really talk. Would that be alright? Can you tell me how you feel? Now?"

"About what?"

"About us. The baby. All of it."

"You really want to know how I feel?"

"I really want to know. The good, the bad, the ugly." His smile couldn't hide the trepidation in his eyes. She knew he was terrified of losing her, especially with a baby on the way. But then he should have thought of that before he slept with Angie Hansen!

"I don't know if I can ever trust you again. I'm terrified that I'll lose this baby from all the stress in our lives. I'm so angry at you for getting us into this mess in the first place, but I'm trying not to let myself go there, for the sake of the baby. Is that enough, or do you want more?"

"It's a start." He flashed her his pretty boy smile but she wasn't having it.

"How could you sleep with another woman, Nick? How *could* you? After all we've been through? After our perfect trip?"

"I don't know! It was meaningless to me. And stupid. And I don't mean to speak ill of the dead, but she really did come on to me. I was tipsy when it happened the first time. And that was all it was ever going to be for me. I regretted it right away. But she got the wrong idea. I never gave her any indication that I was interested in a relationship. I tried to let her down gently. Close the sale. Move on. I swear. But she wasn't getting it. It was a mistake, I know. But she meant nothing to me. I love you, Victoria. Only you. From the minute I saw you."

"Then how could you *sleep* with her? I could never tell you I love you and then go sleep with another man!"

"And I could never be in an emotional relationship with another person! But you've been in one the whole time we've been together. And I take a back seat to him. All the time."

"What on earth are you talking about?"

"Charles!"

Was he actually serious? "Charles? Charles is gay!" She certainly did not see this one coming.

"But you're not!"

"What exactly are you getting at, Nick?"

"He's a handsome man. He's from your social circles. He's the one you confide in about everything. You're telling me that if he wasn't gay, you wouldn't be married to him?"

"That's ridiculous! I don't even think of him in that way." She couldn't believe it. All these years? Had Nick been jealous of Charles? This whole time? Or was he just grasping at straws? Trying to throw the blame back on her?

"Are you sure about that, Victoria?"

"Yes, I'm sure! He's my business partner. My good friend."

"Most people don't text their business partners while they're lying in bed at night. Or first thing in the morning. They don't have cute little inside jokes. You talk to him about how you're feeling, but not to me. I heard you on the phone with him.

Even after Hawaii. It was back to good old Charles, your prime confidant." She had to admit, he had a point. But still! This was different.

"So I pushed you into another woman's arms because I'm secretly in love with my gay best friend?"

"That's not what I'm saying."

"And this isn't the first time you've cheated. I've already given you a second chance."

"We've been over this! We weren't even married then! We'd just started dating. And if you remember, that happened right after I met your family for the first time. You didn't prepare me at all for that. I had no idea you were from that kind of money."

"What difference does that make?"

"Oh, come on, Victoria. You know exactly what kind of difference it makes. That's why you didn't tell me in the first place. You don't think it would be a bit intimidating to me? And by the way, Charles was there that day too. Sizing me up. I could see then how close you two were with all your inside jokes and your long history. I knew I'd never be able to replace him. It was all a different world. I didn't fit into it and I knew I never would. Then I ran into an old flame. It felt familiar. I went with it. Frankly, I didn't see us working out at that point. I thought you were just slumming it with me."

"*Slumming* it? I can't believe you would think that. I didn't even want my family money. You know that!" This was all quite a revelation, but she couldn't help but wonder if it was all an act.

"I figured that was just fashion. Youthful rebellion. That you'd come around."

"Then why did you stay with me? After you knew?"

"Because I was in love with you. And when I saw how upset you got about Gina, I finally believed that you loved me too.

And then you told me about what happened to you. With your advisor. How your mother reacted to it. Your disappointment. And I started to understand you better. I started to understand what you saw in me."

"I see."

"Look, Victoria. We have to at least try to make this work. We have a child to think about."

"I know that, Nick. You think I don't know that?"

"Yes, Victoria. I know that you know that." They both paused for a while—Victoria with her head in her hands, Nick staring off into space—knowing that they needed to walk carefully through the next few moments.

"Speaking of which. How is it going? With the baby? When was your last check up?" Nick asked.

"Two days ago. And the baby is perfectly healthy so far." She absolutely could not tell him that Charles went with her! What if he found out? She'd need to take that one to the grave.

"That's fantastic news. And how are you feeling?"

"Better. I had morning sickness but it's going away now. I'm hungry all the time. And tired."

He took her hand in his and she let him. "I'll be here for you. The whole way. And I'll do whatever you want me to do to fix this. Marriage counseling. Marriage retreats. Take out the garbage. Bring in the garbage." He paused. "Ankle bracelet?" Nick flashed that cheeky grin of his and she couldn't help but smile back at him this time. "Ankle bracelet it is," he said.

"*Stop!* Look, Nick. I know you'll be a fabulous father. I have no doubt about that. I've always known that. I know we'll be a great team as parents, whatever happens with our relationship. But that's about all I can give you right now. I can't promise you anything about us or our relationship. I can promise you I'll try to get past this, but I can't promise I'll be successful. I'm just taking it one day at a time."

"I'll take it. It's more than I deserve. Now, are you getting cravings? What kind of cravings? Should I go get pickles?"

"Gross! Not pickles!" The thought of it was enough to make her sick.

"Okay no pickles."

"Get me some decaf coffee. This tea isn't doing it for me."

"You got it."

"Now why don't you tell me more about that business idea of yours?"

"Gladly. There's this house, like I said." He went on to tell her all about it. But she wasn't really listening to the words. It was more the cadence of his speech that struck her. Even in the face of all this, his eternal optimism shined through. It's what had attracted her to him in the first place, and she needed that in her life now. More than ever.

SEVENTEEN

Victoria was almost at her destination, Mount Vernon, a town about twenty minutes away. Sam Coleman was right. She was out of practice, and that needed to change. She'd come here many times with her father, years ago. He was big on teaching his daughter to defend herself. He warned her constantly about the dangers of being from a family like hers. Stranger danger, even from a young age. The thought of a kidnapping, in particular, made him lose sleep. He'd waited until she was in middle school to really drive it home to her. She remembered the day.

"Victoria, families like ours, we have a great deal of advantages, with the kind of money we have. Not everyone lives like we do.

"I know Dad. I think that's why it's hard to make friends sometimes. It's awkward when they come over. And you don't like me going to my friend's houses."

"I'm sorry about that. But there are also certain dangers you should know about. Real dangers, Victoria."

"I know how to take care of myself, Dad! I'm not a kid."

"Victoria, I didn't tell you this when you were little. But you need to know. We've gotten threats before. If someone wanted to get at me, or get at our money, taking you would be the perfect way to do it. You're my only child. They know I'd pay anything, do anything, to get you back."

"We've had threats?" She remembered how her entire world view had shifted that day. What good was all of it? The money? The house? If they had to live in fear? She longed to be from a regular family, on a block with other kids her own age who played in the street.

"People like us, we have to be more careful. But I can't keep you in a cage forever. So I want to make sure you can defend yourself."

"Defend myself?"

"You're going to learn to shoot a gun. Today. I'm going to take you, and I'm going to teach you. I also want you to start a self-defense class. You'll be headed off to college before we know it, and I have to make sure you're as protected as possible."

She pulled into the parking lot of Patriot Shooting Center, grateful for those afternoon memories with her dad. Maybe it wasn't the classic father and daughter pastime, but it was special to her. And it did give her confidence. She'd been able to arrange for private training outside of normal business hours. Money couldn't fix all her problems, but it certainly helped. She was planning to meet Sam Coleman at her mother's house later, and she was mulling over whether or not to tell her about the baby.

She sat in her car alone with her thoughts. Who killed Angie Hansen? And who was out to get them? Was it the same person? Different people? What if it was just a random burglary gone bad and all of these incidents were unrelated? The photos, Jackman. The spray paint, a harmless prank. Was it all just random? Or was it all part of a larger plot to bring them down? Would it all just die down and fade away? Or were they on the edge of total disaster?

———

Nick was on his Peloton, getting in a good cardio sweat. He was tired but the bike ride was helping to reinvigorate him. He'd awoken last night from a recurring dream around three in the morning. He'd had it a few times over the past few weeks. He couldn't remember all of it, but it always involved a barking dog. A big dog with a deep, throaty bark like a German Shepard. He didn't remember seeing a dog, just hearing it bark.

"Woof! Woof! Woof." *"Woof! Woof! Woof."* He could still hear it now, in his mind. *"Woof! Woof! Woof."* *"Woof! Woof! Woof."* It was nagging at him.

He couldn't get back to sleep after the dream woke him, so he got up and at it. Painted over the horrific message on the garage door. Started to crunch the numbers for the flipping project. He was going to look at the house again today. Take more photos for Victoria. She seemed pretty eager to get going on it. Maybe she just wanted him out of her hair. He needed to be busy and they both knew that. They had a lot of fun renovating their place. He thought it might be a way to find their way back to each other. Hopefully she thought so too.

He was squarely in the zone, pedaling his head off, looking out the window at the gnarled trees and dense foliage across the river. All of a sudden it clicked. *A dog barking!* He'd heard it. While he was sitting in his car in the driveway that night at Angie's. He closed his eyes and thought back to make sure. He pictured himself sitting in the car, the engine running and the windows down. The smell of pine and musty leaves. Yes, he could hear it now, faintly. A dog. Barking in the background. Did it mean anything? Did it relate in some way to the feeling that someone had been watching him? But what good would it do if it did? He couldn't tell anyone about it or he'd have to tell them everything. And he certainly couldn't do that.

———

Her mother insisted that she meet Sam Coleman at her place after her session. She wanted to keep up on the case. Victoria could tell she was beside herself with worry. She wanted them to move in with her. Her mother was also turning out to be one of Nick's greatest champions, and Victoria was a bit skeptical about her newfound support for him. She'd never really liked him, yet she was paying for Sam's services and seemed eager to help clear him. There had to be more to it. Maybe Dr. Mason had told her about the baby. She wouldn't put it past her. Or maybe her mother had figured it out on her own. No alcohol at the function. No coffee today. The nausea.

"How are things with you and Nick?" Her mother wasn't beating around the bush this time.

"That's a big question." She hadn't expected her to launch into it so fast, but then Sam would be there any minute.

"It's an important one."

"He's trying."

"I guess that's something. And how are you feeling?"

"I'm fine. I told you. It was just mild anemia. And the stress."

"I mean emotionally, Victoria."

"Right. I'm sort of numb really. I just want this legal mess over with. I can't really deal with the relationship issue right now."

"Sam will get to the bottom of it. He's the best."

"So why are you so keen on helping Nick all of a sudden?" If her mother could be direct, then so could she.

"What do you mean?" Her mother was playing coy but Victoria knew she understood exactly what she meant.

"Come on, Mom. You never liked him."

"I never liked him *for you.* That's different. I have nothing against him personally. But he hurt you. Badly. When you were just dating. How am I supposed to like a man who hurt my only child?" She touched Victoria under the chin.

"But then why are you helping him now?"

"Because you married him! He's your husband now. And I know he's not a murderer. And so do you. Whatever happens between you and him, you have to clear his name. Or it'll ruin your lives forever." Victoria wasn't buying it.

"And that's the only reason?"

"If there were another reason, let's just say I wouldn't want to bring it up until you were good and ready to talk about it." Her mother knew about the baby. Well, that explained her sudden fondness for Nick. A grandchild would do it.

"I see. Well, I'm not. Good and ready to talk about it."

"I gathered. So let's change the subject then?"

"Okay. Sam Coleman. Why have I never met this mysterious man who seems to know so much about me?"

"There was never an occasion for you to meet him."

"It's weird, Mother. He says he's known you a long time. He knows all about me."

"We're old friends."

"What kind of friends?"

"*Friends* friends Victoria!"

The buzzer sounded and her mother dashed off to answer it. *Friends* friends? What on earth did that mean?

"Sam! Please come in. It's great to see you."

"It's great to see you too, Sandra. It's been too long. You look wonderful." As they walked over, she didn't notice any sort of chemistry between them. If he were an old flame, it seemed to have died out. Anyway, she was pretty sure she'd seen a ring on him last time.

"Hello Victoria! How are you doing after last night? That had to be awful for you."

"It was, but we're doing alright." She looked down. Yep, he had a ring. Too bad. Her mother could use some companionship. "Do you have any thoughts on who might have done it?" Victoria had filled him in on everything Stark had said, last night.

"I agree with Detective Stark. It's not likely to be Jackman. It's beneath someone like him. I also agree with him that it's not a teenager on a lark. Unfortunately, that leaves us with someone who knew Angie, the killer, or some random vigilante. I did check out Higgins and I'm confident he's harmless. But all of the options are potential dangers for you. I'm going through all of her relatives first. Given the turn of events, I really think you should consider moving here. Until it dies down."

"No. Please, not yet. We've increased our security. They'll arrive at four, before the sun sets. And we'll have two now, one in front and one out back. Let's give it a week or two. If something else happens, we'll reconsider."

"Victoria, I'm just not sure that's a good idea. You're so vulnerable there." Her mother was right, but she still wasn't ready to move in. That was too much for her right now.

"Mom. Sam. I'll be careful. We'll be careful. Nick is there with me. I'm not alone. We'll be fine. We have a great security system. And I know how to defend myself. And yes, Sam, I've started training again. Just please get to the bottom of this so we can all move on. Speaking of which, have you gotten anywhere on the case?"

"There's some good news. They found the murder weapon. It was a lamp. They found it in the woods, out back, down the hill. There's a path that winds down the hill and back out to Bedford Road behind the house. The killer ditched it, on foot. So they're now looking more seriously at the possibility that it was a random break-in that went bad. They're canvasing the area, trying to get camera footage down there, to see if they can spot someone getting an Uber or a cab. It's going in the right direction as far as Nick's concerned. I called Sylvia Murray and discussed it. She's pleased. She thinks it's enough for reasonable doubt if it comes to that."

"Oh my God! That's *great!*"

"Don't get your hopes up too much. These sorts of cases are hard to solve. Even if they don't arrest Nick, we may never know who did it." She knew that was bad. If it never got solved, there would always be cloud hanging over him. Over them. Still, it was better than facing a murder trial.

"Well, it's something. After last night, the garage door, I'll take any positive news. Do you think one of Angie Hansen's relatives did it? Or do you think it was someone else?"

"That's what I'm trying to find out. It could have been a random prank. Seems like someone out to get you would be more subtle, but then you never know. It could be a sign of a brazen personality. I'll let you know as soon as I have anything. I probably should get going soon."

"Oh no! I made some lunch for all of us. You two can get to know each other better. Please stay!" Her mother looked hopeful.

"That was thoughtful of you. Lunch sounds good," Sam replied.

Lunch? Victoria thought about what a strange turn her life had taken. She was pregnant. Her cheating husband was a murder suspect. Any number of people might be lurking outside their home, wanting to harm them. And she was about to have lunch with a man she'd never met before who was supposed to fix it all.

"Victoria?"

She looked over at her mother. What did she have to lose? "Lunch sounds good Mom."

———

Nick was back from his fact-finding mission at the property and Victoria was still out somewhere. His phone rang. Good timing. "Hey Pops."

"Is this a good time?" His father wasn't big on small talk.

"Yes. What's up?"

"I had my people check out the Rossi family. It wasn't them. They got no beef with you."

"You're sure?" Nick instantly regretted that question.

"*Nick!* Who're you talking to here?" His father's tone was sharp.

"Right. Sorry Pops."

"So what are you thinking?"

"Probably someone closer to you. Out of my reach. I don't like it. I don't like it at all."

"We added more security."

"You had security last time and look how close they got. Maybe you should come here. Send Victoria to her mother's house until this all dies down."

"No, Pops. We'll be okay. It was probably an isolated incident." Nick doubted that. But what good would it do to worry him?

"If you change your mind, let me know."

"I will."

"How's the legal situation?"

"Quiet."

"Good. Have you thought any more about coming back into the business?"

"Not now, Pops. Too much going on. But thanks."

"We're here for you if you change your mind."

"Thanks."

Nick couldn't really pinpoint the first time he'd realized that there was something special about his family. On some level, he'd always known. He'd grown up around hushed phone calls. Side glances from his grandfather that told him to bud out. An innate feeling to not ask too many questions. As the youngest, they shielded him longer than they needed to, like parents who held out too long on the truth about Santa in an effort to try and stop time. Maybe that was why he had distanced himself from all of the family business.

His late grandfather had been a well-respected and powerful man in the neighborhood, the kind you didn't cross if you had any sense, and Nick's father had grown up in his shadow. Today, his father lived on the periphery of that old and faded power structure. Mostly he just ran a construction business. But he had connections. Powerful ones. Useful ones—inside and outside of the official power channels. And today Nick felt comforted by that.

Then he took a look around their stunning home with its spectacular views. They'd been so happy when they found this place. It needed work, but the view of the Hudson was everything Victoria had ever wanted. And he loved the modern, clean lines that dared to defy the traditions of the area. It stood out. It made a statement. He and Victoria, forever their own people. They'd turned it into their dream home. Now it was turning out to be somewhat more of a nightmare. They were so exposed here, and it had never even crossed their minds that it would be an issue. And it was all his fault.

It was late afternoon. He got the remote and shut all the shades, sealing them in for the evening as best he could as the security officers took their posts outside for the long, dark night ahead.

EIGHTEEN

Victoria was starting to adjust to their new reality. A week had passed with no further incidents. She felt more secure with the officers there in early evening, but it did feel a bit claustrophobic, accustomed as she was to the wide expansive view that they now closed off on a nightly basis. Still, she wasn't complaining.

It was Sunday morning and she was looking forward to a relaxing weekend. She was doing some light jogging these days which felt good. And she'd taken up Tai Chi which was supposed to be good for managing stress. It seemed to be helping a bit. But what really helped was her weapons training. It gave her confidence that she could defend herself and her child, if it ever came to that. Her next session was later that day and she was looking forward to it.

She heard Nick come through the door, back from his run, as she sipped her decaf on the sofa. He was still sleeping in the guest room and she wondered how long that could go on until it would just get too awkward to ever go back to being a real couple.

"Hey!" Nick was a bit out of breath and his cheeks were red.

"Hi. How was it?"

"A little brisk at first but perfect after about a mile."

"How far did you go?"

"About eight miles." He came and sat with her. "What's on your agenda for the day?"

"I thought we could go over to that property together." She knew this would make him happy and it felt good to want that again.

"Really? You think I should pursue it? I haven't gotten an answer yet from Mark."

"I think *we* should pursue it. I'm not sure it's a good idea to bring in your brother now. With all we have going on. You can just hire him to do some of the work."

"How exactly would that work? I don't have enough cash for that." He was biting his bottom lip, looking skeptical.

"I do. We can partner on it." She knew that Nick would want to do this on his own, but it just wasn't practical. Hopefully he could put his ego aside.

"By partner, you mean you'd buy the house for me?" He shook his head and waved a hand back and forth. "No. No way. You know how I feel about that."

"I know you have your pride, but this would still be your thing. You know construction. I don't. I'll buy the house and you do the renovation. It's fair. And I want another option, just in case. This place. We're so exposed here. And it's also a good investment. For our future." She put her hand on her belly.

"Speaking of being vulnerable, what do you think about a dog? They're good protection." He'd always wanted a dog. It was a nice try, but she wasn't falling for it.

"You know how I feel about that. Not with the baby coming." She'd read dogs could get jealous of new babies. That it was better to bring in a dog after a baby. But really, she also thought about the burden. And the mess.

"You'd feel safer," he offered.

"I can't think about that right now. Can we go see the house soon?"

"I'll try and set it up. Any news from Coleman?" Victoria and Nick had shared with each other what they'd learned. They were both guardedly optimistic. About the murder weapon messing with the timeline and creating reasonable doubt, and about his father's reassurance regarding on the Rossi family.

"Nothing but what I told you."

"I guess no news is good news?"

"Let's hope so."

————

Victoria was done with her tactical lesson and was practicing her aim. She looked out to the target clipped on its metal frame as she steadied herself in her spot. She fired three shots. Not bad, but not good enough. And the gun seemed to be sticking a bit. She would take it in to be serviced. Her accuracy had always been good, and with some practice, it was getting even better. But she had on her ear protection. She was calm. This wasn't real life.

She thought about what her trainer had told her. Real life is different. It's much louder, for one thing, and the target is almost never still. Adrenaline is pumping, especially if you feel that your life is in danger. It's easy to overreact. She thought back to that night in college, years ago. She remembered clearly what it felt like. The adrenaline rush. Being in danger. If she'd had a gun then, would it really have made any difference?

He was her senior thesis advisor. He wasn't her first choice, but the professor she'd been working with went out on maternity leave. He was the type who liked to get chummy with students. His stringy hair was long in the back and he wore it in a ponytail. It looked out of place with his receding hairline but it was a perfect match for his aging hipster attire. He'd asked her to meet for drinks, to talk about her thesis, the implication being that if she didn't, her grade would be in jeopardy. He drank scotch on the rocks that night. She had wine. Too much of it. She was uncomfortable. He wanted her to include some articles he'd flagged for her in her thesis before he would sign off on it. He was married, so when he insisted she come to his apartment to pick them up that night, she wasn't overly concerned. He lived in faculty housing, so it wasn't too out of the way.

He closed the door behind them with a slam and locked the dead bolt. She looked around at the dark, dingy interior cluttered with papers and books. It didn't seem like anyone was home. It was a tiny one-bedroom apartment and all the lights were off except the one he'd turned on. She didn't hear anyone.

"Where's your wife?"

"Out of town. Why?"

"Oh, I was looking forward to meet her. That's all." She was hoping that her inquiry would make it clear that she had no intention of sleeping with him. But he didn't seem to get the message.

"Come on, Victoria. Don't play coy with me. You know how the world works." He ticked her under her chin with his finger. It made her skin crawl. "Let me get us a nightcap. What do you want?"

"Just some water for me, thanks. Do you have those articles?"

"What's your rush?" He was toying with her.

"It's just, I need to get going. I have an early day tomorrow." She took a step back.

"I'll get us some drinks. And you can have a seat." He said this with authority, pointing to his worn mustard-colored loveseat. Was he counting on the fact that a student would be intimidated into staying, or would he get physically aggressive? To hell with her grade, she thought. To hell with her degree. The minute he went into the kitchen, she would bolt. She had to be fast. He was only few paces away and he was tall. Her heart was racing and her palms were sweaty. She tried to breathe, calm herself down. His back was to her now. This was her chance.

Go! She bolted for the door and grabbed the knob. Her damp palm slipped off of it on the first try. She turned and pulled, then she realized she'd forgotten about the dead bolt. She tried to turn it but it stuck a bit. She heard him behind her. Soon his wiry body enveloped her, his arms reaching around like tentacles pulling her back in. He spun her around and pushed her up against the wall, smiling, his face close to hers. His breath reeked of cheap liquor.

"So you want to play hard to get? Is that it, you little tease?" He was surprisingly strong for a thinner man. He had her arms pinned up against the wall. He started to kiss her, his gross slimy, tongue probing her mouth, and then his arms were everywhere. Groping her. His hands were under her t-shirt. Her bra. Moving down into her pants with such force he popped her zipper open as he plunged his hand in. He stopped for a moment to open his own pants. She had to get out of this. But how?

"Wait! Please! I want to slow this down. Your wife's away right?" She tilted her head, trying to look innocent yet seductive.

He took a deep breath and backed off a bit. It seemed to be working.

"Right." He was running his spidery hands through his hair, calming himself down.

"Get me that drink?" she said sheepishly. "I'm just nervous, that's all. This is a big step for us. What's the big rush?" She rubbed the side of his arm, trying not to gag, feigning a shy smile.

"Sure babe. I'm here to please." He smiled again, exposing his coffee-stained teeth. He started to walk away and then turned back to her. "What can I get you?"

She had a clear shot but she would only get one chance. Drawing on muscle memory from karate class back in high school, she shot her leg out towards him as hard as she could, kicking him squarely in the crotch. His eyes bulged out of his head as he let out a guttural scream. He fell back on the floor and curled up into the fetal position, holding his privates. She moved for the door.

"*You bitch!* If you tell anyone about this, *you're dead.*" He said this in a low, angry rumble that only she could hear. It was very effective.

She got the door open, closed it softly behind her, and walked away as fast as she could, trying not to attract attention to herself as she struggled to hold up her pants. She took a leave of absence the next day, loaded up her car, and drove the five hours back home, taking him at his word.

———

Jack was in again on a Sunday sitting at his cold metal desk. But then he didn't really have anywhere else to be. He'd told

Lexi to take the weekend off. He'd spent Saturday away from the office but all he could think about was the case. He wasn't getting much sleep either. So he came in. He was enjoying the quiet as he went through the case files over and over again. He knew when they found the weapon in the woods that it was going to be a long haul to an arrest.

They only had one viable suspect. And if it wasn't him, it could be just about anybody. And facts were facts. They knew Mancusio was at the store at 8:31 and was home by 9:15. They'd confirmed it with video camera footage, witnesses, and the store receipt. There just wasn't enough time for him to have done it and ditched the weapon. Unless the time of death was off or he was missing something. What he needed was a break.

"Hey Stark, someone's here to see you. They have information on the Hansen case," the front desk officer called out.

"Send them in." He wasn't holding his breath, but he could hope.

"Hi Detective Stark. I live in the area, off Bedford, and I just got back into town. I have some security footage that might help with the Hansen case." He handed him a flash drive.

Thanks for coming by." Jack connected the flash drive to the computer and loaded up the video. "Son of a gun," he said, as he rubbed his forehead. "I'll be damned."

NINETEEN

Nick had moved quickly on his business idea after his talk with Victoria earlier that day. He wrote up their offer on the house, a major fixer upper in the sought-after Chappaqua neighborhood of Hemlock Hills. They decided to offer quite a bit under the asking price, but Nick figured they had nothing to lose. It would easily sell for much more once they had renovated it, but they weren't going to pay a penny more. They didn't need to do this, and he was counting on the fact that most buyers didn't want to deal with a renovation with the price of supplies and labor so high. Victoria found him in his office and signed off on it. And that was that. He wasn't quite sure where her head was at, but he wasn't asking any questions.

"Do we want to celebrate, maybe? Go out to eat?" Victoria offered. It was nearing dinner time and both of them had been too busy to think about it.

"Sure. Where do you want to go?"

"I don't know. Surprise me. I'll go get ready." Victoria was certainly in a good mood. What was up with that? He knew she'd been over at her mother's. That wasn't likely the reason. But her attitude towards him seemed to be shifting. This was very good news. Finally, things were going in the right direction. They had a baby on the way. The case seemed to be stalling—fingers crossed. Victoria was warming up to him, and he had a new business venture to keep him busy. He hoped his luck would hold.

———

Victoria went upstairs and looked at all the clothes in her enormous walk-in closet. Soon—hopefully—none of these clothes would fit her. She was getting more confident as the pregnancy progressed, daring to think of her future, but only little bits at a time. She picked out an outfit and went to the bathroom to shower and primp.

She hadn't thought about that horrible night at her advisor's house in a long time. It was always somewhere, in the back of her mind, but she usually managed to block out the actual event, along with his name—Timothy Sutton. He'd been on her mind the last few days because of the security tape from the night of the Halloween fair, when her garage door had been vandalized. The way the man moved, it reminded her of him. But that was impossible. Why would he come after her now? It was probably just her imagination.

She'd told her mother about what had happened and her mother insisted she not report it. She said it would only hurt her reputation. She arranged, under some unknown pretense, for her daughter to finish up her senior thesis and get her degree from home. And it was all swept under the rug. They never spoke of it again. Victoria wondered what would have happened if her father had been alive. Would he have gone after him or would he have followed her mother's lead?

Reliving it made her remember something else. How Nick was the one who had brought her back to life. She didn't have a relationship for over a year after that. Some casual dating, but nothing substantial. Nick was the only person she'd told besides her mother. She hadn't even told Charles the whole story, just that her advisor was a creep so she left school. Nick had been so wonderful with her. Patient. Loving. Gentle. He made her laugh and forget her problems. As she thought about the good times, she found herself warming up to him again. She was hopeful that it would continue. She was even thinking of asking him to sleep next to her tonight, finding herself hungry for the familiar comfort of having him next to her while she slept.

———

"You look beautiful!" Nick looked truly awestruck. She'd really done it up. Tight black dress—short, that showed off her fabulously shapely legs. High heels, which she rarely wore. A bit more make-up with a darker mascara that made her blue eyes pop. And the necklace that Nick had bought her in Hawaii at the hotel shop, a large, dark gray Tahitian pearl framed with diamonds in a white gold setting.

"I'm in the mood to celebrate. Plus, hopefully, I won't be able to dress like this for very long! I plan to get horribly, wonderfully big. So take a good look, Nick Mancusio. You may not see this body for a while." She did a model pose and spun around for him.

He walked up and put his hands on her cheeks. "Get as big as a house. I can't wait!"

She looked up at him, trying so hard to think positive. "I'm not sure I have much choice. I'm so hungry all the time. This baby's a foodie."

"You know, the other day I thought about the first time I saw you. In the quad. Do you remember? That windy day?"

"I do! I thought you were full of it." She smiled as she thought back to it, a nice memory.

"Maybe I was. But I also thought I'd never seen a more beautiful woman in my life. And I hadn't. Until now. You're positively glowing." Nick kissed her gently on the lips, and it felt right.

"I'm so afraid to be happy."

"Don't be, Vic. We deserve it. We're going to get past all of it. Trust me. I love you."

"I know you do," she replied. He looked a bit disappointed by her response, but that was all she could give him right now.

"Should we go then?"

"Yes, I'm starving. I'll go get my purse." Victoria walked into the kitchen as Nick waited for her in the living room. Then all hell broke loose.

Boom. Boom. Boom. The pounding on the door reverberated through the living room, obscuring the words of someone outside, yelling. Her stomach lurched. What was happening? Were they under some sort of attack? Was the security team being overrun? Then they heard the words more clearly.

"Open up! We have a warrant to search these premises."

Nick headed for the door.

"What's happening?" Victoria asked.

"Stay back, Victoria!" Nick commanded. She obeyed, ducking behind a wall. She heard him open the door.

"May I see that?" Nick asked.

"We have a warrant to search your home. Please stand back." It was Stark's voice. It seemed safe, so she came out to see what was going on. One of the uniformed officers addressed her. In this context, she didn't think it wise to address Stark at all.

"Ma'am, please stay to the side and let us do our jobs." About a dozen law enforcement officers descended on their house like a swarm of angry bees, shattering their fragile fairytale. They looked at each other, helpless, as they watched the officers fan out and proceed to upend their home. It surprised her that they were polite and methodical, but that didn't make it any less stressful.

Nick took out his phone and dialed. She assumed it was Sylvia Murray he was calling. Victoria felt ridiculous standing there in her sexy dress, but she couldn't very well go change. She remembered that her gun was being serviced and thought that was probably a good thing, even though it was legal. She didn't want them to take it. And she would be sure to remember to go pick it up soon. She sat down on the sofa and waited until an officer asked her to get up so they could check between the cushions. Maybe this was all just for show. She sat back down when they were done. Nick joined her.

It went on like this for a long time. She and Nick were just sitting there. Waiting. Not really talking. Sylvia was on her way over. An officer was standing guard near them. They couldn't see Stark.

"I've got something!" one of them called out from outside the front door, and Stark came out from wherever he was to meet up with him. The officer came in and handed him something. "We found a cell phone. Buried under one of the potted plants." The officer handed it to Stark. He took it, put it in an evidence bag, and walked over to Nick.

"If this is Angie Hansen's, you've got a big problem." Stark looked genuinely surprised, which only added to Victoria's distress. "Any other explanation as to why there's a cell phone buried in your yard?"

"If that's Angie Hansen's, I'm being framed!" Nick looked shocked.

"Nick, don't say another word! I'll call Sylvia and get her over here." Victoria knew she'd fall apart soon, but right now she was functional.

"You can tell her to meet him at the station," Stark said. "Nick Mancusio, you're under arrest for the murder of Angela Hansen. . ."

"Victoria! Get Sylvia to meet me there."

"Let me come with him!" Victoria yelled out.

"You should stay here until they finish. It'll be a while. They'll give you a receipt for everything we take." Stark said this as if that made it all okay.

"No, Victoria, stay here. It's too stressful," Nick said.

"I'll meet you there later, Nick. Don't say a word until Sylvia gets there."

She got the phone to call Sylvia as they cuffed Nick and took him away, leaving her with a house full of officers combing through her private life. It went to voicemail but she left a message. It would be a miracle if this baby survived all of this. She was trying so hard not to crack, to stay calm, but how much could one person take?

Of course Nick was being framed. He wasn't stupid enough to leave a murdered woman's cell phone in his own yard. Was he? And what did they suddenly have on him to bring this on? A feeling of complete and total dread shook her to her core. Just when she thought it couldn't get any worse, an officer came over to her.

"Ma'am, I'm going to need to take your cell phone."

PART THREE

TWENTY

Two days later

Victoria had been lying in bed for about an hour, trying to avoid getting up and facing reality. It had been two days since Nick's arrest. She looked around at her tidy bedroom, everything in its place—the bamboo floor free of Nick's dirty socks, the Tamo Ash dressers and nightstands clear of clutter and showing off their sheen. It was nice, having it all to herself. She'd been pretty calm over last two days. Instead of feeling lonely, she actually felt relived. She hadn't realized how much the marital situation had been stressing her out.

She was going over it in her mind. They had evidence that Nick had gone up to the house again, around nine that night—camera footage from a home owner who had been out of town for the past few weeks. Sylvia insisted that they would never make a second-degree murder charge stick. They still only had circumstantial evidence and the timeline was all wrong, even with the fact that the cell phone had been found on their property. Victoria wasn't so sure.

The arraignment was later that day. Sylvia told her to free up about a million in cash. She expected him to make bail but it wasn't going to be cheap. Victoria had always taken her wealth for granted, not really giving it much weight, even rebelling against it at times. Now she realized just how fortunate she was to have all that money at her disposal. She wasn't a billionaire or anything, but she could afford bail. A second home. How did people manage a crisis like this without those kinds of resources? It usually made her feel guilty but at that moment she just felt grateful.

———

Normally, Jack would be thrilled after making an arrest on a case like this. But he wasn't. There were too many things that didn't make sense. Why had Mancusio lied about the second drive to the house if he was innocent? But then why would he keep the cell phone at his house if he was guilty? And how could he have ditched the murder weapon and gotten home when he did? He'd wanted to wait on the warrant, but the higher ups were pressuring him. They needed progress on the case so he appeased them with the search. He really hadn't expected to find much at the house. He was as shocked as anyone that the cell phone had been found outside their home. And anyone could have planted it there. The arraignment was later that day, and he didn't feel very good about it.

"Penny for your thoughts," Lexi said.

"I'm going over it again. It just doesn't make sense to me."

"Not if you look at it logically. But if you look at it from the perspective of someone who was very frazzled, maybe it does."

"How so?" He looked over at Lexi, slouched over her notes. She looked up at him.

"If we agree he's not a dangerous predator, that this was out of character for him, maybe it goes like this: it was a crime of passion. She threatened to tell his wife. He panicked. He grabbed her by the throat and then came to his senses and let go. Then he's in too deep. She's hysterical, turning and running away from him. He grabs the lamp and *bam!*" She hit the table. "He's a murderer!"

"Okay. And then?"

"He's frazzled. He takes the lamp and the cell phone. Ditches the lamp later. Keeps the cell. Maybe there's something on it he doesn't want anyone to see?" She shook her head, seeming to immediately realize the flaws in her own argument. "No, that doesn't make sense. The cell phone just corroborates what he told us. He texted Angie and she didn't text him back, so he went up there again to see if Victoria was there."

"Right. It's possible but it doesn't make much sense. Go back and put the lamp in the woods? A robbery gone bad is just as likely, if not more so at this point. With all the publicity, everyone knows he's a suspect. The real killer could have ditched the lamp and then planted the cell to throw suspicion on him. His comment about hearing the barking dog that night. It fits. Someone ran down there and there's sure to be some dogs along the way. We need to look into it."

"Then why didn't he tell us this earlier? The first time he was here? He admitted the affair. Why leave this part out? He has to be hiding something. But what? We both feel it. We've done our jobs, Jack. It's up to the courts to do the rest."

Lexi was young. Idealistic. She hadn't yet had the experience of putting away an innocent person only to have them exonerated years or even decades later. Even if it didn't go that far, a 'not guilty' verdict didn't necessarily clear a person in the minds of the public. Lives were ruined by going after the wrong person, especially if the real killer was never found. Not to mention the fact that the real perpetrator was still out there in cases like that, getting away with murder. It was a heavy burden to bear. But he was too tired to lay all of this on her right now.

"Courts aren't perfect." It was all he could muster.

"I know. But it's out of our hands now." She was right about that as far as Mancusio was concerned. But he was going to keep looking. He would start with the houses down the hill from the victim's house, looking for any big, barking dogs.

———

People might have thought Victoria callous for working at a time like this, but she didn't care. It got her mind off things. The morning was flying by and she'd done nothing on the case yet. She had to leave soon for the arraignment. She took out Higgins' card and sent a text asking for a meet up the following morning. She was pretty neutral regarding psychics. Maybe he was and maybe he wasn't. But she still wanted to meet him face to face. Stark told her he wasn't dangerous, but she wanted to see for herself. She was also banking on the fact that if she acted like she believed him, she'd be on his good side—just in case.

"Victoria? Jeff Malone is here to see you," her assistant announced.

"Send him in, Nate." She needed to find out more about Angie Hansen. Who was she? What did Nick see in her? Who would want her dead? Jeff Malone seemed like a good place to start.

"Victoria! How're you holding up?" He looked good, like he'd lost a few pounds. Nick seemed to look up to Jeff but she could never really understand why. Nick was far more handsome but then Jeff did have a certain kind of alpha male energy that could be intimidating. He also made more money than Nick and liked to live in it. The suit he wore to her office——a custom Kiton—probably cost upwards of five figures.

"I'm doing alright. Thanks for coming." She closed her laptop but stayed behind her desk.

"No problem. Glad you're doing okay. Tough situation."

"I'm made of tough stock. The rugged old Dutch. We just carry on." She stood up from behind her desk and started to walk around to the sitting area.

"It's admirable. You look great." Maybe it was the pregnancy. Charles claimed she was glowing.

"Thanks."

"So, what's happening with the case?" Jeff asked.

"Nick's getting arraigned this afternoon. That's about all I know right now. Sylvia doesn't think they can make it stick. She doesn't expect the grand jury to indict him, but that won't be for a few weeks at best. We expect he'll make bail and be out in the meantime. But I'm afraid that even if he doesn't get indicted, this will hang over him forever. If they don't find the real killer, that is."

"Do they have any other leads?"

"Not as far as I know." She thought about telling him about the murder weapon complicating the timeline, but then thought better of it.

"So how can I help?" Jeff leaned back in his chair and crossed one leg over the other.

"What do you know about Randy Jackman? And his relationship with Angie Hansen? Nick said she was afraid of him."

"She was. Very afraid of him. He was a real bastard and he doesn't like to be challenged. Everyone who works for him says the same thing. There's a lot of turnover. Only the really ruthless can cut it there. It seems like that's intentional. He wants sharks. Like him. People who have no morals but enough brains not to do anything illegal.

"I see." Victoria needed to see this Jackman for herself.

"People who can't cut it are out. But the ones who stay make a fortune, so there's a steady stream of new blood. It seems to be working for him." Jeff shrugged and threw up his hands.

"So what about Angie Hansen? Was she cutting it?"

"That's tough to say. She was almost like a split personality. She had a ruthless edge to her in business. She was driven. Wanted the promotion. Thought she deserved it. I'm sure she would do whatever it took businesswise to get what she wanted. But she wasn't going to sleep with him."

"What was her allegation against Jackman? Or is that not something you are comfortable sharing with me?"

"I can tell you the basics. She said she was outperforming all the men in the office. She deserved the promotion. He met privately with all three candidates. The two others were male. When they were alone, he came on to her. Touched her inappropriately. She wouldn't play ball on that. She didn't get the promotion. She claimed it was because she rejected him."

"Do you think she was telling the truth?" She thought back to what Nick had said about her.

"I'm paid to do what my client wants me to do. She seemed to believe it, and I didn't ask any questions."

"But there was no proof?" she asked.

"Nope. It was a he-said, she-said."

Victoria fiddled with her hair as she contemplated her next move. "What was she like on a personal level?"

"Do you really want to go there, Victoria?"

"I have to know what she was like. Nick claims she came on to him. Not that it excuses him if she did, but do you think he's telling the truth?"

"Look, Victoria, Nick will say whatever he has to say to save his marriage. He loves you. I know that and you know that. But he risked it all, like a spoiled school boy. For what? You know how pissed off I am about this. I warned him she was seductive. And vulnerable. Even unstable. And he went for it anyway."

"I know." She wondered why Jeff would think to warn Nick about something like that.

"Truthfully, when he first told me she was dead, I thought it was suicide. That's how messed up she was." Jeff's expression turned somber.

"You didn't really answer my question."

"No, I didn't." He sat for a moment, his lips pursed, then he started in. "I'll say this much. She had a kind of immaturity when it came to men. That's what I mean about the split personality. She was very alluring, yes. I'm sure she flirted with him. She flirted with me too. That's why I warned Nick about her. Could she have come on to him? Sure. But I also believe the part about her getting too attached to him. And she was definitely the type to go crazy on him for ending it. She liked to call the shots with men. And that's not a good thing for Nick's case, given what happened."

"I see." Victoria didn't like where this was going.

"Frankly, I hope they don't call me as a witness if this goes to trial because being forced to say something like that? About what she was really like? It certainly doesn't help him. But I won't lie for him."

"I'm sure he doesn't expect it, Jeff. You're still upset with him. I don't blame you."

"I'm more disappointed than upset. But I'm trying. He gazed off into the distance with a heavy look in his eyes and then turned back to her. "He's supposed to be my best friend."

"I'm disappointed too."

"I can imagine. Well, I probably should get going now." He leaned forward, looking about ready to get up and leave. "Let me know if you need anything. And are you sure you're safe? At the house alone?"

She stood up and he followed suit. "You sound like my mother! I'll be fine. Don't worry. I can take care of myself. And I've hired private security. I'm probably safer now that Nick's not there anymore."

"That's a good point. But still, don't take any chances. If someone is trying to frame him, they're still around somewhere."

"I know. Thanks, Jeff. Can you see yourself out? I'm so swamped here."

"Yes, of course. Let me know if you need anything." He walked out the door and then turned back to look at her. "Take care, Victoria."

"I will." She went back to her desk and stared out to the Hudson, reflecting on what Jeff said. Angie Hansen was unstable. Vulnerable. Nick went up to the house a second time. Did she buy his explanation? It seemed likely that he was being framed. Why wouldn't he ditch the cell phone if he murdered her instead of leaving it for the police to find on his property? Still, it didn't look good. Even if she believed him, would a jury? Would the public?

———

"All rise." The judge walked in and everyone in the courtroom stood up and then sat back down. Nick was exhausted from two nights of no sleep. The warm wood paneling of the courtroom contrasted sharply with his recent memory of the cold metal cell. He was sure he looked like hell. He could see it on Victoria's face when he walked in and they'd caught each other's eyes. Her look was somewhere between pained and disgusted. He couldn't blame her. This was all his fault to begin with. How could he expect sympathy?

His biggest concern right now was bail. Sylvia assured him he would get out that day, but he knew it was a possibility that he wouldn't. That scared him more than anything. He wasn't thinking about the future anymore. He was taking it day by day. She also told him that she didn't really expect the grand jury to indict him. They wouldn't convene for another few weeks. That was too abstract for him. All he cared about was now. And right now, he couldn't shake the terrifying fear that he might never get out. It was so much worse than anyone could ever imagine. The loss of freedom. The humiliation. The sheer inhumanity of it all.

He listened as everyone introduced themselves and the formalities were taken care of, including his acceptance of Sylvia Murray as his counsel. He looked over at her, her brown bob perfectly coiffed, her fitted black suit accented with a single strand of white pearls and matching stud earrings, looking so professional and composed. He felt like a homeless person next to her. He tried to look engaged but all he could think about was bail. Would he go home or back to a cell?

"Will the accused please rise?" Nick and Sylvia stood.

"Nicholas Mancusio, you are charged with one count of murder in the second degree in the death of Angela Hansen. This carries a maximum charge of life in prison. Do you understand these charges?"

"Yes, your honor." His stomach sank as he heard the words he'd been dreading.

"Do you understand that you have the right to plead guilty or not guilty to these charges?"

"Yes, I understand."

"Do you understand that you have the right to a trial by a jury or judge, you have the right to call witnesses for your defense, and you have the right to question the witnesses of the prosecution? Do you understand also that you have the right to remain silent? Do you understand all of these rights?"

"I understand, your honor."

"To one count of murder in the second degree in the death of Angela Hansen, how do you plead?"

Nick straightened up, his head high, and looked her in the eye. "Not guilty, your honor." It felt good to say that out loud.

"Bail is set at half a million dollars." The judge pounded her gavel and that was it. A rush of relief coursed through his body and his knees buckled out from under him. He was so overcome with emotion, he had to sit. A shower. His bed. He stood up again and hugged a stiff and unresponsive Sylvia. She gave him a polite smile and a firm nod of her head. Maybe she didn't believe him or maybe that was just her way. He didn't care. He couldn't think about the long road ahead. For now, he was going home, and it seemed to him like a miracle.

TWENTY-ONE

Nick was unusually quiet on the way home. She'd never seen him so beaten down. He'd nodded off towards the end of the drive, even sleeping through the boisterous crowd of reporters surrounding their house. Then he'd gone straight up to shower. When she went up to check on him, he was asleep on top of the guest bed in his boxers. She covered him up with a blanket and turned off the light. He was obviously—and understandably—exhausted.

Victoria was filled with a strange mix of pity and apprehension. She wasn't sure how comfortable she was having him here right now. She was in much less danger with him gone than with him home. Whoever did this was out to get Nick. Not her. Not the baby. An obvious solution was for her to stay with her mother, but why should she leave? The lies. They were peeling off the layers of trust they'd built up over the years. Soon there would be nothing left but a raw core of doubt and suspicion. Yet he was still the father of her child. She rubbed her hand over the slight bump that was forming and closed her eyes, envisioning the different paths their futures might take, trying hard not to imagine the worst-case scenario—the father of her child in prison.

———

Nick woke up disoriented. His eyes darted around for dangers, a habit he had quickly picked up during his two-night stay in a jail cell. A flood of relief filled him. He was home. In the guest bed. It looked dark outside, but then it got dark early this time of year. He fumbled for his phone. It was just after five in the evening. He'd been asleep for a little over an hour. He didn't remember falling asleep. He assumed Victoria had put the blanket on him. That was a nice gesture, but he knew things were bad. She was losing faith in him, and he really couldn't blame her. He knew he wouldn't be able to offer a good explanation for his actions. He barely understood them himself. He got up and went to get some clothes on to go face her.

As he walked downstairs, the pungent smell of garlic and tomatoes filled the air. It smelled good. He suddenly realized he was very hungry. He stopped halfway down the stairs to admire their home, the sanctuary he had destroyed for some reason even he couldn't understand. If he ever got out of this legal mess, he would go to therapy. Wouldn't that be a luxury? Therapy. Maybe they had that in prison.

"Hey," he said, as he entered the kitchen.

"Hi. Are you hungry?"

"Yeah, I think I am."

"I made some pasta. Nothing fancy."

"It sounds perfect." Nick went over to the cupboard and got a glass, then went over to the fridge to fill it with ice and water. He chugged it down, realizing that even a simple staple like ice water had quickly become a luxury to him. He felt the sweet cold liquid move through his system. It brought him back to life. He refilled his glass and walked to the kitchen table. Victoria brought over his meal and placed it in front of him.

"This smells good. Thanks."

"You're welcome."

"Are you going to join me?" It had only been two days but it seemed like a lifetime.

She hesitated a bit. "Yes, sure. I'm just getting a drink." She went to get some ice water. "Do you want something stronger than water?"

"No, not right now, thanks." They were so polite. So formal. It worse than an argument. It was like they were strangers. Nick felt radioactive now, the jail stench permeating his being, destined to contaminate the sanctity of their home.

Victoria sat down with her meal. They sat there, eating in silence. It wasn't so bad. Better than the forced small talk.

"So, how are you doing?" she asked.

"I'm fine. It wasn't that bad." He didn't want to burden her with the truth. That he was terrified of going back. That he'd probably rather kill himself than spend his life in prison.

"I'm glad to hear that."

"How are you feeling?" he asked.

"Good. Better. I had another check-up yesterday." He'd missed it again! Damn it! Another one, gone forever.

"And how is everything?"

"Great."

"That's the best news I've heard in a while. You didn't find out . . ." He looked over at her.

"The sex? No. I wanted to wait for you." He smiled. At least that was something. She wanted to wait for him to find out. Still, he wasn't going to read too much into it.

"Speaking of the baby," Victoria said.

"Yes?"

"I think given all the media attention, it might be better—safer for us—if you stayed with your family for a while." He was crushed, even though it had crossed his mind. He was even thinking of suggesting it. But the fact that she suggested it first meant that he was losing her.

"That's probably a good idea. I was thinking the same thing."

"I called the seller's agent and told them to move forward on the house. That way, you could stay there once we close. And we'd be a bit closer." He'd totally forgotten about the house.

"You still want to move forward with that?" That made him feel a bit hopeful, but then maybe there was something he wasn't seeing. He was still a bit foggy.

"Sure. Sylvia is confident they won't indict. We should move forward and think positive."

"So you believe me?" He wasn't sure he wanted to hear her reply. She looked away for a moment and ran her hand through her hair, and then turned back to him.

She let out a sigh. "I believe you, Nick. But I'm confused. There's been so many lies. I don't understand what this all means. Why did you go up there a second time? And why didn't you tell them about it when they first questioned you?"

He hesitated, not sure how she would take all of this. But he had to tell her the truth. They had to start trusting each other again.

"I went up again because I saw you. Or I thought I saw you. In your car. On the side of the road when I left her house. Did you pull over? On the side of the road? On Bedford?"

"Yeah, I did. I was pretty shaken up."

"I wasn't sure at the time. I drove by pretty fast, but it kept nagging at me afterwards. I had a feeling you knew, even before that night. Something about the way you'd been acting. So after I went to the store, I texted her to see if you'd come by. She didn't answer my text, so I drove back up, thinking that maybe you'd driven up there to confront her." He hesitated for a moment, wondering how much to reveal to her. "But all the lights were out, so I figured it was fine. That she'd just gone to sleep early. So I just came home."

"I see. So why didn't you just tell them that?"

"Because I found out she was murdered! And I didn't know what to think. I only knew I didn't do it." He looked away after he said it.

"Wait, did you think *I* did it?" Her jaw dropped.

"I didn't know what to think!" He waited, trying to interpret the wide-eyed look on her face. "There's something I never told you, Victoria. I found your teal blouse. In the garbage. When I was looking for the receipt from the store. It had blood on it. After that, I didn't want to tell them I saw your car on the side of the road. I didn't know what you told them. I thought it might make you look bad. I wasn't sure what happened."

"Oh my God. You thought . . ." she put her head in her hands. She sat there like that for a bit and then looked back up at him. "You thought I killed her?" Her voice was soft. "You were trying to protect me?"

"I didn't know what happened. And yes, of course I was trying to protect you. I'd do anything to keep you safe, Victoria. That's why I destroyed the blouse right after I found it. I'd plead guilty right now to keep you from going to prison. But then you explained it all. About going there and taking the photos. And falling, and ripping your blouse. And then I knew you didn't do it, but I already left that part out at the station. How could I go back and tell them why left it out the first time? I mean, what could I say? Hey, sorry. I thought my wife got into a brawl and killed someone, so I lied for her." They both sat for a bit. "So here we are." Nick let out a sigh while Victoria sat in silence, looking stunned.

"So that's why you were acting so weird when I got back to the house that afternoon, after I went to the police to clear myself. You found my blouse." She sat there, shaking her head, as if trying to reshuffle all of this in a way that made sense. "*Nick?* How could you think that of me?!"

"Not you. *Her!* She was unstable! I thought if you'd gone up there, maybe she could have come after you first. I just didn't know. With her personality and how jealous of her you seemed. And how she wouldn't accept that things were over. I could see something like that escalating. And you were acting really cagey that night. I knew you went somewhere. I knew you were frazzled when I saw your car parked like that, even before I found your blouse."

"Did you tell the police all of this now?"

"No, of course not. I only told them I went up there the second time to find out if you were on to me because I thought I'd seen your car. And I certainly didn't kill her, Victoria! Surely you must see that now."

"Nick. This is a lot to take in."

She seemed to be getting it, but then Victoria was a hard person to read. "I can imagine. But don't forget that I had your back. This whole time. That's what family does. And we're family. I need you now, Victoria. I'm sorry—so, so sorry—that I cheated on you. But I don't deserve to go to *prison* for this." His mind flashed back to the sound of the jail door clanging shut and his heart raced. He took a few breaths, willing his heart to slow down.

"I believe you. I'm doing all I can to try to find the real killer."

"Then let's work together, okay? Like you said, whatever happens with our relationship, we'll be raising a child together. I'll go stay at my parents until we close on the other house. It's true. You're safer with me not here. But we have to trust each other."

She looked off in the distance, and Nick waited as it sunk in. She turned to him. "You're right, Nick. Whatever your flaws, you've always had my back."

"In ways you don't even know, Victoria."

"What do you mean?"

"It's not important."

"It's important to me. What do you mean?"

"I'm not sure if it's something you want to know about."

"Nick? What is it? We said we'd be honest with each other." She was right. But her reaction to this could go either way. But if they were being honest, then he was going all in.

"Remember when you told me about your advisor?"

"Yes?"

"And I suggested we pay him a little visit? And you told me not to?"

"Yes?"

"Well, let's just say I did it anyway. We caught up with him. Taught him a lesson."

"He's not...dead?"

"No! We didn't kill him, Victoria." Nick let out a chuckle. "You've seen too many mob movies. Just gave a good roughing up. Don't worry, there was no permanent damage, but he sure got the message. Maybe he'll think twice about doing it again. By the way, he was pretty hard to find. He'd lost his job. He was working at a Barnes and Noble information desk outside Philly. So maybe someone else blew the whistle on him. No idea about that."

She looked at him with something resembling awe. "You did this for me?"

"Of course. I'd do anything to protect you, Victoria. You're my wife. And soon to be the mother of my child."

"My God, Nick." He was pretty sure that she meant that in a good way.

"So, my master sleuth, who do you think did it?" he said.

"Let me get my files."

"Your files?"

"Yes, Nick. My files." As she walked away, he started to feel a little better. If she was looking for the real killer, did that mean she truly believed him? Optimism was lurking in the depths somewhere and he was tugging at it with all his might, trying to pull it to the surface.

TWENTY-TWO

The next morning when Victoria left to meet Higgins, Nick was still sleeping. She thought maybe she should give him a day or two before sending him off to Brooklyn, but then the longer he stayed, the more he'd get used to it. She would ask him to leave the following day. Regardless of the fact that he'd covered for her, she was still in more danger with him there.

She knew this was a risky move, taking the investigation into her own hands, but it seemed like the only one available to her. Waiting wasn't an option. Higgins had cleaned himself up with a haircut and shave. He was working away on his computer when she arrived. They had an awkward first few moments, but he seemed to be warming up to her. He struck her as reserved with an edgy undercurrent. Not dangerous, but a little persnickety.

"So, why don't you tell me a little about yourself? Are you from around here?" She was hoping to bond with him. Get him to open up.

"Nope. I'm from Michigan. Originally. But I moved to New York City for a job after college."

"Where in the city? I went to grad school at Columbia."

"I worked in Midtown. But I lived in Murray Hill."

"That's a nice area. More of a neighborhood. And you live up here now?"

"Yeah. I used to come up here a lot when I was living in the city. I'd always read a lot about the history of the Hudson River Valley. I'm a history buff."

"Seems we have a lot in common. I grew up in the area. I was always fascinated by its history too. And the art, the folklore. It's such an amazing place."

"Aren't you part of its history in a way? Doesn't your family go way back? To the original settlers?" He wore a cheeky smile on his face, the expression of a show-off.

"You've done your homework, I see. On my mother's side, yes. You know Philipsburg Manor, I take it?"

"Of course. I've toured it. And filmed it. I do walking tour videos on my You Tube channel. It's sort of a side gig. Pretty good extra money, if I don't say." He sipped his coffee and leaned back in his chair.

"Oh. Interesting. Well, my mother's from a family like that. She's from one of the original Dutch miller families, but not that one. We even have relatives buried in the Old Dutch Burying Ground."

"So, you're related to slave owners?" He gave her a smirk, seeming to enjoy giving her a little dig.

"Most wealthy people back then did own slaves, unfortunately. I'm afraid my family is no exception." She remembered the first time she'd learned about the history of the region, when they'd toured the mill in elementary school. She hadn't been singled out, and she was sure most kids didn't make the connection, but it was the first time she remembered feeling guilty about her family lineage. It just got worse from there.

"And your father? He's Dutch too, I take it? Vander Hofen?"

"He is, but he's not from the original settlers. There was a smaller wave of Dutch who came in the late seventeen-hundreds, inspired by the Revolution. Many of them helped. They had no great love of the British, as you can imagine, since they'd taken New York from them.

"Right."

"This entire region was in a crucial position during the war, on the border between Patriot-and British-held territory. There was a lot of action here, and that only added to the legends and folklore."

"Yeah, I know." He paused to sip his coffee, looking less than enthralled with her history lessons. "So what do you make of all the supernatural stories here? It goes further back than the Revolution. Do you think there's anything to it, or is it all just small-town gossip?"

She was happy to move the conversation back in that direction. "It's always had that kind of reputation, as you probably know, even with the Indian tribes of the region. Before the Dutch came. Then everyone added to them. Europeans. Africans. It all sort of blended together and the stories fed off each other. Then Irving's works really etched it all into stone. I was always fascinated by the stories as a girl."

"Have you ever seen anything? Like for yourself?"

"No Headless Horseman galloping around, if that's what you mean," she said. His forced laugh was followed by an awkward silence. This was getting positively painful. She needed to move things along.

"But there was this one time. When I was hiking at Rockefeller. You know the trails there? I run there all the time."

"Yeah. I hike there sometimes, but I don't run. Not my thing." He gave a dismissive wave of his hand.

"Have you heard about Raven Rock?"

"Yes! The woman in white who died there?" He perked up a bit and leaned in.

"That's the one. She moans and yells to warn off people to stay away."

"Right."

"I was doing a hike there one time. It was really windy, and I swear I thought I heard her. I actually looked around to see if someone was hurt, I was so convinced I'd heard moaning. But nobody was there. Of course, the power of suggestion is pretty strong. And so were the winds. It could have been a trick of the mind."

"The power of suggestion. So you're a skeptic?" His sly smile dared her to admit it.

"I'm neutral, but I'm open to the possibility."

"Remember what happened in Irving's tale? To the disbeliever? Old Brouwer?"

She shook her head. "No. I'm sorry. It's been a long time. Refresh my memory."

"The Headless Horseman chased him. Then turned himself into a skeleton and nearly scared Old Brouwer to death. And then Brouwer went plunging into the river. Now, I'm not saying that'll happen to everyone, but who wants to chance it, right?" He smirked.

"Right. But now, if I remember correctly, Irving ended his story in ambiguity. At least as far as Ichabod Crane's fate was concerned."

"Sure, he leaves it open to the possibility that it was all a hoax. That Crane left town with a broken heart and lived a long and productive life. But what fun would that be?" He smiled. "So the legend persists."

"And so it does," she said.

"Come on, Victoria. You're you telling me that if you were walking in the woods, late at night, those stories wouldn't be lurking somewhere in the back of your mind somewhere... freaking you out?"

She thought about the night of the murder, creeping along in the dark, feeling like she could disappear into the woods never to be found. It made the hair on the back of her neck stand up. Did Higgins know something?

"It's just I don't think things like that are so sensational. When, or if, they really happen, I think it would be a bit more subtle. More personal, if you will."

"Yeah, for sure. I'm just messing with you, Victoria!" A smile lit up his face and he let out a chuckle. Had she passed his test?

"So, is that why you moved up here? From the city? Because you were interested in the folklore and history?"

"I moved up here because I figured people in this area would be more open-minded about topics like this. And they are. I have a gift of sorts and I feel more comfortable telling people about it up here. I don't feel like a freak. It can be more of a burden than anything, the way some people react."

"And what kind of gift do you have? Are you psychic?" She was starting to see him in a different light, as an oddball who didn't quite fit in. She'd felt that way her whole life, even though she had everything going for her on the outside.

"Not quite. I feel feelings. It's not like I read minds, I just feel feelings of other people and then I have to make sense of them. The first time it happened it was my dog. I was eight. She was lost. She ran away and we looked all over the neighborhood for her. I could feel she was scared. She was outside and the open spaces were freaking her out." His eyes widened. "There was this large park in our town. Far from our house. We never even went there with her. But I convinced my father to drive there. He thought I was nuts, but he did it anyway." He smiled at the memory. "And then we found her. I didn't think much of it at the time. I was just glad to have my dog back."

"Kids are very attached to their dogs. It makes sense that you'd be in tune with her. And what about me? What did you feel that had to do with me?"

His look turned to one of genuine concern for her. "I got a feeling the night of the murder. I had no idea what it was at the time. It was just random. He was a male. He was angry, trying to restrain himself. But then he couldn't hold it in anymore. He gave in to his anger. And he's had these angry urges for a while. He's probably got some past history somewhere along the line. That's about all I got from that night. And it didn't make any sense until I read the news reports. Then it clicked, so I went to the police."

"So why did you come to my house? That afternoon?"

"Because I found out your husband was a person of interest. If it was your husband, I thought he might be dangerous for you. And the police wouldn't listen to me. They even stared investigating *me!*" He rolled his eyes.

"That's terrible, Wade."

"Can you believe it? I was just trying to help!" He threw up his hands and let out a sigh.

"Yes, I know. And I appreciate it. But I know for sure that my husband didn't do it. I'm not in any danger from him, I assure you. But whoever did this is obviously out to frame him. Your advice is well taken. And I appreciate your going out of your way to tell me. Someone's been on our property recently, so your warnings are relevant and timely." She was sure now that Higgins wasn't a danger to her, but she also wasn't putting much stock in his warnings. They were pretty generic. Still, maybe he could be useful to her.

She continued. "So how did you find out where I live? And the information on my background?"

"That's easy. I can find out pretty much anything. About anyone. It's my job," he said.

"Your job?" she asked. He nodded. "And what do you do exactly?"

"All kinds of things. Programming, forensics, research. It's a mixed bag."

"Research. Like . . . hacking?"

"I prefer the term 'investigation.'" He smiled.

"Do you take private clients?"

"Yes, of course. I have one large programming contract that's sort of my bread and butter. I fill in with side gigs and revenue from my YouTube channel."

"Could you do something for me?"

"Maybe."

"I need to run into somebody. I need to know his schedule. Is that something you could do for me?"

"Probably. Especially if they use an online calendar that's web-based. Mostly every office does these days. Who is it?"

"Randy Jackman, CEO of Jackman Capital." She knew Sam would have a cow if he knew she was going to spy on Jackman. It was also a big risk to trust Higgins, but she was desperate to figure this out. And to do that, she had to see him for herself.

"Angie Hansen's boss?"

"You're up on the case, I see."

"Everyone's up on this case, Victoria. I charge three hundred an hour for this sort of thing."

"I'll double it if you can get this to me by the end of the day."

"Consider it done."

"I need to get going now. It was nice to meet you, Wade."

"You too, Victoria. Take care."

She was pretty sure he didn't have any gift, but what he said about the killer having a past made sense. She made a mental note to call Sam Coleman and instruct him to dig further back. If something was buried in Jackman's past, she would find it.

———

Jack couldn't sit back and do nothing when his gut was telling him they had the wrong guy, so he went back to the scene of the crime to go over it, once again. He stood back and took a good look at the front of the house. He could see how someone would be enamored with it, at least initially, especially a person fed up with the city looking for space. By day, it was a peaceful oasis, rolling hills in the background and mature trees ensuring privacy, the kind of place where you could sit and write the next Great American Novel. By night, it was more like the setting of the next Great American Horror Story.

The thick, knotty woods surrounding the area served as the perfect hiding place for a psychopath, a formidable buffer against any noisy neighbors, a situation where nobody could hear you scream. At the very least, a woman living alone here should have a dog. And probably a gun. And for sure a security gate. He understood Vince Rossi's regrets. Truthfully, he'd never let his own daughter move to a place like this. But then she grew up with a police officer for a father and tended to take his advice on safety very seriously.

If someone from the outside had arrived on foot, they most likely came from the Bedford Road direction, unless they knew the area. If it was a local, they could have come from any direction. The rain had washed away much of the footprint evidence from that night, so he figured focusing on the killer's exit was a better use of his time. He went around to the back of the house where the back door exited out of the laundry area. He started there and then walked through the back yard along the path. It seemed to end at the point where the lawn stopped and the woods began. But then he cleared away some of the brush. There was a path of sorts still there.

He started to walk it. It led out to one of the many horse trails that wound through the area and then back out to Bedford. His plan was to walk down in the direction of where they found the lamp and see if he heard any big, barking dogs to corroborate Mancusio's recollections.

He got the equivalent of about five houses down when he heard a dog barking. It sounded like a German Shepard—a big, throaty bark like Mancusio said. It was close enough to the house to be heard in the driveway. He stepped up his pace and jogged down to where they found the lamp. It was about a quarter mile from where the dog was. It all fit.

Of course, this wasn't proof that Mancusio didn't do it, but as far as Jack was concerned, he was pretty convinced they had the wrong guy. He went back up and down again, this time more slowly, looking for the missing wine glass. That was easy to get rid of, like the cell phone, so he wasn't holding out much hope, but it gave him purpose and had the added benefit of getting him some exercise in the process. Who was it who'd been running through the woods that night, if it wasn't Nick Mancusio? Was there any way that Jackman could have pulled this off? Or was it a random crime, destined for the cold case files that haunted him in the middle of the night?

TWENTY-THREE

As Victoria made her way over to her table to meet her client, she felt the power of old money at her disposal. Higgins had made good on his promise the day before, and she was already acting on his information. The Cosmopolitan Club was her territory, and it was a stroke of luck that Randy Jackman frequented it as well. With its restrained Renaissance Revival exterior and lush French Baroque interior, its stunning views of Central Park and its long and storied history dating back to the Gilded Age, it was a living testament to old New York, and all the new money in the world couldn't trump her status. It couldn't eclipse the fact that her family had been frequenting this exclusive establishment since its founding in the late 1800s while Jackman's waited back in Europe for their turn at the American dream. New York was like that, and it worked to her advantage at times like this. The baroque décor. The white marble with gold trim. The wood paneled walls and the dark brown studded leather seating. It all seemed to be frozen in time, except for one major addition—women.

Sergei stood up as she approached the table. He pulled out her chair as she took off her coat and sat down. She needed a pretense to be at the club, and her client-turned-friend was the perfect decoy. He loved this place.

"Victoria! It's lovely to see you." Sergei was in his early fifties, attractive enough and notoriously well groomed. A proud Russian aristocrat descended from a nobility stripped of its wealth and power during the revolution only to rise again. He appreciated great art, but he was also an unabashed speculator in anything that could turn a profit—even NFTs. They'd sparred a few times about the risk involved, but he liked to live on the edge, even if it meant getting stuck with something he found hideous.

"It's great to get into the city. I didn't realize how much I was missing it."

"It's hard not to miss this." He held up his palm and motioned to the room.

"This isn't really my style." She ran her hand through her hair, adjusted her scarf, and ordered a club soda from the waiter.

"Oh come on, Victoria. Look who you're talking to. It's okay to admit you like it. Everyone here likes it. That's why we're here."

"I suppose."

"This little guilt trip you have. It's annoying. Your revolutionaries had the good sense not to mess with the existing power structures. Don't rub it in." Sergei was smiling but she knew he meant it. She didn't argue with him. Plus, he did have a point.

"I guess it's all about perspective." She thought about what it would be like. To lose everything. To have nothing and have to start all over.

"You've done your penance. It's time to enjoy life, Victoria. Don't be such a bore!" His voice reverberated around the room, his faint accent adding a touch of intrigue.

"I'll try to lighten up." She genuinely liked Sergei and enjoyed his company. They were cut from the same cloth. Both from wealthy backgrounds, but both of them driven and successful in their own right.

"So how was your trip to Marfa? Did you pick up anything interesting?" Marfa. A small town in middle-of-nowhere West Texas that had become a haven for contemporary art. Collectors flew in on their private jets, adding to the eclectic mix of artists, bohemians, ranchers, agricultural workers, and tourists that made for a one-of-a kind experience. It wasn't for everyone.

"Nothing I saw fit the bill. Much to your delight, I'm sure."

"It's your money, Sergei." She shrugged her shoulders and he smiled back at her. "How are you liking the Cole?"

"I'm *loving* it."

"I'm glad."

"So why are we really here? You didn't come to ask about my road trip. Something to do with the trouble you're in?"

"I'm doing some 'research'" Her fingers flew up into air quotes and then back down to her club soda. She fiddled with her straw as she thought about how much to reveal.

"Regarding what? The murder?" He took a sip of his coffee.

"Sort of." She looked away and then back at him.

"You don't think Nick did it, I take it?"

"I know he didn't do it!" She hoped he would just leave it at that and not ask any questions.

"So who did it?" he asked.

"That's what I'm trying to find out." She rolled her eyes. "Nick's lawyer doesn't think they have enough evidence to indict him, but unless they find the killer, this will haunt us forever."

"And you're not the slightest bit bitter? I didn't peg you for a liberated woman, Victoria. Most women would be vengeful. Why are you so concerned about what happens to your unfaithful husband?"

"It's complicated."

"I see you're drinking a club soda today. That's an unusual choice for you. No coffee? I guess it is a bit early for wine."

"I decided to try something new. For a change."

"I see." Sergei was a pretty smart guy and she knew he could read between the lines. "So what have you found out?"

"Randy Jackman leaked those photos to the press. And he has a strong motive."

"And Randy Jackman is a member here. Impressive, Victoria. So I'm part of your little scheme, eh? Very exciting. Maybe you're not such a bore after all. But Randy Jackman knows better than to give in to vengeance."

"Probably, but I have to start somewhere. He also knows the truth. About Angie Hansen. He claims she was making it all up. About the come on." She looked towards the door. "And here he is now."

"What a nice coincidence." They both watched as Jackman was seated at a table across the room, alone. "So what's your plan now?"

"I didn't think that far in advance," she confessed. Her stomach was in knots. It was a big risk coming here. She could make an idiot of herself. Or worse.

"What did you think you would accomplish? By coming here?"

"I just wanted to look him in the eye. See him for myself. Get a read on him."

"Is that all?"

"I guess I want to know more about Angie Hansen. What she was like. Nick claims she came on to him. Jackman claims she was lying about his come-on. I want to know what kind of woman she was."

"Then just ask him. Go over to him and ask him. Don't accuse him of anything. He'll understand why you want to know. Trust me, it'll be okay. Call me if you need anything. I'm impressed, Victoria. Very bold move. I like it." Sergei went on his way, leaving her to her little mission. She called the waiter over and instructed him to send Mr. Jackman a drink.

———

Jack's legwork at the crime scene the day before had paid off. After he'd located the barking dog, he'd gone house to house looking for any camera footage from that evening they may have missed. A few houses down from the barking dog, he found something that changed everything.

The video was grainy, but he could see someone running past, then stopping, backing up, and then disappearing from view. Then the person popped up again, looked around, and continued down the hill. Jack played it over and over in slow motion trying to glimpse anything of value. It was really dark, and some of the view was obstructed by the trees, but it clearly showed someone was in the woods near the barking dog, about a quarter mile before the spot where they'd eventually found the murder weapon. Short hair, close to six feet tall with a masculine gait. It could be almost anyone. Except for Nick Mancusio. The video stopped at 9:07 about the time Mancusio was almost home.

"What do we do now?" Lexi asked.

"We give it to the DA."

"And we keep looking?"

"Yup. We're back to square one. It could be anyone. A burglary gone bad. A murder for hire. Anyone except Mancusio."

"Or Higgins. Hair's all wrong. His was longer at the time."

"Right. So anyone except Mancusio or Higgins. That narrows it right down. Nothing from Uber or the local cab companies for pick-ups around that time? No drop offs at her house earlier?"

"Nothing so far," Lexi said.

"I hope to God it wasn't random. If it was, we could have a bigger problem on our hands. If this wasn't personal, then we could have a murderer in the neighborhood, hiding in plain sight." Jack sat there for a long moment with his head in his hands. He was exhausted. The insomnia was getting worse, and it was a vicious cycle. The more he worried about sleeping, the more he couldn't sleep, and the more he worried that he'd be too spent to solve the case.

"I don't like this. I don't like it at all." He went to get another coffee, knowing it would only be a short-term fix, but what choice did he have?

————

Randy Jackman wore a suit jacket and tie, as required, but Victoria could tell it pained him. He was the irreverent type. The type who wore jeans to a board meeting just to make a statement. But his bad boy façade wasn't fooling her. If he was really that much of a rebel, he wouldn't be a member here. He was kidding himself, and that gave her confidence.

"It's uncanny timing. You reaching out to me now. I was just thinking that maybe I should add to my art collection. I'm surprised you're taking on new clients, with all you have going on." He was leaning back with a cocky grin on his face, but that didn't surprise her. It didn't intimidate her either.

"I'm capable of compartmentalizing. Like anyone in business for themselves. What are you interested in?" She could play this game all day.

"I'll mull it over and get back to you." He sat up straighter.

"You do that." She noticed a flicker of movement, like maybe he was going to bail on her. But then he settled back in.

"So do you need some investment advice? Or is there another reason we're sitting here?"

"We're both busy, so I'll be direct."

"I'd appreciate that. Time is money."

"Angie Hansen."

"Right. What do you want to know?"

"What was she like?"

"What was she *like*? She was delusional. She thought she was better than she was at her job. She wouldn't accept constructive criticism. She complained that men hit on her but dressed like a bridge and tunnel party girl."

"And you deny that you hit on her?"

"Categorically!" He reached for his wallet and pulled out a photo. "This is my wife. Does it look like I need to hit on someone like Angie Hansen?"

She'd seen his wife before. They were in the public eye all the time. A model-turned-fashion entrepreneur. That meant nothing, as far as she was concerned. "She's quite lovely."

He shot her a sideways glance. "Angie Hansen hit on *me*. Tried to sweet talk her way into a promotion she didn't deserve. Her and that jackass Malone. They made my life a living hell."

"Did you have her followed? Was it you who leaked those photos to the press?"

"Do you think I would tell you if I did? But it's not illegal. And if I did, you should thank me for exposing the truth. And I can tell you this. She probably came on to your husband too. She liked married guys. I think it she took it as a personal challenge."

"My husband didn't kill her."

"Neither did I."

"Was there anyone else you know who had a grudge against her?"

"You're worse than the detectives with all these questions! She had a track record so yeah, I'm sure there were some wives out there. Jilted lovers. That kind of thing. Nobody in my office cared enough to kill her, if that's what you're asking."

"That's what I'm asking."

"I have to go now. My client is here. Nice chatting with you, Victoria."

"Let me know when you're ready to make an acquisition." She leaned back and casually crossed her arms. He flashed her a thumbs-up as he walked away. Jackman was everything people said he was. Cocky, irreverent. Bold. But one thing he wasn't was flirtatious. She'd sent him a drink. A player was a player, and he was all business. She believed him. Angie Hansen was lying about the sexual harassment. And it may have gotten her killed.

TWENTY-FOUR

As Victoria expected, Sam Coleman wasn't impressed with the amateur detective work she'd done the day before. He wasn't the type to get emotional, but she could tell he was upset. It wasn't in the tone of his voice, but rather the tight lips, the furrowed brow. And the tie that was a bit askew from the way he was rubbing his neck with his hand as he paced around her mother's living room.

"I'm sure that Angie Hansen was lying about the sexual harassment. That has to mean something, Sam!"

"Victoria, do you have any idea the kind of dangerous situation you're putting yourself in? Confronting these men alone?"

"I can handle myself, Sam. I'm not some damsel in distress. I can take care of myself. You told me yourself that Higgins was harmless."

"That's not the point. You hired me to do the investigating. They've got the entire Tarrytown Police Department on the case. But you think you're going to solve it yourself?" He seemed a bit offended by the implication.

"Not solve it. Just do what I can to help. I'm not the kind to sit around and wait. I have to do *something!* This is my life.

My future. Did you find out anything about Jackman's past? Anything at his high school? Or college? Any unsolved cases?"

"Nothing turned up, but then a lot of juvenile records are sealed." He looked off in the distance, then looked back at her.

"What, Sam? Is something wrong?"

"Sit down, Victoria. There's something I need to tell you." He motioned to the sofa.

"What is it?" She sat, leaning forward, her stomach in knots.

"When you told me to run background on Jackman, I decided to do the same thing for Nick. Just in case."

"And? Did you find something?"

"Not exactly. Not about Nick per se."

"Then what?"

"It seems there was an incident at his college around the time he was there as an undergraduate. It very well might have nothing to do with him, but I had to let you know. I found an article in the student paper about sexual assaults on campus. There were other incidents besides this one, as I'm sure you can imagine. But something about this one stood out.

"What?" She leaned in.

"A female student in the article. She was quoted, anonymously, regarding an assault. A potential date rape situation. The male student wouldn't take no for an answer. She tried to fight him off. Then he started to strangle her. But for some reason, he let her go. He pushed her down on the bed and ran out the door. She wouldn't report it or say who it was, but she wanted to warn other women. Here's the article." He handed it to her. "Given what the police told you about Angie Hansen and the marks on her neck, I thought you should know."

Victoria's heart sank. "But it could've been anyone, right?" Nick had never been violent with her, she assured herself. But then she remembered what he'd told her about her advisor. That was different. He did that to protect her. A woman. Wasn't that the opposite? Or was she just telling herself what she wanted to hear?

"Sure, Victoria. I said it probably isn't relevant. But I wanted to let you know."

She wasn't sure what to do with this information, so she just moved on. "Can you do a little more digging for me on someone else?"

"That's what I'm here for."

"Timothy Sutton. He's a former professor of mine. Can you find out what happened to him? And where he is now? It's a long shot, but he could have it in for me. Now that Nick and I are all over the media, he would know where to find me." She noticed a flash of recognition on Sam's face.

"Timothy Sutton?"

"Yes. Do you know him?"

"I think you might want to ask your mother, Victoria. She should be back soon. I'm not sure how comfortable I am explaining all this to you. But yes, I know who he is."

"How do you know who he is?"

He hesitated. "Because your mother hired me. After what happened to you. To take care of the situation."

"Hired you? To do what exactly?" Victoria was shocked. No wonder Sam knew so much about her and her family. He'd been in her life for over a decade. Why had her mother kept it a secret?

"To expose him for what he was. And have him suffer the consequences."

"What? *How?*" Her mind was reeling. Maybe the sinking feeling she'd felt when viewing the security tape wasn't just her imagination after all. With all the media publicity, Sutton had likely seen Nick's photo. Maybe he'd put two and two together.

"I was able to get photos and other proof of him doing what he did to you to other students. We gave it to the administration. And we gave it to his wife. Anonymously. He lost his job. His wife divorced him. And he had no idea it was because of you. Your mother insisted about that part of it. To keep you out of danger."

"I can't believe this, Sam! My mother did all this?"

"Yes she did, Victoria. To protect you." Victoria felt a wave of regret for misjudging her mother. All this time, she blamed her mother for sweeping it under the rug. For letting Sutton get away with it. But he didn't really get away with it. Why had she kept it a secret?

"How can you be sure he doesn't know we were responsible?"

"Well, nobody can be totally sure, Victoria. But we timed it like that to protect you. It was a good while after you were gone."

"Did you know about what Nick did, too?"

"Nick? No. What are you talking about?"

"Nick went looking for him. With his brother. After we met and I told him what happened. They roughed him up a bit. I only learned this yesterday. From Nick. He told me that Sutton had lost his job. He was working at a Barnes and Noble help desk."

"We keep tabs on him, but I didn't know about the incident with Nick. Anyway, he moved to Arizona years ago. He's no threat to you now." Sam seemed confident about this, but Victoria wasn't so sure.

"Why didn't my mother tell me all of this?"

"You'll have to ask her that yourself."

"This is a lot to take in, Sam. But thanks for letting me know." She took a deep breath as she mulled all of it over. "Is there anything else you're working on as far as the case?"

"I'm going through all of the cab companies, Uber, Lyft, anyone who could have dropped off or picked up someone near the house that night. I don't think they'll indict Nick, and even if they do, I think it's almost impossible to convict him based on what they have. But finding the killer is another matter. I'm working on it."

"Do you think Jackman could have hired someone to make it look like a robbery gone bad?"

"He could have, sure. But an actual robbery gone bad makes a lot more sense."

"Maybe, but not if he was truly offended by her allegations." She knew she was grasping at straws with Jackman, but the idea of a robbery gone bad and a case that would never be solved? She couldn't accept that outcome.

"True. Let me think about it and look at it again from that perspective. See what my sources turn up."

"Of course. Thanks, Sam. For everything."

"Just doing my job, Victoria." They said their goodbyes and Sam left her sitting there struggling to process the flood of emotions she was feeling. Why had her mother and Nick hidden the truth from her for so long? Why did the people closest to her think she was so fragile that they had to shield her from the truth? She had fought Sutton off, after all. She was a formidable business woman with a lucrative career and the CEO of a successful non-profit. She was grateful for the covert support, but she couldn't help feeling bit offended. Why did the people closest to her see her as someone who needed protecting?

———

"So where does this leave us?" Lexi was standing back from the white board, arms folded, taking in all the evidence when Jack walked back in to the conference room. The harsh lighting made Jack long for a warm, dark room and some good sleep.

"Let's step up the efforts to vet everyone in the area. I know you checked the sex offender registry in the immediate area, but let's widen it a bit. Go out a few miles. See if anyone stands out. Look at unsolved burglaries in the area. And keep going on the cabs. Uber. Lyft. Widen the search area. Either they live in the area or they got dropped off and picked up."

"I still can't believe his wife is standing by him. She hired a private detective!"

"Marriage is complicated, Lexi."

"Oh crap, Jack." Her hand went to her forehead. "I didn't mean anything by that."

"Let's just get this all out in the open, okay?" Jack was tired of skirting around the issue.

"Get *what* out in the open?" Lexi asked. Jack knew she was playing dumb.

"Come on. You know about my divorce. My affair. Everyone knows about it."

"It's none of my business." She looked away.

"Maybe it is. And maybe you need to stop being so judgmental about Nick Mancusio and his affair. It's slanting your powers of analysis on this case."

"What? *No!*"

"You're letting your biases affect your thinking. You think Nick Mancusio committed a mortal sin by cheating. You think his wife's a fool for staying with him. It's clouding your judgement!" He threw up his hands in exasperation.

"No it's not!" she insisted.

"Let me give you a piece of unsolicited advice about marriage."

"I'm not slanting my view, Jack. I can separate my feelings from the facts just fine. I'm not a child! But fine. What's your advice?"

"Marriage is hard. Nobody really knows how hard, until they're in it."

"That's it?" She gave him a curious look.

He took a deep breath. "Sit. Please. Give me a chance to explain myself." He pointed to the chair and they both sat.

"You don't owe me any explanation." Lexi was trying to avoid his gaze.

"Look, I loved my wife. Very much. And she loved me. But we both strayed. She was first, if you must know, but I don't tell people that. Because it was probably my fault anyway."

"Jack, you don't have to do this. I'm sorry . . "

"*Let me finish!* This job, it's a burden. You see things. Horrible things. Every day. And then you go home and get the question, 'How was your day?' And all you can say is 'fine.' Because anything more would be a burden on them. Twisted limbs, blood everywhere, the images that haunt you. You can't tell them about it. The rotting stench of a dead body. The sleepless nights when you can't solve a case. And then the distance grows, because after time, you don't really know each other anymore. You can't. It's impossible."

"I never thought about it like that."

"It's no surprise that my affair was with a colleague. I didn't love her. We liked each other. Respected each other, for sure.

And we knew each other really well. It was just nice to finally be able to just be myself. I'm not proud of it. And I would have done anything to save my marriage. So I can relate to both of them. How he could cheat with someone he found familiar. How she could stand by him."

"Jack. I'm sorry. I don't know what to say."

"You're not supposed to know what to say. Just take it for what it is. Lessons from the school of hard knocks from an old dog like me. No extra charge. And keep your personal feelings out of the office. Understood?"

"Understood." She got back up and turned back to him. "And Jack?"

"Yeah?"

"Thanks. It's good advice. On all levels."

"Sure, Lex. That's what I'm here for."

———

Victoria had filled her mother in on the details of her detective work when she'd gotten back from the club later that morning. Like Sam, her mother was quite perturbed that she was taking matters into her own hands.

"Victoria, you have to be more careful! Let Sam and Detective Stark do their jobs. You always were so headstrong." She shook her head.

"I don't want to talk about it anymore, Mom! I get what you and Sam are saying. But what's done is done. And I have to talk to you about something else. Can we change the subject?"

"What is it? Is it the baby?" Her mother's face went ashen.

"No, nothing like that. Sit. Please. This is important." Her mother obeyed her, for once. "We have to talk about Timothy Sutton."

"Timothy Sutton? Why? Is he bothering you again?" Her mother sat up on her haunches like a lioness ready to pounce.

"No! Nothing like that. Nick brought him up recently. He told me that he'd caught up with him. Right after we met and I told him what happened. He and Mark gave him a little roughing up. On my behalf. He also mentioned that Sutton lost his job. They had a hard time tracking him down. So I asked Sam to look into him and find out more. And he told me what you did."

"I see. And Sam told you everything?"

"Yes. Well, I think so. He told me what happened but he didn't tell me why. He told me that you'd hired him to discredit Sutton. To get proof that he was doing this to other students. To ruin his career and his marriage."

"That's all true."

"And he lost his job and his marriage because of Sam's findings."

"Yes."

"Why didn't you tell me? Why did you let me think you didn't care?"

"Oh Victoria! Is that what you thought? That I didn't care?" Her mother put her hand over her heart as her body curled in on itself.

"I thought you didn't want me to report it because it would tarnish our name."

"Victoria! *No!* I didn't want you to report it because I didn't want him to blame you! He's a dangerous man. If he knew it was you who'd ruined his life, I was afraid he might retaliate. That's why I wanted to put some distance between your incident and his downfall." Her mother covered her face with her hands and shook her head back and forth. That made a lot of sense to Victoria.

"Mom. I'm sorry. I was young. Rebellious. I misjudged you."

"I suppose I should have just told you. But you were so traumatized. You were having nightmares. I heard you, crying out in the night. I just didn't want you to have to think about it anymore. I was just trying to protect you."

"I see it now, Mom. I really do." She really did. She remembered what Sam had said about her mother. She cares more than she lets on. But how did he know that? There had to be something more between them. An old boyfriend maybe? She reached over and hugged her.

"I can't stand the fact that all this time you thought our family name meant more to me than getting you justice."

"I'm sorry, Mom. It's just how it seemed at the time."

"I know. Your father would have known what to do. He was so much better at these things than I was. I had just lost him. We both had just lost him." Her voice was breaking, and then she started to tear up. She hugged her mother close again and they both sat like that for a while.

Her mother had known Sam for over a decade. She'd hired him to discredit Sutton. That explained why he knew so much about her and she knew nothing about him. Still, she still felt like there was something more her mother wasn't telling her about Sam, but she decided to let it go. She'd heard enough revelations for one day.

Her mother pulled herself together and straightened up. She patted her eyes with her fingers and fluffed her hair. "So, Nick went after him for you, did he?"

"He did."

"Well, that's something. Good for him! Maybe he's not so bad after all."

"Yes, maybe he's not so bad." She wasn't going to tell her the rest of it. That Nick had stayed silent when he thought she might have been responsible for Angie Hansen's death. That he'd even destroyed evidence that could have helped clear him. He had her back. She knew that now, and so did her mother.

"Are you going to give him another chance?"

"I'm trying."

"That's all you can ask of yourself." Her mother was more complex than she'd realized, and Victoria was sure there was more to her story. Another day, another time, she'd dig deeper. For now, she had to press on with the case.

TWENTY-FIVE

It was official. They were dropping the charges against Nick Mancusio. The DA decided after reviewing the tape Jack had given them yesterday. It was mid-morning, and Sylvia Murray was getting ready to hold a press conference at his parents' house in Brooklyn where Nick was staying. They were officially back to square one.

On the one hand, Jack felt relieved. It was the right thing. He knew all along that they couldn't make the charges stick. But on the other hand, he was starting to get nervous about the fact that a killer was still out there, hiding in plain sight. If this was a burglary gone bad or a pervert who got his kicks putting his hands around women's necks, the perp was close by. He rubbed his temples and then looked up again at the board. What were they missing? His head snapped around as he heard Lexi came charging into the office with a vengeance, looking like she'd just found the secret to eternal life.

"Jack! I just got off the phone with an Uber driver! He said he picked up a male fitting our description around nine forty-five that night, about a mile from the crime scene."

"That makes sense. Getting picked up close to the crime scene's too risky. It fits with the timeline."

"Finally! A break. He's headed in after he finishes his shift."

"When will that be?" The day had only just begun, so Jack figured it might be a while—which wasn't good.

"He said around five."

"Let's try to see if we can get him here earlier."

"I'll try."

"And we'll give him photos of all of the obvious suspects. If it wasn't any of them, we can get our sketch artist with him. Make sure we've got someone who can stay late, in case he's delayed."

"You got it!"

———

"Victoria! They're dropping the charges!" Nick was still in Brooklyn. She could hear his mother in the background, talking about what a miracle it was. The news shouldn't have come as a shock to Victoria. They had expected it. But she still felt weak in the knees with relief. She had to sit down when she heard Nick say the words out loud.

"Nick, that's fantastic! I'm just speechless. I can't imagine how you must feel."

"I'm still in shock, I think."

"So, what happens now?"

"Sylvia's going to hold a press conference soon. Around eleven-thirty. I'll make a short statement. We're working on it now." She thought that was a good thing, except for the fact that the real killer was still out there somewhere. Would this make them back off of Nick? Or would they turn up the heat?

Whoever did this had planted that cell phone—right outside their door. Were they in even more danger now?

"Were you planning to come home after that?"

"I guess? I mean it's up to you."

"What are you going to say in the press conference?"

"I'm not sure."

"Whoever did this. They're still out there. They'll probably be watching. Just remember that, okay?"

"That's a good point. Why don't stay at your mother's house tonight? I'll stay here until we talk to Stark?"

"I'll think about it. Let's talk later."

They said their goodbyes and she gave herself a rare moment to feel a sense of satisfaction and relief. The worst was over. They could always move away if they didn't feel safe here. Her husband was a free man, and that part of this nightmare was officially over.

———

Victoria was working in her home office when the gate buzzer sounded. It was just after one in the afternoon. It was Jeff Malone at the gate.

"Victoria! I heard the good news about Nick. I wanted to come check on you. I know Nick's still in Brooklyn. Can I come in?"

She figured Nick had asked him to check in on her and make sure she was safe. It seemed like they were finally putting this behind them too. Maybe their friendship would survive all this insanity. Still, she wasn't expecting him and she didn't like surprises. She went to the door and asked him in.

"Hey, Victoria. How are you?" He gave her a hug. Then he took off his coat and casually draped it over his arm. Was he planning to stay awhile? She wasn't really in the mood for company, but she didn't want to be rude.

"I'm relieved. Very relieved. Naturally." She backed up a bit.

"I can imagine." He started to walk towards the sofa and she had no choice but to play the gracious host, although she felt a bit weird having him in her home with Nick gone. Maybe she shouldn't have met him at her office that time. She was just trying to get information on the case, not strike up a separate friendship with him. Perhaps he'd misinterpreted her intentions.

"So what happens now?" Jeff asked. He plopped himself down on the sofa. Victoria seated herself on the edge of an armchair, a respectable distance away from him.

"I suppose Nick's a free man, technically. But if they don't catch the person who did this, I know this will hang over us forever. I'm going to keep trying to find out who did this. I've hired a private detective. I'll keep him on the case."

Jeff's eyes widened. "So you're planning on staying with him? After what he did to you?"

"That's sort of a personal matter, Jeff. Isn't it?" Victoria was getting a bit uncomfortable. Obviously, Jeff was still holding a grudge against Nick. She wondered if Nick had told him about the baby. It didn't seem like it.

"I mean, it's your call, Victoria. It's just that I've known Nick a long time. Longer than you have. That's sort of why I came to see you today."

"I don't understand, Jeff."

He pursed his lips and took a deep breath. "This isn't easy for me to tell you. But I feel like I owe it to you to let you know." He paused. "There are things you don't know about him."

"What kind of things?" She thought about the article from the school paper and her heart started to race. She didn't like where this was going.

"Let me try to explain." Jeff's look turned serious and she suddenly found herself grateful for the company.

———

It was just past one in the afternoon. Jack and Lexi were waiting at the precinct for the Uber driver to come in and hopefully give them a break in their case. Jack tried to get him to come earlier, but the driver wasn't responding to Jack's calls and texts. It had been almost a month since the murder, but instead of growing complacent, he was getting more obsessed with this case. He hadn't slept more than three hours in a row for the past week and a half and it was taking its toll on him.

"Stark. There's someone here to see you, out front," a uniform officer announced.

"Who is it?"

"A woman named Sherry Wilson. Says she wants to talk to you about the Hansen case." Angie Hansen's friend. That perked him up. Maybe she remembered something. An angry boyfriend. A dating app meet up. Something.

"I'll be out in a minute." He went to get Lexi and they walked out to greet Sherry. She was alone. No attorney. He thought maybe she'd come with Malone.

"Hi, Ms. Wilson. Thanks for coming in. Let's go somewhere where we can talk." Jack noticed she looked like a nervous wreck. She was avoiding eye contact. He took her into an interview room.

"So, Ms. Wilson. Thank you for coming in today. Please have a seat. We can use all the help we can get." The three of them sat down. "What did you want to tell us?"

She took a deep breath and folded her hands together as if in silent prayer. "There's something I didn't tell you the first time we met. But it might be important, so I want to tell you now. I saw they dropped the charges against Nick Mancusio today."

"Is it something related to him?"

"No it's not." Sherry looked down for a moment and then back up at Jack. "It's more related to me."

"To you? Why didn't you tell us the first time we talked?"

"I didn't really think it was that important at the time. And I thought it might make me look bad. I thought I might get in trouble." She looked away again and then back at him. "I didn't lie to you or anything. I just didn't tell you everything. About my case."

"So then why are you telling us now?"

"Because the more I thought about it, the more I thought it might be important. Or relevant, for Angie's case. I want to know what really happened to my friend. And I wanted you to know the whole story."

"Okay, so, what did you want to tell us?"

"Well, Jeff Malone, the attorney on my case?"

"Yes?"

"I met him through a friend who also used him. For a similar situation. As you know, I was having problems with my boss. At work. He was saying a lot of inappropriate things to me. He was a creep. A jerk. Very difficult to work for."

"Yes. Isn't that why you hired Malone? To sue your boss? For sexual harassment?" Lexi asked.

"Yes. But I accused my boss of groping me. And that didn't really happen. Jeff encouraged me to exaggerate. To get a bigger settlement."

"Malone encouraged you to exaggerate? Can you define encouraged? You mean he told you to lie?" Jack said.

"Not exactly. He told me to think back carefully. See if there was any time when my boss had done anything that could be construed as 'touching.' And there was. Sort of? I think? He brushed against me one time. It could have been an accident. Calling it groping was a stretch. But Malone said we could use it. To get them to settle. He said that it wasn't really lying. It was up to me, as the person who got touched, to say what it was."

"Well, but if he was actually saying inappropriate things, that should really have been enough. To get some sort of settlement. Why did you have to exaggerate?" Lexi said.

"I thought so too, but Jeff said that the comments were open to interpretation. If he'd touched me, we'd have a stronger case." She let out a sigh. "And we could ask for more money."

"Okay. I see. And what does that have to do with Angie Hansen?" Jack already thought he knew where this was going. If so, it was a game changer.

"Well, when she started having problems with her boss, I suggested she talk to Jeff, as you know. She told me she thought her boss was sexist. He said demeaning things about women. She thought she didn't get the promotion because she was a woman. But she never said anything to me about sexual harassment or a come-on. But then you told me the suit was about sexual harassment, so it made me think. Did Jeff tell her to make stuff up too?"

"That's a very good question, Sherry." Jack's mind started reeling, going over the information again from a different angle.

"I mean, it's possible she didn't tell me everything. Maybe her boss did it. And I don't want to call my friend a liar." She hung her head for a moment. "But something like that could really infuriate a guy like her boss. My situation was different. It's a big hotel chain. They have procedures for this sort of thing. My boss was a harmless little nobody. But hers? He's ruthless. If she was lying, he'd be even more angry."

"That's very helpful information, Sherry. Thank you for letting us know." It was all starting to make sense to Jack. What if Malone was some kind of me-too ambulance chaser? Getting women to lie or exaggerate to get bigger settlements? Jackman swore all along she was making it up about the come on.

"One last thing. She called me earlier that day. I told you that. But I didn't tell you all of it. She sounded upset. We made plans to meet later that week, like I told you. For lunch in the city. She said she wanted to make some major changes in her life. She wanted to clean up her life. Make things right."

"Any idea what she was referring to?"

"Not really. She never told me anything about the affair, which I already told you. But when it all hit the media, I figured that's what she meant. Swearing off married men. This wasn't her first time. But please don't judge her. It was sad. She went for what she couldn't have. It's a self-esteem thing. She needed help. I'd been telling her to get therapy. I thought that's what it was all about, like she finally saw the light. And she wanted to get help. I didn't say all that because I didn't want to make her look bad."

"I see. You're a great friend, Sherry," Lexi said.

"She was a great friend too. She was always there for me. Any time of day or night. She was like that for her friends. I feel horrible making her out to be some kind of home wrecker. It wasn't like that." Sherry cradled her head in her hands.

"We're not judging her, Sherry. We want her killer brought to justice as much as you do," Lexi said.

"Am I in trouble? Are you going to say anything? About my settlement?"

"As far as we're concerned, it's not a criminal matter. You didn't even go to court. Whatever settlement you got, it's none of our business." Jack smiled and her face softened.

"Thank you." She seemed happy to finally get that off of her chest. He thought of Angie's parents and their grief, and all the people whose lives had been wrecked by this case. But most of all, he thought about what this meant. He and Lexi looked at each other and he knew they needed to move fast.

"This is all great information, Sherry. You've done your friend a great service by coming down here. But we have to get going on the case. Can you see yourself out?" Lexi said.

"Of course. Thanks." She got up and left without another word.

"Are you thinking what I'm thinking?" Lexi looked at Jack, wide-eyed.

"Check the phone log again. See who else she called after she called Sherry."

"I don't have to check. I remember who it was."

Jack looked at her. "Malone?"

She nodded. "He told me she called him to check on the case." Lexi put her head in her hands and took a deep breath.

"Oh my God! We never even asked to listen to her message on his phone. I just took him at his word."

"He said he was flying back from Chicago that night. How did you verify it?"

"His assistant gave me his itinerary. I didn't even think to check further. He could have caught an earlier flight. There's so many of them. He probably took a cab there from the airport. I'm so sorry!" Lexi's hand went to her forehead.

"There's no time to beat yourself up. Get the phone logs and the records. Check with the airlines. We'll try to get a warrant. With Mancusio off the hook, he might be on the prowl again. We have to move. *Fast!*"

———

Victoria was in the kitchen. Stalling. And her mind was swirling. She didn't know what to believe anymore. Jeff had shown up at her house, uninvited, insisting that there was more to Nick than she knew. Even with the article about the assault, which she'd kept to herself, she just wasn't buying it. Was she just not wanting to see the truth about her husband, or was there something off about Jeff's behavior? But then it was true. Jeff had known Nick longer than she had, and in a different context. They'd known each other since college.

Then it hit her. Jeff and Nick were at college at the same time. Jeff knew Angie Hansen. Could it have been Jeff? This whole time? But why? He had everything to lose from her death and nothing to gain.

"Need any help in there?" Jeff called to her.

"No, I've got it. I'll just be a minute, Jeff." She didn't believe what he was telling her about her husband. That he had a temper. That she didn't know him as well as Jeff did. This was getting weird.

"Why are you standing by him? He doesn't deserve it." Jeff's voice sounded closer now. He wasn't on the sofa anymore but he wasn't quite in the kitchen either. The back of her neck was tingling and her heart was racing. All of her danger bells were going off, just like the time her advisor shut the door behind them and bolted it. She didn't care anymore if she offended him. She could be wrong, but she had to trust her instincts. Something was off. She picked up her phone and sent a quick text to Stark: Malone is at my house. Acting strange. Help me.

"I'm not standing by anyone, Jeff. I just want to find out the truth," she called out, as she listened for footsteps. Was he just standing there? Outside the kitchen? He was so quiet, it was eerie.

"He's dangerous, Victoria, I'm trying to warn you. He stopped himself with Angie but next time his hands could be around your neck. Don't be a fool."

All at once it clicked. Lightning fast, she bolted for the pantry with her phone, slamming the door shut and locking it. The only people who knew about the marks on that woman's neck were the detectives, herself, Sam, and the killer.

"Victoria?" Jeff was coming closer. "What're you doing in there? I'm just trying to protect you. I'm trying to help you. You have to trust me!" He was trying to keep up his ruse.

"Stay away from me, Jeff! I'm calling the police." She tried to call 911 but there was no reception in the pantry. She had to think fast. She pulled up her voice memo app, pressed record, then placed the phone high on a shelf, in back of some grocery items. If she was going to die, it wouldn't be in vain. Then she grabbed the gun she'd stashed there and readied it for fire. Even with a gun, she could be overpowered. She had to be clever. Calm. Careful. Buy herself some time. Then his voice hardened as he changed his strategy.

"I never took you for a sucker, Victoria. I thought you had more fire in you. He was cheating on you! *It's humiliating!* Even if he didn't kill her, he betrayed us both. We should be sticking together, but he's driving a wedge between us." She could hear Jeff pacing around the kitchen.

"I know you're upset, Jeff. But we can work this out. Let's just take a step back and calm down."

"She was dropping the law suit! She left me a message. Said I forced her to lie! That she had to come clean! She was gonna tell everyone that I put her up to it! *She was gonna ruin my life! All because your stupid husband couldn't keep it in his pants!*" He was losing it. She could almost see the vein pulsating in his forehead as he started to rage.

"Jeff, I know you're upset, but this can all be explained. Tell the police what happened. It wasn't premeditated. You were emotional. Anyone would be. People will understand." She was desperately hoping for a better ending to this than the one that was running through her head.

"I went over to talk some sense into her! Not to kill her! We had a glass of wine. She calmed down. Then she just started freaking out again! Blaming me! Saying I was messing with her head! It was Nick, not me, who messed with her head. *And he's gonna pay for what he did!*"

"Jeff, we can work this out. Please."

"I can't let you go now, Victoria. Why couldn't you just play along? Why did you have to back him? *He doesn't deserve your loyalty!*" Jeff started to pound on the door and then he retreated. She thought she heard him walking away. Was he trying to calm himself down? Or was he getting something to pry open the door?

Victoria knew this lull was her only chance. She steadied the weapon in her hand. Thank God she'd listened to Sam and gotten some training. She thought about what her trainer told her and took a deep breath. Then she quietly opened the lock and gently nudged the door open with her foot as she held the gun steady in her hands.

He was a few paces away when the door opened, walking back towards her, their fireplace poker firmly in his grip. His eyes widened when he saw the gun. He froze and a defeated look washed over his face. For a few moments, she thought she might not have to pull the trigger.

"Don't move, Jeff. The police are on their way." She held his gaze and neither of them moved. It felt like an eternity but it was probably just a matter of seconds. Her hands started to sweat and she worried about losing her grip on the gun.

Suddenly his face reddened and he exploded into a crazy, violent rage. *"I'll kill you!"* He lunged at her, the fireplace poker raised in the air, ready to strike her. She pulled the trigger when he was just paces away, hitting him squarely in the chest. It didn't stop him. She fired again. He staggered back and dropped to the floor. She heard the rush of cars pulling up to the house. She didn't move a muscle.

Then she heard him on the floor, moaning. He wasn't dead! She had enough bullets left to finish the job. She heard Stark call out to her from outside the house. They were breaking down the door. She needed to move fast. She walked over and looked down at him, the gun pointed at his head. His eyes were closed and he was still moaning She thought of her baby. What if he didn't get convicted? What if he got out of prison? What if he came after them again?

"*Victoria! Stop!*" Stark was standing at the kitchen entrance. "*Drop the gun!*" She could see Stark's gun pointed at her out of her peripheral vision.

"He's guilty! He was trying to frame Nick. He would have killed me! It's all recorded. On my phone. In the pantry." She darted her head back in that direction.

"We know. We figured it out. Drop the gun, Victoria. He's not worth it. You don't want his death on your conscience, trust me. It's a horrible burden. Don't let him do that to you. We'll take it from here." She knew she should drop it, but she just couldn't bring herself do it. She was frozen to the spot.

"*Drop the gun, Victoria! Or I'll have to shoot you.*"

Reality hit her like a gut punch. Her baby. What was she thinking?

"I'm putting it on the counter." She looked sideways at Stark. "Is that okay? Can I put it on the counter?"

"Sure, Victoria. Nice and easy does it." She reached over, placed it on the counter, and put her hands up as she watched Malone bleed out all over the kitchen floor. She heard sirens in the background. And then she just collapsed.

TWENTY-SIX

The ambulance had taken Malone to the hospital already. It was likely a flesh wound but he'd lost a lot of blood. Still, they expected him to make it. They had also checked out Victoria Mancusio. She was fine. She was also pregnant. That certainly explained her continued support for her husband. He was the father of her child. It all made sense.

Jack felt a sense of satisfaction and relief. He liked it when things added up. Maybe he'd finally get some sleep. It had been less than a month. They'd caught the killer. The town could rest. He still needed to bring Victoria down to the station for formal questioning, but it could wait. The recording on her phone pretty much sealed Malone's fate.

"That's some fancy detective work you did there, Dr. Mancusio. Maybe you should join up with us." Jack thought how easily this could have gone another way, but she didn't need that stress right now.

She smiled. "Why don't you call me Victoria?" She was sitting up now, her husband at her side. He'd arrived about fifteen minutes after them. They'd called him to get the gate code and he was already on his way home. He'd gotten concerned when she hadn't answered his texts or calls.

"How are you feeling?" Jack asked.

"I'm fine, thanks. But I'd like some water." She looked over at her husband.

"I'll get it," Mancusio said.

"Let me get it. Your kitchen's a crime scene now. You stay with your wife." Lexi went to get the water and check on things in the kitchen.

"I guess congratulations are in order?" Jack said. She looked at him, confused.

He patted his belly. "The baby."

"Oh, right. Thank you."

When are you due?"

"I'm due in May." A faint smile graced her pale face. Jack could tell she was still in shock.

"Nice time of year for a birthday."

She nodded. It probably seemed a lifetime away. "And Detective Stark?" she said.

"Yes, Victoria?"

"Thank you. For what you said to me in there."

"Sure, Victoria. And why don't you call me Jack?"

"Okay then. Jack." They both turned to the sound of voices at the door.

"It's my daughter! You have to let me in!" It was Sandra Vander Hofen. He'd know that voice anywhere.

"It's my mother," she said.

"I know." He walked over to the door. Sandra was there with some man.

"Jack! How is my daughter?"

"She's fine, Sandra. Just fine." He put his hand on her shoulder. "And who is this?"

"I'm Sam Coleman. Private detective. Former FBI." He handed Jack his card and they shook hands. Jack instructed them to sign in. Then Sandra ran over and embraced her daughter. Coleman hung back by the door, staying out of their way. Jack could tell he was former LEO, and he appreciated his deference.

"I'm fine mom."

"And the baby?"

"Fine, we're both fine." Sandra started to shed tears of relief but then quickly pulled herself together. She was as lovely as he remembered.

"I still don't understand. What happened?" Sandra looked over at Jack. Nick Mancusio stroked his wife's hair and held her tight against his chest as Jack proceeded to run through the story with Sandra.

———

Nick sat there listening politely, but he felt a burning rage inside. It made so much sense now, but why hadn't he seen it before? Why did he have such a blind spot to Jeff's flaws? That bastard! Nick was furious. Jeff had almost killed his wife and child. He tried to frame him for murder, then pretended to be on his side. It was an unthinkable betrayal.

He knew Jeff had always been a little jealous of him back in college. Jeff did okay with the ladies back then, but he had a habit of aiming too high and getting shot down while Nick always had a slew of women falling all over him. But he thought that was all over with long ago. Was it Jeff who'd almost strangled that girl at college? Or were the two violent incidents just a coincidence? Was Jeff's obsession with money just an extension of his insane inferiority complex? An unspoken competition with him to even the score?

It wasn't his imagination that night. It was Jeff, waiting in the shadows. Nick was sure of it. He must have heard Nick drive up after he ran out the back door and then bolted down the hill to plant the weapon. And then he tried to frame him. And guilt trip *him!* It was all so clear to him now. Then he thought of Angie. Poor Angie, caught up in all this. It was Jeff who manipulated her. Messed with her head. All out of greed. And he had the audacity to blame him! She didn't deserve to die at the hands of that sociopath, and he had contributed to it. It would haunt him for the rest of his life. And Jeff was going to pay for this. If it was the last thing he ever did, he vowed that Jeff Malone would never threaten his family again.

———

As Victoria listened to Stark tell her mother the story of what had happened, she finally started to grasp the gravity of the situation. The shock was wearing off and she was starting to feel the stress. She took a few deep breaths and tried to remind herself that she was safe, for now. Except she didn't like the fact that Malone might make it. What did that mean for them? He had money. He could get a good lawyer. Stark assured her that this was a slam dunk. Still, it was a lose end, and she didn't like it. And how long would he even get for something like this?

Then she looked over at her mother, focusing in on her conversation with Stark as she came back to reality. Did Stark and her mother know each other? They'd called each other by their first names. They seemed pretty familiar with each other. If she didn't know better, she might even call their behavior flirtatious. When there was a lull in the conversation, she jumped in.

"So do you two know each other?" Victoria asked.

Her mother looked over to her. "We met at your function."

"During last call," Stark added.

"I told you it wasn't my son-in-law." Her mother sat up straight and gave her head a smug-looking shake.

"You certainly did, Sandra. You should team up with your daughter. Start a detective agency. The Hardy Girls." Much to her surprise, her mother let out a hearty laugh. Victoria hadn't heard her laugh like that since her father died.

"If you're feeling better, we should probably get down to the station and take care of business, so you two can get on with your lives," Sanchez said.

"Good plan," Stark added. "Are you up to it, Victoria?"

"Sure, let's get it over with." As she stood up and looked around, she knew they couldn't stay there. They needed a fresh start. She loved this place, and it would break her heart to give up the view, but she couldn't live in a place filled with so many bad memories. But that was a good problem to have, she reminded herself, deciding which lovely home to live in. They would figure it out together, one day at a time.

————

Jack was still in the office, wrapping things up. The Mancusios had left a while before, their names cleared. Most of the other detectives had left for the day. He looked over at the white board, thinking he'd wait for Lexi to take all their work down and file it. She ran out to get something to eat and was on her way back. It was a rare treat, to close a case this fast, and she deserved to share in the spoils. He leaned back and poured himself a scotch from the victory bottle he stashed in his desk. After a bit, Lexi returned to the office, beaming. He remembered that feeling and thought maybe there was something to beginner's luck after all. He had a similar experience on an early case—and then went on to face a string of frustrations over the decades.

"So, you feel like we got the right guy this time?" Lexi asked.

"Hard to argue with a confession…" Jack replied.

"I sense a 'but' in there."

"The front door. Why was it unlocked? Wouldn't she have locked it?" Jack asked.

"I don't know if she would've locked it. Seems like it would be a reflex, but then it's a new home. And her head was all over the place. Maybe she just forgot."

"Probably. But why were there no prints on it, if she opened it and left it unlocked?"

"I guess we'll never know." Lexi sighed. "And the wine glass. That's a loose end too."

"Right. The wine glass. I wonder where he stashed it?" Jack pictured Malone, tramping through the gnarled woods, his eyes darting around in the dark, trying to get away with murder. Not this time.

"He could have thrown it out the window of the car, dumped it in the river, the trash, anywhere. That's a pretty easy thing to get rid of."

"Sure. We wrapped it up tight enough. Angie Hansen got justice. And so did her parents." Jack felt truly satisfied about that part of it.

"It's a sad story, even though we solved it." Lexi said.

"It is." Jack stood up and made his way over to the filing cabinet. He pulled out a stack of files, walked back over, and plopped them down in front of her. "But not nearly as sad as the ones that don't get solved."

"What're these?"

"My cold cases, Lex. The ones that got away from me. I pull them out and work on them from time to time. Try to see if I can see something from a different angle."

"Can I have a look?"

"Be my guest," Jack said. "We need all the help we can get. We've got over a hundred and thirty cold cases in Westchester alone." That gave him an idea. He grabbed his phone and dialed.

"Hi Victoria. No, nothing's wrong. I was just thinking about something. That hundred grand you wanted to donate for a reward? There may be a good use for it, if you're open to the idea that is. There's this group called the Cold Case Foundation…" Jack continued as Lexi started to clear the board and put this case to bed, once and for all.

EPILOGUE

Six months later

Nick was sitting in the living room of their new home reflecting on his talk with Father Patrick. He'd found it rather comforting, being in a confession booth again. He was planning to talk to Victoria about raising their children Catholic. Kids needed a moral compass these days. He didn't expect her to object. And it would please his mother to no end. He'd gone about a month before, and his nightmares had dropped off after the visit.

"Forgive me father for I have sinned. It's been twenty-one years since my last confession."

"That's a long time." Father Patrick smiled. Nick would have known him anywhere, but he wasn't sure if he remembered him or not.

"Yes, I know."

"What brings you here today?"

"I committed adultery." Nick hung his head. He couldn't face him just yet.

"And you regret this?"

He looked up at Father Patrick. "With all my heart."

"Has your wife forgiven you?"

"I think so." Nick looked past him, off into the distance.

"If you are truly sorry in your heart, then the healing has begun in God's eyes. Do you promise to be faithful and spend the rest of your days atoning and making things right with your wife?"

He looked Father Patrick in the eye. "I do, Father. I really do. We have a child on the way." He felt a warm glow inside as he thought about it.

"Then there's no more you need from me. Stay true to that promise and to your wife."

"Thank you. I will." Nick paused. "But that's not all."

"Go on."

"There was a murder. You may have seen it in the news. In Westchester."

"Yes. I know who you are, Nick. But her killer was brought to justice. Or so I thought."

"I didn't kill her."

"But you had an affair with her."

"Right."

"So you feel guilty about her death? That you contributed somehow to the circumstances?" Father Patrick seemed a bit perplexed.

"Yes, but there's more." Nick hesitated as Father Patrick waited. "I didn't kill her. But I may have let her die."

"I don't understand."

"I was there the night of her death. Right after she was attacked. I went back to her house because I thought my wife may have gone up there to confront her. Angie wasn't answering my texts, which was weird, so I went back up to see if Victoria was there. I told the police this. But I didn't tell them everything."

"Go on."

"I felt like something was off. I felt like she wouldn't have gone to sleep so early. So I went to the front door and opened it. It was unlocked. The lights were all out and there was this horrible metallic smell. I shined my phone light into the room. And then I saw her there. Lying at the bottom of the stairs. In a pool of blood. She wasn't moving. She looked dead. But I didn't call the police." He cradled his head in his hands. "I just wiped the doorknob and left."

"And why didn't you call the police?"

He hesitated. "Because I thought my wife may have been responsible for her death."

"You were trying to protect your wife."

"Yes. But what if Angie was still alive? What if she could have been saved?"

"That's something you'd have to ask the police. From what I've read about the case, it's unlikely that she could have been saved. But what you did is still a crime. Leaving the scene like that."

"I know that."

"I can help you make this right with God, but it's your decision what to do about the law. And your wife. Does she know?"

"No, I didn't tell a soul. Except you."

"That's what I'm here for, Nick."

From what Nick could find out about her death, she likely died fairly instantly. He'd asked Stark, claiming he wanted to know if she suffered. He concluded it wouldn't have made much difference if he'd called the police. As far as Angie was concerned, he let himself off the hook. He could live with it. And he certainly wasn't telling the police. But he and Victoria had agreed on a fresh start. No more secrets. Could he burden her with this? Or were some secrets better left in the shadows?

———

Victoria was sitting in her colorful, blooming garden, full of purple azaleas and yellow daffodils, surrounded by tall trees and blue sky. She felt as big as their new house. She was due any day now. The new place was working out fine. She missed the view of the Hudson, but this home was perfect for raising children. A cul-de-sac, a big yard, great neighbors. No nefarious history to speak of. It was calm. Peaceful. Joyful. She planned to get pregnant again as soon as possible. She wasn't wasting any time. She didn't want her child to grow up lonely and alone.

Malone had taken a plea deal. He'd gotten fifteen years, which hardly seemed like much for what he'd done. About a month before, he was knifed to death in prison by a lifer. She thought that a strange coincidence. But she wasn't asking any questions. She knew Nick's father had the connections to pull something like that off. Or maybe it was the Rossi family. Or maybe he just pissed someone off. She didn't care, and they never talked about it. It was better that way. He was gone, no threat to them now, and that was all that mattered.

The revelation about Sam Coleman still stung, even though she'd known all along that something was up. She thought back to that earthshaking conversation with her mother. It was her mother who'd brought up the subject, about a month before, when Victoria went over for a visit.

"Victoria, remember when you asked me about Sam Coleman?" Her mother looked serious, even for her.

"Yeah. That was quite a while ago Mom. Why are you bringing it up now?"

"It's time I told you how I really met him. Come sit, Victoria." Her mother sat on the sofa and patted the space next to her.

"O-*kay?*" Victoria wasn't sure she was ready for this.

"Your father and I. At one point, we had a sort of . . . we kind of . . . took a break. In our marriage."

"You took a break? What does that even mean?"

"We separated for a bit."

"For how long is a bit?" She didn't like where this was going.

"A few months."

"And what does that have to do with Sam Coleman?" She thought she knew the answer, but she felt like she had to say something.

"I took a trip to Quebec City. With some friends. And I met a man there. At the bar at the Hotel Frontenac. It had such a lovely view of the river. It was magical." She had a faraway look in her eye. This couldn't be good.

"Don't tell me. Sam Coleman."

"Yes, but that wasn't the name he gave me. He was with the FBI, working under cover. We had a little ... fling!" She waved her hands and gave her shoulders a shrug.

"Mom! A little *fling?*" Was her entire life a façade? How many secrets could one family have?

"I'm sorry Victoria. I know it's hard to hear. But your father and I were separated. It wasn't an affair. Not technically." It came out as more of a question as her mother fidgeted with her hair, unable to look her in the eye. "And I'm sorry to have to tell you this, but there's more."

Victoria's stomach was already in knots. "This is all a lot to take in, Mom."

"I know. I'm so sorry." She put her hand on Victoria's shoulder. "Do you want me to continue?"

"I don't know. *Do I?*" Victoria looked at her and then turned away.

Her mother continued. "When I got back, your father and I reconciled."

"When was this, exactly?"

Her mother hesitated. "About two years into our marriage."

"That was about the time. . ." Victoria's stomach lurched. It felt as if the very ground beneath her had shifted.

"Yes." Now it was her mother who looked away.

"Oh my God. Mom! Is Sam my *father?*" A wave of nausea washed over her.

"Victoria, whatever the biology, your father was your father. Don't think of it like that. And the truth is, I really don't know if he is or not!"

"Mom! What the *hell!*"

"I'm so sorry, Victoria. After the fling, I realized it was all just a terrible mistake. The affair. The separation. We both did. We'd been together since high school. I think we both just needed confirmation that we weren't missing out on anything. We got back together, and that was that. But your father and I had a lot of trouble conceiving, as you know. I couldn't get pregnant again after you. I always knew there was a chance, but I just didn't want to believe it. And I couldn't have even found Sam if I'd wanted to. The name he gave me was fake. So, I just let it go."

"Did Dad know?"

"No. Never. He never even suspected, I don't think. I didn't want to break his heart. You were his world."

"Oh my God, Mom. All this time? You kept it to yourself?" Her mother nodded yes.

"Does Sam know?"

"He knows now. I found him after your father died. And I told him."

"How did you find him?"

"By coincidence. When I was looking for a private investigator, to go after your advisor, I found his firm. Online. I recognized his photo right away. I figured he'd make sure to protect you. If I told him about my suspicions. Your father wasn't around anymore to do it."

"So he knows about all of this?" Her mother nodded. "Doesn't he want to know the truth? If I'm his or not?" The news was devastating, but she also felt like things finally made sense. It gave her confidence that she should trust her instincts.

"We both agreed to leave it for the time being. He has a family. There was nothing to gain by finding out. But it's up to you now if you want to know or not."

She didn't talk to her mother for a few weeks after that. It was all such a shock. She felt so betrayed. But eventually, she reached out to her. She still wasn't ready to find out the truth. If Sam was her father, she also had two half-sisters and she certainly wasn't ready to meet them. It was all too much for one year. She'd leave it for another day.

For now, she was focused on the immediate future. Their baby. Their plans to finally open the art gallery she'd always wanted. As partners. And all of this insanity had made her even less likely to complicate her life with a divorce. Although there was a part of her that would never feel the same way about Nick, she had forgiven him and she was trying to move past it. She looked around and envisioned her little nuclear family, safe and snug and cozy, like she'd always wanted—except for one major loose end.

She thought it was ironic that Nick and her mother felt she needed protecting. She could take care of herself and she could take care of her child. And it was clear that she would have to be the one to finish what they'd started with Timothy Sutton. They meant well, but she'd probably be in less danger right now if they'd done nothing. With Nick's face plastered all over the media, she was certain her former advisor knew by now who had ruined his life.

Trusting her instincts, she'd done a little detective work herself and found out that Sutton was in town the night her garage door was vandalized. And she also discovered that there was a string of unsolved sexual assaults near his home in Arizona, starting about the time he moved there. He was a vicious predator—vindictive and highly intelligent—and that wasn't going to change. She could still hear the last words he said to her, rolled up in a ball on the floor with that menacing look on his face—"if you tell anyone about this, *you're dead.*" And now he had nothing to lose—making him all the more dangerous. Victoria had connections too, and the will to put an end to this once and for all. And sometime soon, one way or another, Timothy Sutton would no longer be a threat to her or her family.

———

Nick got up and walked over to the French doors, looking at his wife sitting out in the yard. She was positively radiant. She seemed to love it there. She'd even made a new friend, a woman her age next door with a one-year-old boy. He decided right then and there. She had finally found peace. He'd take his secret to the grave.

"Nick!" She stood up and called out to him, eyes wide and mouth open. His stomach sank as his head darted around, looking for dangers.

"What is it, Victoria?" He felt his heart race as a flood of scenarios ran through his mind. She looked down and then back up at him.

"I think my water broke!" Her face lit up with that smile of hers and he breathed a sigh of relief, placing his hand over his heart to steady himself. It was the same smile she wore in the photo on the mantel he'd taken all those years ago. And he vowed to spend the rest of his life trying to keep it there.

———

One year later

Sandi Reston, one of the top ten real estate agents in Westchester county, was driving a young computer geek around, looking at houses. He wanted a deal, and he had to stay under a million.

As she drove up Bedford towards the turn off to Shady Hill Road, they noticed a real estate sign pointing off to the left that hadn't been there a few days before. She knew the house.

"What about that one?" he asked as Sandi drove by.

"It must have just come on the market again. It was in escrow."

"Is it priced too high?"

"No, actually. It's priced at seven-ninety-five."

"That's a steal! Can we go in and have a look?"

"Sure, whatever you want." Although the leaves had already peaked, the remaining ones added some color and the sun's rays poked through the bare patches on the tree branches, brightening up the dark road a bit. Sandi pulled into the driveway, imagining it pitch black in the dead of night. It made her shiver.

"Can we go in?" he asked.

"Sure." Sandi wasn't obligated to tell him the gory details of its recent past, but she knew that she probably should. When they entered the house, she looked over toward the stairs and couldn't help but picture a body lying there in a pool of blood.

"Why did it fall out of escrow?"

"Listen, there's something I have to tell you about the house. A woman was murdered here. About a year ago. Sellers aren't required to disclose this kind of thing in New York, so beware of that. It was all over the news. Maybe you heard about it. She was new to the area. It was a big scandal."

"Yes, of course. I know all about it. Has it been on the market ever since?" he asked.

"No. It sold a few months after that. The market was really hot. It was a young couple. New in town. The husband traveled all the time."

"And they're selling now?"

"Yes."

"Why?"

"Keep in mind that there's so many stories about haunted houses, haunted rocks, haunted caves in this area. Every house around here probably has some kind of story. Most people usually don't give it a second thought."

"So, what happened here?" he asked.

"Now, I'm not saying I believe any of this, mind you. But from what I heard, the wife claimed she could hear a woman, wailing in the night. It freaked her out, being home alone much of the time." She shrugged. "I'm sure it was nothing, just the power of suggestion, or maybe the wind. But they moved out a few months in. It's been vacant ever since. It was in escrow but it must have fallen through. I'd have to check on that."

"I see," he said. They were both silent for a few moments.

"So do you still want to have a look around the place, Wade?"

"Absolutely!" Wade replied.

ACKNOWLEDGMENTS

My thanks to the many people who helped me along this journey. Thanks to my husband Rick who read countless drafts, offering many suggestions, large and small, which helped refine and improve this novel. Thanks to my father and grandmother who seem to have passed the mystery lover gene on to me. To my friends Susan and Donna who graciously read drafts and gave me valuable feedback, thank you for taking the time and energy to help me improve and refine my novel and for encouraging me to keep writing. Thanks to Hedi Lampert for helping me turn my rough ideas into a solid first draft and to Jordan Kanty for his thorough editing services.

Thanks goes out to the Cold Case Foundation for their data base of cold cases and their expert advice. The foundation provides funding and advising to local law enforcement agencies to help them solve cold cases, and they rely totally on donations for support. I also highly recommend *Police Procedure and Investigation: A Guide for Writers* by Lee Lofland which helped me understand the law enforcement perspective and provided valuable information on forensics and police procedures.

And finally, thanks to the many mystery writers out there who have kept me turning the pages late into the night over the years, leaving me at once perplexed and satisfied up until the end. I hope to have done the same for my readers.

ABOUT THE AUTHOR

 Dr. Bonnie L. Traymore is an accomplished historian and educator with a Ph.D. in United States History. She is an award-winning non-fiction writer with a love of mystery novels and films. Originally from the New York City area, she and her husband have two children and reside in Honolulu, Hawaii. *Killer Motives* is her debut novel.